Penguin Books
A Painted Devil

Rachel Billington was educated at a Catholic
convent and at Oxford University where she took
a BA Honours degree in English Literature and
Language. She then went to work for Associated
Television as a researcher. In 1965 she moved to
New York to work for the American Broadcasting
Corporation on documentary programmes. Six
months researching on drug addiction also gave
background material for her first novel, *All
Things Nice* (1967), which she wrote on her
return to London. Her other novels include, *The
Big Dipper*, *Lilacs*, *Out of the Dead Land*, *Cock
Robin* and *Beautiful*, which is also published in
Penguin. She has also had short stories and
features published. She spent a year as book
reviewer for *Cosmopolitan* and at present reviews
for the *Financial Times*. She has also written
plays for radio, and her first television play, *Don't
Be Silly*, was produced in 1979. A second will be
shown in 1980. Her latest novel is *A Woman's
Age*.

Rachel Billington is married to film and theatre
director Kevin Billington and they have four
children.

Rachel Billington

A Painted Devil

Penguin Books

Penguin Books Ltd, Harmondsworth,
Middlesex, England
Penguin Books, 625 Madison Avenue,
New York, New York 10022, U.S.A.
Penguin Books Australia Ltd, Ringwood,
Victoria, Australia
Penguin Books Canada Ltd, 2801 John Street,
Markham, Ontario, Canada L3R 1B4
Penguin Books (N.Z.) Ltd, 182–190 Wairau Road,
Auckland 10, New Zealand

First published by William Heinemann Ltd 1975
Published in Penguin Books 1981

Made and printed in Great Britain by
Hazell, Watson & Viney Ltd,
Aylesbury, Bucks
Set in Intertype Baskerville

For my mother and
my father

'The sleeping and the dead
Are but as pictures; 'tis the eye of childhood
That fears a painted devil.'

Macbeth, Act II, scene ii

They first saw each other, like Dante and Beatrice, on the Ponte Vecchio. It was winter, early in the morning, and the outlines of their bodies were blurred by a mist rising off the river. They didn't speak as they passed, but stared intently.

Fenella saw a tall thin young man with pale gold hair and a high narrow forehead come thrusting towards her. His footsteps clicked sharply on the pavement. He was wearing a green military cloak that swung behind him and carried a sword-stick that he used like a baton to sound the closed wooden shutters of the small shops that bordered the bridge. As they came level with each other, he frowned at her. Fenella was not at all insulted by the frown, for a smile would have been a vulgarity. In Florence one didn't smile at strangers.

Edward saw a tall dark girl wrapped in long reddish furs appear mysteriously on the crest of the empty bridge. As she reached him, she hesitated, either as if she thought to turn back or perhaps to speak, but finally did neither, merely paused, looked, dark blue eyes in a white face stared almost absent-mindedly. He was filled with a desire to paint her. He concentrated his excitement into a frown. At which she moved on swiftly, though not in alarm, as if she had forgotten something and must hurry to find it.

Then Edward, who had not broken his stride, was the other side of the bridge and she had vanished behind him into the city's centre. Neither looked round. There was no need, for both had guessed the other was English and both knew they must inevitably meet again.

This second meeting came a few days later at a lunch party in the *palazzo* of an English expatriate aesthete.

Edward cried out the moment he saw Fenella.

' "I saw Eternal Beauty wandering on her way and now I find her captured!" '

'Yeats,' contributed their host, who did not expect his only woman guest to be singled out for such public homage.

'I like walking early,' said Fenella tranquilly.

After that, it was not difficult to persuade her to sit for him.

Edward was staying in the top floor of a fifteenth-century tower chosen for its picturesque qualities : the view over the pink curling rooftops, the wide unfurnished space, the copper-coloured tiles, the twirling stone staircase, the changing light that came in December wisps through the wide windows, and the golden doge's chair. He didn't notice the lack of heating, of curtains, of carpets, of furniture, of bath, of cooker.

Fenella came in every other morning and sat before him, wrapped in her sweeping reddish fur. Their white breath sailed about the room as they talked, he energetically, she languidly, about Ghirlandaio's restrained use of red and pink in the Church of Santa Trinità, about Filippo Lippi's decadence compared to the spirituality of Fra Angelico, about the supreme merit of Masaccio who had lived only twenty-seven years. But never about themselves. They remained as ignorant about each other's background as they had been that first morning on the Ponte Vecchio.

*

Then just before Christmas, Tristram came out to stay with Edward. Tristram had been Edward's only real friend since their public school days when they had drawn close over Bosch and Beerbohm. Too close eventually for the school's comfort. But disgrace was averted by Edward, despite his lack of enthusiasm for the academic life, winning a scholarship to Cambridge, which success cancelled out his irregular personal habits.

At this time it was not clear which boy would be the dominant character. Tristram's relaxed almost adult manner made him more popular than Edward, whose reserve gave the impression of shyness. Even the teachers enjoyed Tristram's exuberant talent as a painter more than Edward's concentration. Without such a friend, Edward would have

8

found school unbearable. It was Tristram who had firm plans for the future. He enrolled at the Royal College of Art. Yet Edward's secret knowledge that he was cleverer than Tristram gave him more choices. He knew he must become a painter, but wondered whether first to train his mind.

'... *fabrum esse suae quemque fortuna.*' He was a Classics scholar. But one year at Cambridge convinced him that it was, as he disdainfully informed his surprised parents, 'a mausoleum peopled by butterflies'. The image pleased him and he illustrated it with a careful pen-and-ink drawing which he sent to Tristram on the postcard which announced his departure from academics. Tristram was naturally exultant, feeling his own course of action justified. 'They're all eagles here,' he welcomed Edward to London. But Edward was only passing through.

'It's not people I care about,' he looked quite cross at the necessity to put it so badly into words. 'It's painting. I'm going to Florence for a year. Afterwards I may join you.' Tristram, having seen himself change from pawn to queen, became pawn again. 'You may visit me at Christmas,' continued Edward grandly, but with an edge of fondness.

'Of course I shall,' Tristram became romantic at once. 'We'll meet beside the Arno.'

But in this he was rather upstaged by Fenella.

*

Fenella was seated in the doge's chair when Tristram arrived. Although it was evening, she still seemed to be posing, and did not move as he crossed her line of vision. She saw a fragile boy with pale vixenish face, large green eyes, and a mass of red-brown hair. In many ways he was more feminine than herself.

Tristram saw a long-faced girl with a straight back enthroned in a round room lit by candles. Her bony pallor and large frame were softened by the misty blueness of her eyes, by the curls and bird's wing blackness of her hair and by the flowing fur coat. The view through the window behind her of illuminated domes, towers and palaces created a fitting backdrop.

Edward stood between them. 'This is Fenella. Who I'm painting. She's another habitué of Florence.' He turned to Fenella. 'Tristram has come on a visit.'

'*Ben venuto.*'

When Fenella spoke her voice was low, even masculine. This, together with her appearance, made Tristram realize she couldn't be dismissed with the sisters of friends that he and Edward had historically despised. He found her calm graceful manner immediately sympathetic. Being clever about people, he even identified the reason – her resemblance to Edward. Physically, though one dark, one fair, they shared the same angular height, long pale face and strong, in Edward's case almost jutting, chin beneath very red full lips. This forestalled any obvious jealousy, for two such similar beings could never form the halves of a whole.

He danced up to Fenella and executed a clever little bow.

'Your hand, m'lady.'

Fenella smiled; she thought this mocking very apt. Here was someone who could provide the lightness, the intimacy that Edward lacked. It was obvious that *they* were already intimate. Although, in her virgin innocence, she did not analyse what this feeling implied in sexual terms. Already she saw it was part of Edward's nature not to explain people.

Fenella extended her hand to Tristram. He separated each long cold finger and touched it lightly with his mouth. Fenella, concentrating hard, for she was not used to physical contact, did not pull away.

'I hope your journey was easy.'

'Heavens, no!' Tristram laughed. 'It was dreadfully tiresome. The aeroplane was filled with drum majorettes.'

'How tiresome!' echoed Fenella understandingly.

'*Vino,*' he said, hanging out his tongue. 'And then you must explain yourself.'

Fenella blinked. She saw that the coming of Tristram would make the atmosphere more personal, more daring. She wondered how she would explain her life in Florence.

She had taken a year off from the Courtauld Institute to study Florentine art. She lived in the Pensione Adria which was on the top floor of a *palazzo* the other side of the Arno.

A walnut-veneered lift took guests lugubriously to the top floor where tall windows opened onto the river. Her next-door neighbour was a seventeen-year-old English girl called Tish Skeffington-Smith who had somehow landed up in Florence instead of at a finishing school in Switzerland. She could speak no Italian, knew little about painting and admired Fenella in a dogged sort of way which showed a certain strength of character. She often followed Fenella about the galleries so that Edward, who thought her pink cheeks and yellow curly hair quite ridiculous, christened her 'Little Lamb'. Certainly her bouncy cheerfulness, contrasted with Fenella's dreamy languor, made it seem an unlikely relationship.

Fenella and Tish were two of many English girls at the pensione, for it was run by an Englishwoman married to an Italian. She had been a friend of Fenella's mother when she had in her turn lived in Florence, and when Fenella had arrived the spring before, the rooms were filled with great bowls of lilac, as if Signora Foscari thought wistfully of an English garden. Fenella suspected her tall Amazonian mother, who had returned to a life of Sussex gardens and charitable occupations, had a willowy romantic past which she had given up for Mr Frith-Peacock. Who farmed. Fenella noted that often talented but unself-confident women threw in their lot with ordinary even stupid men, apparently equating conventionality with security. It was a mistake she was determined not to make herself. Her father had tortured her mother by stamping on her imaginative nature and raiding the county ladies with the finesse of one of his own bulls. Fenella often meditated on this as she lay on her high mahogany bed, or crossed the Ponte Vecchio on her way to her college. Her first sight of Edward had actually displaced a vision of her father's solid brick face. It had been like seeing a silvery steeple arise above a brick Victorian factory.

Some of this she told Tristram. Edward, who didn't know it either, listened attentively. Then he turned to Tristram.

'I've bought you a campbed. At a flea market. It's under mine.'

Tristram looked at Edward's high ornate bed covered with a magnificent, though slightly moth-eaten tiger skin.

'Would you like to sin –'

'Tristram's a painter too,' Edward interrupted him, 'though he behaves like a jester.'

'You are lucky. I can only admire.'

'That's an art too.'

'Colour, at the moment.' It was a relief for Fenella to return to art. Tristram dashed back some wine.

'Colour's like rhyme in poetry, an inessential extra!'

'Don't be so cruel. Pictures are people. You can wound them.' Edward was firm. 'Portraits especially are people. That's why copies, though apparently identical are frightful Frankensteins; why a pieced-together statue is nothing whatsoever.'

'A mosaic?' Tristram grinned.

This first evening was typical of those which followed. They became a threesome, inseparable until far into the night, drinking *chianti* out of goblets, taking on all the problems facing the aesthete and the painter. Tristram, more self-conscious than the other two, spiked Edward with *faux naïf* questions and goaded Fenella into overblown statements. Sometimes they would temporarily abandon art and, still in abstract and literary terms, ponder the meaning of life and death.

One evening, Fenella produced a leather-bound volume. She sat enthroned with her foxy furs flaring round her thin ankles and opened it at a page marked by a striped ibis feather.

'Listen,' she said, 'remember what I said about searching the obscure. This is a lesser seventeenth-century playwright's view on death.' She read slowly :

> 'Death is the privilege of Human Nature,
> And life without it were not worth our taking.'

She paused for some time and then read it again even more slowly. 'It comes from *The Fair Penitent*.' She shivered and hugged herself. Her eyes glittered. 'Terrifying.'

Neither Edward nor Tristram reacted so strongly. But they

looked at her emotion with interest and somehow the lines became fixed in their imaginations, so that in those dreamlike early morning hours they would sprawl with drooping lids, quoting Nicholas Rowe backwards and forwards. One of them would begin,

'Death is . . .'
'Death is the privilege.'
'The privilege of death.'
'The privilege of Human Nature.'
'And life were.'
'And life without it were.'

And altogether they chorused, 'Not worth our taking.'

Then they would fall back crying out, if it was late enough and they had drunk enough, 'Oh! Glorious! Ultimate! Sublime!'

Thus Nicholas Rowe's thoughts on life and death became a password for their friendship. They did not interpret them in a Christian sense, as referring to an after-life, but in the sense of tragedy in the shape of death heightening and giving meaning to the ordinariness of life. This was not death that came as a negative force at the end of a decaying life, but death as a god snatching and ennobling a young spirit. This idea suited their youthful romanticism, their adolescent death wish.

*

That was their night-times. In the daylight, their trio became more complicated. Their differences were more obvious.

One morning, it was only a few days before Christmas and the weather had become colder than ever, Tristram who somewhat earlier had been rolled unwillingly from Edward's bed and fallen among a twisted red rug to his campbed beneath, awoke to the sound of leather-clad knuckles on the door.

'Oh.' Fenella stayed poised at the doorway. She often seemed dazzled by her own arrival.

'It must be cold,' Tristram pulled a sweater over his head. 'Your nose is pink and your face is white and your fur is standing on end. Edward's been out since dawn.'

'It's the snow. Nearly snow. Big round blobs one at a time. Unconvincing but dramatic. I'd better wait. He wants to paint me.'

She came further into the room and stood silently for a moment.

'Shall I make your bed for you?' She was polite. This was the morning.

'I just push it under Edward's.'

'I'll help. Oh.' Fenella stopped in a crouched position. Tristram thought admiringly that with her huge fur coat sweeping around her she looked like some yet-to-be-invented animal. A winter unicorn. 'What ever is that?'

'What?' Tristram was not curious by nature. He liked inventing things, scenes, people, animals, not discovering them. 'A cardboard box.' He decided he was curious after all. 'Pull it out.'

Together they dragged it towards them.

'Do you think we should open it?' Without waiting for a reply, Fenella took off the lid with her bony fingers. Tristram began to laugh.

'His silk handkerchiefs. How superb! He's always had an inhuman passion for coloured silk handkerchiefs but I never would have thought he'd have so many here.'

'Florence is filled with silk handkerchiefs,' Fenella sat back primly. 'It's a very sensible place to buy them.'

'Oh, I know.' Tristram still smiled. 'But it's not sensible to have so many. Stuffed under your bed. Like a body.'

Suddenly the door was thrown open and Edward stood brisk and glowing in the threshold.

'I'm late,' he cried, 'but look.'

Tristram and Fenella started round guiltily. Fenella nudged the box back with her elbow and Tristram jumped up. Edward didn't notice. He only wanted their attention. At the end of his arm dangled a huge chandelier. A sudden flood of wintry sunshine came through the windows and lit on the mass of glass so that it glittered in a thousand colours. Edward shook it slightly and red, green, blue, yellow sparks flew across the room pinning Tristram where he stood and piercing Fenella's wide blue eyes. She closed them defensively and when she opened them again, the chandelier was still, Edward was still, and instead of the fiery darts, she saw a multitude of tiny faces, Edward over and over again, mirrored on every glassy surface as he peered over it admiringly. Fenella was awed; she had never understood the power and beauty of a chandelier before. This was not the dead ungainly object that hung in her parents' hall in Sussex. This was a living creation.

'I shall put candles into it.' He moved swiftly across the room and set the chandelier down on the bed. Fenella watched sadly as the darker corner turned it back into a crumpled piece of glass.

Edward began to squeeze careful blobs of paint onto his palette. Fenella went over and touched it.

'That's made of glass, too.'

'I like glass. It's a unique material. It must be treated with respect. I would never humiliate glass by putting it over a picture. Like the Filippo Lippi's in the Uffizi; all you can see are people coming into the gallery behind you. It does its best to spoil the picture. Glass can be mean-minded.'

'I suppose you want to start painting?' Although he was still not the slightest bit jealous of Fenella, Tristram was immediately jealous of Edward painting her.

At school Edward had drawn him often : intricate spidery compositions in brown pen and ink which they dubbed his Dürers. Often he would make them ghoulish, with a lock of hair turning into a snake entering at his ear and coming out through his nose; or grotesquely comic, with a fly perched on his nose, or three arms coming around his head and one ending in a bird's claw. Or sometimes sexual in an insinuating sniggering kind of way, with eyes for nipples and a slow-worm for a penis. But this portrait of Fenella was different. The composition showed no signs of disturbing surprises. In fact the effect was undeniably romantic. Tristram stared at the picture with inquisitive concentration. It seemed that Fenella had inspired Edward towards some new phase of his development.

'I'll be off to Paradise then.' He decided to take a walk to the Baptistery. He would place himself in front of Ghiberti's bronze doors. Perhaps genius would communicate itself. 'And afterwards to Doney's,' he added.

Tristram closed the door behind him.

Fenella, sitting warmly among her furs, stared out at the city, now half veiled by misty clouds. She would have liked to have gone with Tristram. Already she realized that one of his greatest gifts was for enjoyment, which made him an excellent companion. They had been to the Uffizi several times together and she had been impressed by his understanding of her great loves, of Giotto's Virgin, of Leonardo's Nativity. His critical sympathy was very different from Edward's approach.

Once, when she had been sitting mesmerized in front of Piero della Francesca's double portrait of the Duke and Duchess of Urbino, she had felt a hand on her shoulder. A loud voice she hardly recognized had cried.

'Like Patience on a monument. I thought you'd seen Medusa at least, and now I see it's only the good old Duke and Duchess.'

She had swivelled round nervously. 'Oh, Edward.'

Edward was febrile. As if the sight of her calmness was unbearable to him, he had pulled her up and started to propel her down the long wooden floor of the gallery. Her protests were ignored. He strode along, noisily discussing points of art, more often than not unconnected with the pictures on either side of them. Every now and again he stopped unexpectedly, so that she cannoned into him. She found it an unnerving experience and couldn't understand how someone as sensitive as Edward could behave in such a way. Then he said something about a painter 'needing pride', and she realized that his violent reaction to the Uffizi was a safeguard against being submerged under greatness. He felt himself in competition with della Francesca, Botticelli, Leonardo da Vinci, and all the other stars in her firmament.

Now she smiled indulgently at such arrogance.

'No,' objected Edward.

'Sorry.' She was glad he didn't like her to smile, although he probably didn't like any woman to smile. She guessed he was unrealistic, well, perhaps romantic about women, wanting them to be heroines of tragic opera; which was why he admired her height, her pallor and her long black ringlets. 'I don't expect you know many women,' she said, without having meant to.

Edward, dabbing purplish black, was interested in the idea. For she was, of course, quite right. 'My mother,' he grinned, 'is a fine Swedish expatriate, ageing now to a new maturity. I have painted her several times, but last time I put an ice-cream cone i.. her mouth and she was offended.'

'I hope you won't put anything in my mouth.'

'She's pale and cold. It was appropriate.'

'Inevitable.' Fenella thought how he had answered her question 'knowing' women in terms of 'painting' women.

*

Tristram had ordered a first plateful of *lasagne* by the time Edward arrived at Doney's. Edward was invigorated by the progress he had seen in his painting and by a fast swinging walk. Tristram, on the other hand, after his morning of critical appreciation and with a glass or two already inside him, was entering his afternoon mood of lazy satisfaction.

'I'm ravenous.' Edward sat opposite him. 'What's that you've got?' He peered at his plate.

Tristram pulled out a strand of *lasagne*, as if he was pointing a long green tongue. 'Where's Fenella?'

'Gone.'

Edward was glad. She reminded him too vividly of his portrait. How could he relax with her sitting at the same table? Those huge misty eyes, that long elegant nose, that curious flat body under such a welter of black hair. She was a problem he was trying to solve on canvas. He had already admitted defeat over the body, preferring to disguise it under the luxuriant fur, rather than try and understand its femaleness. And yet the richness, the femaleness of her hair and manner was in peculiar contrast to the hardness of her body, the flat sterility, like cardboard.

'She might come back. With her little lamb.'

'Baa.'

But Edward had another reason for wishing Fenella out of the way. He looked down at the table seriously.

'We only have one chance to build a life.' He broke up a packet of *pan d'oro* and stacked a bonfire in the middle of the white tablecloth. 'One must choose the right spot for the match. And fan the flames.'

'Baden-Powell's boy scout handbook. Rule number 8980, para 6a, Do not burn down forests without advance warning to chipmunks, weasels, ants, woodpeckers and other interested rodents.'

Edward ignored this. 'I really can't join you at art school. One must make one's path. After all, it's the mind that creates paintings, not the body.'

'Not even the hand,' Tristram tried to be funny. He put on an Irish accent and, hiding his hands behind his back, nodded his head vigorously at his plate, 'Sean O'Shaunessy, the look-no-hands painter, says brains are enough.'

'The mind.' Edward would not be distracted.

Tristram lifted his head sharply and a waiter produced his second steaming bowl of *lasagne*. He watched, depressed, as it was liberally covered with crumbly cheese. '*Basta*,' he advised sooner than usual. And then thinking better of it, waved him back again. '*Mi scusi; più; ecco. Va bene*.'

His Italian was bad but the waiter liked his spirit. He kissed his fingers at the plate. '*Ah. Ottimo!*'

Tristram was nearly restored. He had been looking forward to Edward joining him at art school, but he saw now he had never really expected it. Edward was so trail-blazing. He blew at the *pan d'oro* bonfire. 'Just fanning the flames.'

'The point is,' said Edward, who had been carrying on his own train of thought, 'it could only hinder my progress. I'm learning so much so fast that I can't spare the time.'

'Ah.' Tristram attempted half-heartedly to reconcile this view with his own desultory attendance at college, which he tried to make up with sudden obsessive spurts at home. 'I expect I only go to keep my mother happy,' he suggested, with false humility. In fact, his ever-optimistic philosophy was that genuine talent – which he never denied himself – could replace determination.

'Oh no.' Edward was firm. 'Your painting needs the discipline. You need the discipline.'

Tristram thought the atmosphere was like a headmaster's study. 'My mother loves to tell her friends her son's at art school,' he said. 'It explains my long hair and velvet trousers and all the silly things that excite and upset middle-aged ladies. A sort of house-trained Chatterton.' As Edward smiled at the image, Tristram relaxed.

In fact there was some truth in his explanation. Maggie Brown, Tristram's mother, had been a widow from before his birth and was a lady of strong views. She had auburn hair which had given her son his reddish aura and a sharp vixen's face which rose somewhat oddly from an ample bosom and flowing hips. Her waist, however, was still small.

'Why did she never marry again?' Edward allowed himself to be diverted. He saw that Tristram had accepted that their futures would diverge.

'Because she's in love with me.'

'Oh, shocking.'

'You're lucky to have disengaged parents,' Tristram sighed, but not very convincingly. It would be foolish to spurn adoration – even in a mother.

'Quite. I can do what I want. However, I've decided to join the Courtauld.'

This time there was no *lasagne* to distract Tristram. Edward was joining Fenella.

'Traitor,' he said dourly.

Edward ignored him. He leant back and his pale bony face under its border of pale straight hair became intense. 'I like education as long as it doesn't distract one from oneself. Life is not long enough for such a lack of seriousness.'

Tristram digested this bit of philosophy and found himself in no position to call it self-centred. Instead he pretended to misunderstand.

'The proper study of mankind is man,' he said.

'Of course, one presumes talent.'

'Genius,' murmured Tristram, who used the word freely.

'Genius?' echoed a girl's voice at his elbow.

Tristram jumped. He was annoyed. He had no time to

accept Edward's decision graciously. Here was Fenella, already pawing like a cat for her victim. He looked at her long intelligent face with disapproval. Worse still, Tish was there too.

'*Ben venuto,*' he said, meaning to be ironic.

But Fenella looked pleased, and said quite humbly, 'Oh good. Then we can join you for ice-cream and coffee?'

'It's so cold outside,' said Tish, whose sense of inferiority made her determined to speak before being overwhelmed. She was trying to decide which boy she loved. Although Tristram laughed at her more openly, he seemed more approachable. She couldn't even begin to imagine Edward kissing her.

'So you want to be freezing inside too.' Tristram cleared his coat from a chair and pulled her cold fingers. He shook them from the wrist. 'Like icicles. Listen how they jangle.' Tish sat down quickly. She was confused. She blushed.

'Oh, thank you. I'm so ... It's so ...' Her love became fixed.

Fenella, sitting beside Edward, watched and was jealous. Sometimes she felt so old, so world-weary. She thought of Byron's lines :

> I stood
> Among them. But not of them, in a shroud
> Of thoughts which were not their thoughts.

She looked at Edward and was about to speak when he turned his back to her and shouted across the room.

'*Cameriere. Ancora vino bianco.*'

Tristram drummed his fingers on the table. '*Ancora. Bravo.*'

Tish laughed excitedly.

Fenella imagined how outside the restaurant dusk was already coming down like a mist on the Florence she loved : the sudden dungeon walls, the secret courtyards, the canaries that sang from their dangling cages, the cobblestones that sabotaged a brisk English stride, cafés that smelled of coffee beans, the rooftops, the churches, the palaces, the campaniles, the piazzas where pigeons scavenged ...

'Dreamer.' Edward poured wine into her glass. 'That's how you look when I paint you.'

... And the pictures. The paintings. The frescoes. In galleries. On altars. In refectories, in monastic cells. They were most real of everything to her. More real than people. She turned her wide blue eyes on Edward. Even more real than Edward.

2

1967

Edward found Florence in June too hot and dominated by tourists. The temptation to sip iced drinks in the villas round Fiesole was corrupting. Fenella disappeared to San Sepolcro, a small town in the Apennines where she intended to sit daily before Piero della Francesca's Resurrection.

London, though cooler, was also filled with tourists, so without even stopping to find Tristram, he took a train to his parents' home in the country. There, after nearly a year of Italy, he was amazed by the luxurious greenness all around. It was as if a huge brush, loaded with green paint, had dolloped it over earth, bushes, walls and houses. It seemed to reflect upwards into the sky. Edward felt encased in its brilliance and determined to transfer some of it onto canvas.

It took him some time to feel the need for company beyond his parents. They respected him, as he respected them. It had been a relief on both sides when he became an adult. They admired his painting of Fenella, identifying her as *jolie laide*, and the portrait as a cross between Romney and Chagall – no Florentine influence at all – and they asked kindly after Tristram. So eventually Edward sent each of them an invitation to stay.

*

Fenella and Tristram met on Wormley Station which was small and quite astonishingly picturesque, enclosed by high banks of grass filled with wild flowers glowing in the deep golden sunlight of a late August afternoon. Beyond the banks, the Somerset countryside opened out into corn fields mostly cut and patterned with bales and divided by rich green hedges. Behind them stretched a deep violet sky. There was no sign of their host.

Fenella and Tristram had not seen each other since Italy

and were separately and secretly taken aback by the other's appearance. Edward, with some wickedness, had let each think that he was to be a solitary guest.

Fenella, clasping shut her handbag, saw a raffish-looking youth in grubby sneakers, streaky jeans, wavy silk scarf and a wild shock of shiny hair. She could hardly see his pale vixen-ish face, but she couldn't think that they had ever been friends. He looked so casual, so slipshod, so unfeeling; when she knew herself to be so caring, so aware of every moment of life.

Tristram, stubbing out a cigarette under his foot, saw a stiff matronly figure totally encased in a long linen coat. The formality of her face, its long nose and prominent cheek-bones, were accentuated by her hair drawn back to the nape of her straight neck. She wore expensive green suede shoes over fine-textured stockings. Tristram, who seldom compared, thought of Cherry with nostalgia.

Since his visit to Florence, he had discovered the attractions of a new breed of slim young girls in jeans and T-shirts. The art school swarmed with them, the ragged ends of their long manes catching on their studded belts or stencilled bottoms. They seemed altogether another sex to the know-ing sisters who had visited his schooldays. It was a kind of simple narcissism for they looked much more like him than most of the men he knew. One, called Cherry, with chestnut-coloured locks and etiolated breastless body, stared at him in life classes and brought him cups of coffee in the college snack bar. Tristram's male fidelity, even in principle not a virtue he rated high, did not survive long.

Cherry lived in a bedsitter in an unrenovated Georgian house. The walls were covered with bright patterned cushions and there was one rug-draped mattress. She was a very silent person. They had hardly ever exchanged more than a word. Sometimes a smoke. Sometimes a pill. But seldom a word. There was another form of communication. After a while, Cherry would put her slightly grubby hand onto his jeans. Tristram liked her little fingers covered with sharp silver rings. As Cherry and he began delicately, like butterflies, to make love, he would think about painting, he found the preliminaries of heterosexual love-making a very good moment for artistic planning. His body being so exquisitely tuned seemed to free his mind from those complex bonds that descended at the sight of a sheet of paper or a canvas. For the last year he had been experimenting with watercolours. He would progress to oils. When the two bodies were naked, slim legs and arms entwining, like Columbine, he thought about Turner. Perhaps he was a Turner. Blake or Turner. Cherry crawled over him, her long hair swishing across his chest. People would call him great. People would call him a genius. Tristram would float off into the most delightful dream.

He almost regretted his haste to answer Edward's summons. Fenella bent gracefully to the bank on her left and plucked from the overflowing grass first a spiky white daisy and then a scarlet poppy. She caressed them with her fingers.

'Oh,' she sighed ecstatically, aware of Tristram's gaze, 'is anything more beautiful than an English wayside flower?'

Tristram would not be outdone. At once he sprang forward and, as she straightened, pressed his cheek against hers. So close, he saw only her huge floating blue-green eyes and for a moment he shut his own.

'Magic.'

At that moment Edward appeared on the other side of the railway line. He was dressed all in white and waved his arms at them in a manner more commanding than welcoming. They were to cross the bridge to him.

'Lazy sod,' said Tristram, smiling.

'My case isn't very heavy,' said Fenella.

'Oh, I don't care about that.' Swinging down and up, Tristram placed a case on each shoulder and jumped onto the line. In a moment he was over on the other side. Fenella wondered briefly about the advisability of threesomes. However she'd always liked crossing bridges.

Edward and Fenella met on top of the criss-crossed iron bridge.

'I'm glad you could come,' Edward said politely, and shook her hand.

Tristram couldn't find his ticket. He searched his pockets enthusiastically but in the end Edward had to buy him another.

'Perhaps you forgot to get one?' Fenella suggested as they wandered towards the car.

'Ah,' Tristram did not commit himself, but curled helpfully into the back of Edward's small car.

'It's my mother's,' explained Edward.

Fenella stared fixedly out of the window. She felt remote and literary, for she had never been to this part of the country before. In San Sepolcro she had stared with the same expression at the face of Christ resurrected. His eyes were extraordinary. Fierce, sad, triumphant eyes that had seen three days of death and lived again. She hardly noticed the Roman guards asleep in ungainly human parody below the tomb; she saw only Christ, poised athletically like a footballer, knee upraised in conquest, pennant in hand. Whether she stood close or far away, he remained a mystery.

And then one afternoon when the heat hung thick and heavy through the soft yellow-stoned town, she had risen early from her siesta and slowly climbed the steps that led up to the gallery. She stood for a moment at the top with the heat and dazzling sunlight behind her and the cool room in front. At the far end, the picture. Christ. She paused and saw it with sudden new clarity. It was Edward. She felt faint, and even swayed. The eyes were Edward's, pale and knowing. It was ludicrous, obscene.

The next day she decided it was time she left for England. She told herself she was becoming like a Henry James spinster. Soon she would be having the vapours. Perhaps that was exactly what she'd already suffered. Her stalwart English stock had uprisen. If she stayed longer in Italy she would run the risk of becoming *déracinée*. Her own mother would never have made the mistake of marrying her father, if she had not spent so long abroad. She had lost the appropriate standard for judging the English male. Perhaps she too had mistaken paint for people.

Fenella had seen how glad her mother was to have her daughter back in England. Perhaps it lessened her jealousy.

Perhaps Fenella's hollow, pale face made her feel better about her own life. She was certainly encouraging about the future and about the exciting jobs she could get, once she had completed her degree. But although at home, Fenella had still felt a wanderer. She walked about her father's fields with a subdued air and, like Edward, wondered at the rich growth of fields and hedges and trees. It was almost too over-bearing. Then Edward's letter had arrived. And once more she was in an unknown land.

'It's like a Samuel Palmer.' She searched for associations.

'The neatness, the order.' Edward was interested.

'The thickness of line. The richness.'

'I've been sketching in the fields,' said Edward.

'It's a pity the harvesting's done,' said Tristram who suddenly had a picture of himself stripped to the waist, forking the yellow offerings of corn. 'I've never been here at this time of year.'

'They still have to be brought from the fields.'

'Some of the leaves are turning,' said Fenella.

'Not yet,' cried Tristram.

'It's the salt. From the sea winds,' explained Edward.

There seemed plenty to talk about even in this wary renewal of intimacy.

*

The house was built of grey stone and, despite its wide windows and bow front, appeared to Fenella cold and unwelcoming. Perhaps it was the thick Virginia creeper which crawled across the façade like a false whiskers and beard.

'We'll have a drink in the garden,' said Edward, without caring to show them their rooms. There, behind a pretty ironwork table, they discovered Gunilla Aubrey who laid aside a pair of horn-rimmed glasses and a large book.

'I was reading,' she said, smiling rather vacantly.

'We guessed as much,' Edward stared at his mother disapprovingly, but Fenella, who knew that unrelated feeling, warmed to her at once.

'Books seem so much better outdoors,' she pressed forward enthusiastically and held out her hand. Mrs Aubrey squeezed it warmly, 'Like food,' she said, and then looked past her to Tristram. 'And Tristram, who we haven't seen for so long.'

'We thought we'd have a drink,' said Edward firmly.

'Of course. Of course,' Mrs Aubrey turned to Fenella appealingly, 'I like you to do just what you want. Tristram knows already but I hope you will too. And stay for as long as you like.'

Edward came back with their drinks. Against the thick foliage of the trees, the deep-coloured grass, he looked almost supernaturally light and bright. Fenella found her heart missing a beat. Yet it was the warmth of Tristram's cheek and the slight dampness of his mouth as he had kissed her at the station which came into her mind.

'You have brought your painting things, haven't you?' Edward asked Tristram.

'I told Maggie you would be painting me. That's why she let me go.'

'How is your mother?' Mrs Aubrey sipped her martini. 'She was always so friendly on those dreadful school occasions.'

'Jealous,' said Tristram. 'She thinks I have more fun with Edward than she has with her accountants and solicitors. They take her dancing.'

'I'm so sorry.'

'She thought of moving to the countryside herself.'

'And what did she decide?' Fenella was curious.

'God!' Edward leapt to his feet. This was the sort of chatter that drove him mad.

'That she's not ready to trade life for a herbaceous border,' Tristram finished blandly. And the three of them watched as Edward fled back across the lawn.

Edward went along to his studio room, dimly lit in the dying sun and wondered why he had chosen to interrupt a delightful and satisfying way of life. What had he to do with a spoilt layabout and an ugly middle-class girl? He should have realized that he had grown out of Tristram and that Florence had cast its magic over Fenella. He moved along to see his picture of her. Had her power all been created by his own imagination?

27

That evening Fenella came down for dinner looking very odd. She wore what appeared to be a pierrot's outfit in shiny red artificial silk, with a floppy collar, flapping trouser legs and white fluffy pompons all down her flat chest. Both Tristram and Edward were immediately cheered by the sight – though for different reasons. Tristram, because he could laugh at her a little and stroke her slippery arm and duck under the formidable light in her eyes. While Edward was intrigued anew by the extraordinary personality which could pick on a costume so at odds with her own aura. His spirits rose still further at the thought of his father's reaction. Her thin elegant ankles, he noted, were clad in multi-coloured socks.

'How dazzling.'

'Exotic!'

'Oh, what? This. Yes. It always makes me feel gay.'

Fenella had become very mournful in her bedroom. It was not the fault of the room which had all kinds of pretty things in it, but she had suddenly lost her sense of identity. It had been quite clear to her that neither Tristram nor Edward had been able to see her. So she had put on her ludicrous pierrot's robe, knowing it would cure or kill. She had initially bought it to annoy her father.

Luckily, Edward's father, unlike her own, judged people on their conversation and Fenella's slow precision held his attention at once. Mr Aubrey liked to talk about works of art. He was essentially a businessman, imposing, in a bulldog sort of way, but his life was enriched by his intellectual wife, his clever son, and his solid collection of Hereké rugs, Chinese jades and various mostly eighteenth-century paintings.

'Ah,' he said to Fenella, 'you're prettier than your picture.'

Mrs Aubrey watched her son. In a way, she was a remote woman, almost cold, and her love for her only son was tempered by this quality, so it was more like admiration for a stranger.

After dinner, Fenella looked about the long dim drawing-room. The only lighting came from above the dark oil paintings which hung along the panelled walls. In one corner she discovered a much ornamented and inlaid baby grand piano; candlestick-holders still swung above the keys. Mr Aubrey saw where she was looking and brought candles from the dining-room table. Fenella in her weird trousers shimmered over to the embroidered stool and seated herself carefully.

'We so seldom use it now,' said Mrs Aubrey.

'I'm not good,' said Fenella in her deliberate way, so that it was obvious she spoke only the truth.

Edward liked Fenella's clear and yet lingering manner of playing. She had found a book of simple Beethoven tunes and she played them one after another, while the candlelight flickered in her eyes.

After a while, Mr and Mrs Aubrey went to bed, but Fenella, mesmerized by her music, played on and on. Edward, who had fallen into a reverie, lounged on the sofa. Tristram sat close beside him.

'Isn't she extraordinary?' he whispered. 'Quite unique. I don't believe she exists at all. However did we find such a girl?'

Edward smiled. 'Do you think she's ever been touched?' Tristram's soft hair brushed Edward's hard jaw. 'It was so odd when I kissed her.'

'You kissed her?'

'Chastely.'

'Her body's so hard.' Edward thought how he had not been able to paint it.

'She has a little moustache. Very delicate,' Tristram invented, knowing how the idea would catch Edward's imagination.

'A moustache. A delicate mustachio,' Edward mused. 'She has all that mass of black hair . . .'

Fenella's fingers stumbled over the keys and her eyes became confused by the white pompons down her front. She looked over to where Edward and Tristram huddled together on the sofa. For the first time she allowed herself to admit that their relationship was more than mere friendship. Yet the awareness did not shut her out from them. She remembered Tristram's kiss again; its eager warmth was not that of a woman-hater. Fenella sensed that Tristram would jump onto anyone's lap and purr for whoever stroked him. She shivered slightly.

'Why have you stopped playing?'

Tristram and Fenella started at the stern voice. Then Edward laughed and sprang to his feet. Tristram, who had been leaning against him, fell sideways.

'Can we go into the garden?' Fenella came slowly towards him and Edward took her hand. Together they walked over to the long french windows covered with a heavy curtain of golden damask. Edward pushed open the doors beyond. For a moment the material bound them together.

'Ugh. It's cold.' Tristram began to pile cushions round himself.

'You don't have to come out.'

'Oh,' Fenella called from the garden. 'There's such a moon.'

Edward joined her on the terrace, lit by the yellow globe of the harvest moon.

'I believe you're a lunatic,' he said.

'Oh, I am. I know I am. The moon has been drawing me out all evening.' She began to dance, weaving her way round the smooth stones. Her white pompons flashed. As she dipped and swayed, Edward had an idea for a painting. He became very excited, though his calm exterior didn't change. Oddly enough, just before he had the idea, he had been thinking satirical thoughts; he had been prepared to laugh at the strange spectacle and now it was all turned to feverish imagination. Although the darkness and the moon was his painting, he wished desperately for the daylight when he could stretch a white canvas.

'I'm going to bed,' he turned abruptly.

Fenella was wondering whether the moon was hot or cold; its rich colour was as warm as the sun, but the light that spread across the house and terrace was as cool as Edward's hand.

*

'Are you hot?'

'Of course we're hot. We're perspiring with heat.'

Edward was driving them into the countryside. They would picnic and shut their eyes against the sun.

'Even Fenella's ivory pallor has a tinge of pink.'

'We'll stop here then and swim.'

The serpentine country lane was just then passing a gate that opened into a sloping field. At the bottom shrubs and small trees sprouted in rich fertility. At their roots ran a stream.

'Nature is so sexual,' Edward noted in an aesthetic tone of voice. He unhooked the gate carefully. 'You take the hamper, Tristram.'

'The ever-willing donkey.'

Looking over the smooth-rounded field, Fenella realized she had quite forgotten to bring a bathing costume. No one had mentioned it and she wasn't the sort of girl who carried a bikini in her hand-bag. She had despised the swimming set in Italy. Only the poor or stupid sat in the sun. Besides, her skin was not suited to sunbathing and she had felt no sympathy for the coastal regions. But the thought of cool woodland water – for she was really very hot – tempted her. She considered her underclothes but they seemed quite inappropriate to the setting.

'I'll race you down the hill,' cried Tristram.

'No, there's champagne.'

'Champagne. Oh. Oh.' Tristram became a buffoon. 'I'll crawl down the hill and lick up the dribbles.'

Fenella felt how ridiculous she was to spoil such a perfect occasion with the sort of preoccupations she despised in other girls.

Edward loved swimming. Although he was thin with no solid covering of adult flesh yet, he never felt the cold. He often swam in this particular part of the river, but he had never brought Tristram or anyone else there before.

'There are willows!' Fenella sat on the bank and undid her sandals. The water was so clear that she could see flashing fishes in the bottom and pebbles shining like jewels beneath them. Delicate fronds of green wound through one or two but mostly the water was clear. She quoted to herself

Milton's Sabrina 'Under the glassy, cool, translucent wave . . .'

'Is it really deep enough to swim?' she asked wonderingly. But Edward had walked away upstream.

'If it's deep, it's cold,' Tristram behind her, still catching sun from the field, shivered theatrically. 'I shall lie down among the buttercups.'

So it was quite simple for Fenella. She slipped off her clothes and stepped down into the water. It was icy. She folded her arms across her bosom and stopped the cry rising to her lips.

Tristram watched her from behind the trees. Her figure was really quite strange, he thought, although he saw it mostly from the back; that long thin torso broadening out unexpectedly to low feminine buttocks and then drawing in again to straight boyish legs. He would like to see her front view when she got out although he could already imagine the scarcely moulded breasts and the flat tummy between the wide angle of her hips. In a way she was quite ungainly, with none of the fluid lines of a Cherry or the other be-jeaned girls in the art school. Idly, Tristram wondered whether she attracted him, and then, since the sun was throwing purple spots against his eyelids, he let them close gratefully.

Edward came swimming down the river. He was like a long white warhead, sleek and shiny, cutting the water with decisive strokes. He, too, had seen Fenella get into the water, but from a distance, so that she had looked like a wood sprite, or even the Sabrina she had imagined. He didn't really want to see her closer, so he was glad when she began to swim with a wide breast stroke in the other direction. But she couldn't bear the cold for long. Her fingers began to turn a banana yellow.

'Tristram,' she called. 'Throw me a towel.' But Tristram, away through the trees in some sunny dream, didn't hear her.

Teeth chattering, she stood up in the waist-deep water. Edward, twenty yards away, took pity on her. Fenella watched as he shot out of the water and in a shower of spray, glittering like the glass of the chandelier he had bought in Florence, bounded up the bank, through the greenery and out into the meadow. His white body with its hard glistening surface did not surprise her at all, but she had not expected the thick fuzz of blond hair which half disguised his nudity. Her teeth stopped chattering and she was quite surprised when a scarlet towel came flying towards her. Forgetting her own nakedness she waded slowly out and only remembered to wind the thick material about her when she saw Edward advancing, toga-clad, towards her. He couldn't avoid seeing her undisguised body which was made to look more startlingly uncovered by her mane of long black hair.

Later, Fenella blushed at the scene but at the time it seemed quite natural. She felt that their relationship did not depend on her body. Edward's reaction was far more straightforwardly male. A nude female body, he found rather to his own surprise, for he had no high opinion of woman's sexuality, excited him. It was a new experience. Fenella's white skin, dark hard nipples which astonished him by their size in proportion to her almost flat breasts, and black triangle of hair echoing the wider triangle of her hips, made him curious and excited.

Tristram, with a feminine sense of order, had made an encampment among the buttercups and daisies. He sat cross-legged in his skin-tight jeans and prodded ineffectually at the champagne cork. Edward who would normally have been irritated by his inefficiency was still concentrating on his new emotions. He tugged the folds of the thick towel closer round his hips, for though he would have joked at his body's vulgarity if it had been Tristram and he together, a woman was different. He glanced at her as, also cross-legged, she held out a glass hopefully to Tristram; of course she could have been any naked woman. And yet it was an astonishing thing to discover this fully fledged heterosexual instinct. Luckily he felt no animosity towards its object as he had sometimes imagined might be the case, but rather an intellectual curiosity. The night before, he had read Donne's poem, 'Love's Progress', and the comparison between a woman's body and a map of the world had seemed gloriously denigrating to the woman, but perhaps it would not seem so now

> ... but yet thine eye
> Some Island moles may scattered there descry;
> And sailing towards her India, in that way
> Shall at her fair Atlantic Navel stay;

'Chuck us a pie, Fenella.'

The satisfying of healthy hunger swept out poetry. Suddenly they all three fell onto pies and salads and custard tartlets as if they had only just realized they were more than ornaments.

'I didn't know I was so hungry,' gasped Fenella, a trifle shamefacedly. She jerked her towel under her armpits in a businesslike manner.

'Aha,' Edward laughed wildly. The food and the sun and the champagne had made the sweat start on his forehead. 'It's the swimming.'

Of the three Tristram looked most composed. But then he hadn't swum and he wasn't wrapped in a towel with nothing underneath, and he hadn't been up since the dew was wet on the ground. 'I adore orgies like this. It makes me feel the English countryside has been gravely misrepresented.' Tristram fell back against the grass. 'All those romantic doodaings about "Where the bee sucks there suck I".'

'But that's fantastically orgiastic!' cried Fenella and she too fell languidly backwards. The energy of eating had quite exhausted them all.

'Orgiastic,' repeated Edward, rolling the syllables round his mouth. 'That's the most superb word.'

It struck Tristram that it could be more than a word on this occasion and looking at the glazed faces of Edward and Fenella he wondered if he had implanted the idea in them also. Slowly he rubbed his hand round his smooth chest. He could do no more, for Edward had always to signal the advance. Besides it was so hot.

But suddenly they were all quiet and Fenella, unexpectedly, went to sleep; her mouth parted in a reasonably graceful manner and her head nodded down, back and down again where it hung in a dead-looking manner. And then

Edward, who didn't really approve of inactivity, decided that he would gather pebbles from the stream. Tristram followed him with a glass.

*

The gleaming stones cascaded round Fenella's face and flattened flowers and grass on either side.

'Oh,' she came to with a small start.

Tristram laughed. He liked waking people up. He waggled his hands above his head. 'What am I? Guess what I am?'

'I don't know,' Fenella was still dazed.

'Can't you see my long ears and hear my braying voice? Hee haw. Hee haw!'

Edward was clothed again and he held Fenella's dress over his arm. The picnic hamper was already neatly packed and the rugs folded.

'Bottom! I'm Bottom!'

'I want to catch the last of the sun in my studio,' said Edward.

Tristram began to run up the hill towards the car.

'Death is . . .' he shouted.

'The privilege of . . .' Edward followed. He had changed back into his white trousers and shirt. They dazzled Fenella as she watched, and she rubbed her face.

'Human Nature!' She sat up and pulled on her dress which Edward had laid out like a body.

'Life without it . . .' Edward and Tristram were climbing the gate now, swinging over the hamper, dropping the rug, and levelling controlled punches at each other's stomachs.

Fenella stood up and the bushy clover tickled her bare feet as she swished towards them.

'. . . Were not worth our taking!' she cried, and clapped the soles of her sandals together, as if they were cymbals.

3

The sunny days grew shorter. Yet the pattern of their relationship remained the same. Fenella and Tristram returned to London as autumn began to haunt the parks with the smell of burning leaves and it seemed as if the countryside had cast them into a net that was gilded with sunlight but ultimately paralysing. Tristram only moved towards Fenella as Edward's jester; Fenella could neither reject nor accept his advances because her face was really turned to Edward, and Edward, the strong side of Edward was turned towards his painting. In a way, therefore, it was a relief to be back in London, however nostalgic the atmosphere.

Fenella occupied herself before the term by finding a flat. She enjoyed it, discovering in herself all the instinct of a home-maker. Tristram did not take long to discover this. At first Fenella only tolerated him. But his pretty languorous form added a glow to her drawing-room rug, and she soon began to take pleasure in his uninvited, unannounced visits. Besides, trained by his widowed mother, he was so appreciative, so ready to oblige, and indeed so genuinely helpful in the various handyman jobs like fixing door-knobs or mending washers, which did not appeal to her. Consequently, Edward's continued absence in the country, far from making a break in their relationship, gave them the opportunity to develop a new understanding.

Away from the master's aura, Tristram's attitude underwent a radical change. Gone was his insinuating manner; gone the excessive fawning, the romantic poseur. In its place was a charming brotherly figure. Fenella had never known a man in quite such relaxed circumstances before. He usually arrived around six, when it was just beginning to grow dark. He came with the cuckoo's instinct, looking for another's nest, but he was nevertheless continually surprised by the comfort of the down. That hard angular girl, who seemed so full of challenges, was curiously absent in this gentle dove.

'Lend me a match, Tristram.' Fenella lit a candle so they could watch the night quietly descending.

He confided in her his ambitions and soon described the sensuous generosity of Cherry.

'You wouldn't stand her for a minute, Fenella. She's so absolutely unresponsive, so perfectly negative – except in one area, that is.'

The knowledge of Cherry's existence further blurred Fenella's concept of the relationship between Tristram and Edward. She was even less likely to set them apart with the label 'homosexual'. She thought vaguely of the boyish traditions of English public school. Now they were both growing up.

'And does Maggie approve?'

The jealousy of Tristram's literally green-eyed mother was a constant source of badinage. 'If she's the devil, you're the deep blue sea.'

Fenella knew this already, and they laughed conspiratorially. Somehow discovering that Fenella was a year or two older than Tristram, Maggie had convinced herself that her darling boy was being vilely used. Apparently her jealousy was more than merely sexual and she sensed in Fenella's calm and striking manner a rival of stature.

'Such a flat-faced girl, darling,' Tristram imitated his mother.

'Flat-chested certainly.'

'Such a clever way of speaking. So careful to pick just the right words. Really, one waits on tenterhooks.' Tristram's falsetto rose to a squeak.

'Most certainly clever.'

'Almost a genius.'

'Edward will be in London soon.' Fenella reverted to her normal voice.

*

In fact, Edward had already been in London for some time. A friend of his father's had offered him one of the studios in

Swinburne Studios, off the King's Road. Its roof was made entirely of glass. He had been making it ready with canvases, paints, brushes, plus a campbed, a chaise longue, a saucepan, one plate, one knife, one fork, one spoon, a kettle and a primus stove.

Fenella first saw him a week later, when he walked into the middle of a class on frescoes of the eighteenth century. The class gasped, not only at his appearance which was strikingly correct in a dark suit and waistcoat set off by a purple silk handkerchief, but also at the daring of appearing half an hour late in front of a notoriously punctilious lecturer. He himself seemed totally unaware of the stir he had caused and became quickly taken up by the subject under discussion. Almost at once, by his questions and occasional longer statements, it became clear that he knew more than anyone else there, including their lecturer.

Fenella smiled to herself. She supposed it made her an intellectual snob but she did love clever people.

When the class was over, Edward who had previously shown no signs of noticing her presence, walked at her side and, fired with enthusiasm at the discussion, continued talking energetically. Walking and talking they crossed through Regent's Park and by the skeleton structure of the zoo's aviary without conscious effort. It was like their first meeting in Florence all over again. Everything seemed possible.

Eventually they arrived at Fenella's flat. It had grown dark and as she looked upwards she saw lights at her window. There could be no doubt who had switched them on.

'Tristram's there,' she said gloomily. She could not blame him for behaving in a manner she had herself accepted, if not encouraged; nevertheless, she was overwhelmed by a fierce wave of irritation.

'Oh, where?' Edward looked round vaguely, as if Tristram might spring from the pavement.

'In my flat.'

'Ah. Dear boy. Heavens, I'm cold.' Edward rubbed his bony white fingers energetically. 'We must have walked for miles. So, Tristram's keeping your place warm. He's good at that sort of thing.'

'Oh, no. I mean.' Fenella blushed. She didn't know how much to understand from Edward's remark and therefore how much to deny. Immediately they were back in the old uneasy state of excitement.

'Let's go up then.' Edward was suddenly impatient. 'I don't suppose you have any whisky?'

'Oh, yes.' Fenella unlocked the door and thought of her father.

Edward now only saw her as the owner of a warmly lit flat and a bottle of whisky. However, as they climbed the steep gloomy staircase, she found a sense of anticipation growing. At least the triumvirate would be against her own design. She was the chatelaine.

Edward examined Fenella's small drawing-room before acknowledging Tristram's presence by a quick nod. He picked up a small china shepherdess from the mantelpiece.

'Fenella collects shepherdesses.' Tristram stood up and turned off the gramophone. He had been listening to *Parsifal*.

'Working hard?' Edward had not spoken ironically, but Tristram turned suspiciously. Fenella went to the kitchen for some glasses.

'Sketches of models mostly. At the school.'

'Really? Female?' Edward began to look interested. He was still annoyed by his failure to give Fenella more body than a fur coat.

'Female. Male. Anything on two legs.'

'Nude?'

'Oh, yes.'

'Do you think you could get me into those classes?'

Tristram revived. 'Or there's always Cherry.'

'A girl?'

'A very juicy fruit.'

'You have a girl friend?' Edward sounded surprised, curious, impressed.

'She's not as good a cook as Fenella.'

'Do you like having a girl friend?'

'Variety is the spice.' Tristram began to smile but stopped at Edward's serious eagerness. 'Only two varieties, unfortunately.'

'I want to know about the female body.'

Tristram became depressed. He could not reconcile this cold-blooded seeking of information with a picture of them falling gaily, lusting onto the tiger skin.

'I want to feel the texture of a woman's skin.' Edward smoothed one hand over the other.

'There's only one way.' Tristran cut his losses bravely. 'Life-class would be a beginning.'

*

In fact he only joined Tristram once. Again his pinstriped suit caused a minor sensation. He sat at the back with Tristram, who introduced him to Cherry. Edward stared at her with curiosity and some disappointment, but she did not seem able to see him at all, as if his formality made him invisible. He was very excited by this new experience, anticipating continually the arrival of the model.

'Oh, God,' said Tristram after many false alarms. 'It's dear Dorothy.'

Dorothy was fat and grey and tired and old. She slouched ungracefully on a wooden chair with her legs apart. She had the unhealthy loose-skinned look of an elephant in captivity. Everyone began to draw. Dorothy humped her back further and half shut her eyes. But after a few minutes, giving a spiteful look to her audience, as if she knew they would just have secured their angle, she got up again and, bending lumpishly, adjusted a fan heater so it blew directly up to her scant pubic hair. She then retired back to the chair and went into a doze.

Edward drew a huge thigh on the paper and then, reconsidering, put some toes on the end. All her limbs seemed interchangeable, like those plastic beings conjurors make by twisting balloons. He drew another loop for an arm. She was like a balloon lady three days after the party when the air was starting to seep away and the rubber was going slack and wrinkly. Even a little dusty. Horrid. Horrid. Nothing at all to do with Fenella's absent body. Stretched and white under her fur coat. Rather like a pristine canvas. Reverting to earlier impressions, Edward drew an elephant's trunk above the balloon arms.

Tristram looked over his shoulder; he laughed merrily. Edward, sounding petulant, retaliated. 'It isn't funny. Women shouldn't be funny. It's disgusting. Meaningless. She should be put down.'

Tristram laughed again. 'You don't know anything about women.'

'Thank God.'

'This is a drawing lesson, not a study in lovely ladies.'

'You can't separate method from matter. A slovenly painting.' Edward was fierce.

'You should be a fashion photographer.'

'Buffoon.'

'No ugliness?'

'Meaningless slovenly lady. That's not ugliness. No power.'

'Toulouse Lautrec?'

'I can paint pain.'

'How do you know she's not suffering?'

'Because she's a balloon.'

'With an elephant's trunk.'

'Think of Simone Martini. Filippo Lippi.'

'Monica Vitti,' added Tristram irrelevantly.

'They never wasted their time painting silly people. Her bottom's like the haunches of a Uccello horse.'

'Every human being has the same soul.'

'Modern crap.' Edward's voice was getting louder. Some of the other students began to look. Edward scrumpled up his piece of paper and threw it onto the floor. 'I will not contaminate myself with second class people.'

Tristram, enjoying such pomposity, shepherded him carefully to the door.

Despite this unfortunate experience, Edward became fascinated by the Nude. He bought books on the subject, looked at his own body and thought about others. Unfortunately, for it made research more difficult, his interest still centred on the female form.

He did not see much of Tristram who consoled himself

with Cherry. Tristram spent long desultory evenings among her purplish cushions, smoking grass. In fact, they hardly needed the drug, for they shared a natural ability to float, but it gave them a reason to invite others. The secret society feeling, as they passed the joint in semi-darkness or quoted disconnected words of poetry or philosophy, was Tristram's answer to Edward and Fenella's growing friendship. The cuckoo had given place to the eagle in the nest. Now the cuckoo needed another home. Tristram had always been dependent. His mother had trained him to it, for the suddenness of her husband's death had left everything in her hands to distribute as she pleased. Perhaps his dependence was a case of *sauve qui peut*.

But Maggie was never mean, and since none of the other students had money, Tristram became the generous provider of hash. He would wander off with a purposeful air to Wardour Street and Frith Street and the pizza houses at Leicester Square. He seldom came back empty-handed. He had never had a very strong sense of what was legal or what was dangerous.

Edward had decided that he could learn from Fenella the Secret of Woman in a cultured painless way. He still didn't touch her or flirt in any ordinary sense, but insisted with constant visits to her flat. They sat in her small kitchen, usually candlelit, and talked about life. Florence was re-created without Tristram.

One afternoon after a class together they were walking to Fenella's flat through Regent's Park as they often had since that first meeting. As usual, they passed the entrance to the zoo but this time, since it was the middle of a bright sunny afternoon, Edward stopped decisively.

'I haven't been in since I was a child.'

'Ah,' replied Fenella as if she understood a lot from his words. And they turned together to the pay box.

'I used to think zoos cruel,' said Fenella, as they ventured out into the expanse of grey concrete and then stood undecided beside a signpost.

'You can't feel sorry for snakes,' Edward led the way to the reptile-house.

'I hated circuses more. Because the animals had to perform as well as live in captivity.'

'At least the reptile-house will be warm,' Edward shivered. The rising mounds of concrete buildings seemed to be cutting out the bright sun. He wondered whether it had been such a good idea to come in after all. Fenella's face had taken on a pinched colourless look and she was shrinking into her large fur coat. 'But you wear a fur coat.'

'I don't object to death. Just captivity.'

Edward cheered up again. It was an interesting line of discussion.

'You must be very Christian.'

'Or just sentimental.' Fenella smiled.

'No. You're right. Death isn't degrading.'

'Life without it were not worth our taking.' Fenella pirouetted a little. 'I didn't say I still think zoos cruel.'

'But you still find them depressing.' By this time they had reached the snakes, set like magic lantern slides in the walls of a dimly lit building.

'Of course, you're right,' said Fenella, looking round and visibly relaxing in the dark warmth. 'Snakes aren't animals. Not animals like us anyway. It's the reflection that really depresses me.'

'Monkeys are usually the most popular captives.'

'That's because we're all narcissistic.'

'And masochistic.'

'Quite. I collected monkeys once.'

'Before you turned to shepherdesses.'

'And became a romantic. What could be less like monkeys than delicate shepherdesses.'

'What did you do with your monkeys?'

'I sold them to buy the shepherdesses. I got quite a lot of money. I have a good eye, you know.'

Edward laughed. He pointed. He had led them to the largest of the monkey enclosures. 'How wicked. To sell away your past.'

Fenella stared seriously at the label fixed to the wire meshing and then read out aloud. 'Hylobates Lar inhabitant of the islands of the Indian Archipelago.'

'How humiliating for them.' But she hardly looked at the actual animals who tumbled about the bars happily unaware of their humiliation. 'It's the pairs that I hate most of all. The married couples, locked up in endless uxoriousness.'

'In the public gaze.'

'Yes. That's terrible. I would hate that.'

'You?' Edward's face sharpened, 'But marriage is made for the public eye. Otherwise there's no point in it at all.'

'I don't think so.' An obstinate look came over Fenella's face. This spurred on Edward who felt the warmth of excitement, of the chase, of the chase after her mind.

'Don't you believe in marriage then? Two people sharing a life? Silver bells and pink confetti.'

Fenella became inwardly confused, although she appeared as composed as ever. He seemed to be mocking her and if that were so, she didn't want to answer him, but if he would be serious, she would be too.

'You're asking so many questions at once. Marriage is not just a question of confinement.'

'But you said it was.'

'Nor of confetti. You see, I believe.'

'Yes. What do you believe?'

Fenella stopped warily and glanced out of the corner of her eyes in an untypical manner.

'I'm a romantic.'

'That's evading the issue.'

Of course it was. She knew that. But now she felt definitely uncooperative. Why should she make all the running while he waited to pounce on any idiocies she might in passing utter? She felt he was serious enough underneath, because he never persevered with a subject that did not interest him. But he must prove it. In silence, she pressed her face to the monkey-cage.

Edward understood her motives for going no further.

'I believe in marriage,' he stated firmly.

'*You* do?' Immediately Fenella turned back to him and she brushed her hair back in a pleased, surprised sort of way. 'You do.'

'Two people encouraging the best from each other.'

'Satisfying the human animal to set free the spirit.'

'Ah.' Edward came close to her and dug his hand into her furry pocket. He felt her cold fingers clutch at his like some underwater creature. He squeezed them tight and looked at her face for signs of pain. 'I didn't know you had an animal nature.'

'You're hurting me,' Fenella stared calmly back at him. She saw he was testing her. Edward gripped harder. He imagined her white skin marked red. 'Most people get married out of boredom.'

'Ah.' Fenella looked disdainful, as if she didn't know what boredom was. She would not give Edward the pleasure of reducing the conversation. Once more she waited. They looked at each other coldly. He was hurting her so much she was afraid tears would come into her eyes.

'I suppose I shouldn't torture you.' Edward brought both their hands out of her pocket and looked at their interlocked rigidity. Fenella turned her head away. Edward smiled. 'If I let go of your fingers, will you marry me?'

Fenella didn't answer.

'There I have anyway.' Slowly he opened his hand. Her fingers stayed crushed together. Fenella took them back and began to rub them gently against her coat.

'Well,' said Edward.

'I'm so cold,' said Fenella vaguely.

'Aren't you going to answer me?'

'Oh. No. I didn't think you were serious.'

'But I am. Really.' Edward pressed forward.

Fenella swayed back but turned to face him. 'You haven't even kissed me!' she cried suddenly.

Edward began to laugh. 'But I don't know how to.'

'You can't not know how. I mean really stupid people do it all the time. In books, film, theatre.' She began to laugh too. Edward was laughing harder.

'It's just that I've never kissed a girl before.'

Fenella rose to the occasion. 'I don't expect it's any different. I don't wear lipstick or anything.'

'Shall I try.' Edward tried to purse his mouth but kept breaking into laughter.

45

'Oh. No.' Fenella started back in mock horror, '*Pas devant. Pas devant.*'

'*Devant*? What? There's no one here.'

'The monkeys. Oh, please. The monkeys.'

And then they both grew serious again. Edward said :

'But I do mean to marry you.'

Fenella said :

'Of course I'm in love with you.'

'Yes.' Edward made no sign that this statement gave him any pleasure, but this was shocking hypocrisy for inwardly he was triumphant. He put his hands heavily on her shoulders and pushed his firm red lips against hers. The two mouths stayed statuesquely together and then Fenella's heart jerked suddenly, and she jumped back defensively.

'There. That was quite easy.'

Edward kept one arm on her shoulder. The whole scene had fulfilled his highest expectations. More than that, their present pose – a courting couple in front of a caged couple of monkeys appeared to him as a superb idea for a painting.

It didn't occur to him he should also declare his love for Fenella. It seemed right to him that the man's offer of marriage should be returned by the woman's offer of love.

4

Fenella told no one that she and Edward were planning to get married. But Edward told Tristram. Who assumed he was joking.

'But you haven't even kissed her!' he cried gaily.

Edward meditated on this.

'I've seen her naked.'

'Whenever?'

'When she was swimming in the river.'

'I saw her then too.'

'Oh, did you? What did you think?' Edward leant forward interestedly.

'Oh, I don't know.' Tristram shifted uncomfortably. He suddenly suspected Edward had not been joking. Or if he was, he intended to carry it through. 'I only saw her from behind actually. I suppose she was quite feminine.'

'You don't seem very excited. At my great news.'

'It's awfully sudden. I only saw Fenella this morning and she ... she ...' Tristram tried to imagine how Fenella's calm exterior should have changed to meet the occasion and, his imagination failing him, merely ended lamely, 'She wasn't wearing a ring.'

'A ring?' Edward looked surprised.

'An engagement ring.'

'Do you think she'd want one?'

'Most girls do.' Tristram tried to console himself. At least Edward was eager to share this new relationship – whether it was real or imaginary. 'Yes. You must get a ring. It's *de rigueur.*'

Edward jumped up and grabbed his coat.

'Let's go then.'

'Now?'

'Ring first. Kisses after.'

'Don't you think you should buy it with her?' Tristram

still hesitated a trifle coyly. Edward pushed his shoulder encouragingly.

'But Fenella so admires your taste.'

'I do have a friend in the Burlington Arcade.'

'And roast beef in Simpson's to follow!' They hadn't got on so well in ages. Arm in arm they swept from the studio.

*

Fenella was trying to work in her small sitting-room. Although it was the afternoon, she had taken off her clothes and instead of a dressing-gown had wrapped herself in a large paisley shawl. Its thick black fringe trailed along her straight white calves. She lay on the rug with her books and papers in front of her and the room became dark. Giving up any attempt at work, she fell into a trance-like state. She supposed it might seem ridiculous to ordinary people (whom she despised) that Edward had asked her to marry him with only a single kiss being exchanged. Ordinary people might not take their contract seriously; might suspect Edward was making fun of her. It was true that one never quite trusted him. She wrapped her shawl closer and turned on another bar of the electric fire whose red coils were the only light in the room. Nearly a week had passed since their conversation in the zoo, and Edward had stayed away.

There was a loud noise in the street below. Laughing. Shouting. She recognized the voices of Edward and Tristram. The noise lessened and the doorbell rang. This was a surprise because Tristram still had a key. Fenella didn't stir and soon heard footsteps coming up the stairs.

Edward came through the door. Fenella looked round. Her face was warm and soft from the fire.

'Where's Tristram?'

Edward had become quiet and mysterious so that she wondered if she had dreamt those wine-loud voices below.

'I've been shopping,' Edward said. He stood above her in a calm accusing manner. 'Why are you all huddled up like that?'

Fenella returned to her remote mood.

'Am I?'

'Yes.' Edward sat down in an armchair with his legs stiffly

48

in front of him. 'I had brought you a present, but I'm not sure I'll give it to you when you look like this.'

'How do I look?'

'Supine. Flaccid. Unintelligent.'

Fenella lay prostrate.

'I had brought you a ring.'

Fenella began to debate her next attitude. She decided she would say challengingly, 'Have you been drinking?' Instead, she drew back the black tassels of the shawl across her white skin and laid it open on the floor.

Edward was looking away, extracting a leather box from his inner pocket. Now he balanced it on the outstretched tips of his fingers and in a semi-arabesque offered it to Fenella. His sense of the dramatic was immediately thrilled by her nakedness. He didn't think it at all forced or absurd.

'I bought you pearls around a sapphire.' He came towards her. 'Tears around your eyes.' He knelt down beside her. Fenella reached out a languid hand to receive the ring and the moment was nearly spoiled for it would not fit her third finger. It was too small. Fenella's hands, though giving the impression of slim elegance, were also broad-boned. Edward, with admirable *sangfroid*, quickly changed aim and slipped it on her little finger where it fitted perfectly. Fenella closed her eyes and waited for his kiss and his cold white body.

Edward was in a dilemma. Tristram waited outside the door. At any moment he might burst in. He looked at Fenella's naked breasts like inverted saucers with a cherry in the middle; he looked at her wide angular hips; at her long legs ending in her thin elegant feet. He bent down and kissed her mouth and her forehead and her shoulders and then her breasts. He began to feel hot in his military cloak. He moved away and undid the clasp. Fenella stirred, opened her eyes.

'I love my ring.'

There was a slight shuffling outside the door. A guilty look crossed Edward's face. At the same time Fenella's large eyes fixed on his hand still poised under his chin.

'I've never seen you with a ring before,' she said, still languidly.

'It's a mourning ring.' Edward was distracted. 'It has a lock of hair in the back.'

'Oh, how ghoulish !'

The shuffling outside the door increased.

'Did you buy it today?' inquired Fenella, apparently unhearing.

'A white lily in a bed of pansies!' Tristram stood nonchalantly at the door.

'I was paying homage.' Edward folded up his cloak neatly and placed it like a cushion on a chair.

'At the altar of beauty.'

Fenella refused to show that she was put out by Tristram's presence. But she was horribly shocked by the cool detachment of their appreciation when she still felt the warmth of Edward's lips on her face and breast. She was trapped into immobility by their remarks as if she was a statue or a painting.

'Modigliani?' suggested Edward.

'No. No. Too pallid.' There was a malignancy in Tristram's manner. All at once Fenella understood that she and Tristram were fighting for Edward.

'Cranach?'

'Oh, good. Yes. Though a touch more flesh.' Tristram waved his hand to illustrate Fenella's outline. 'Though never a Dorothy.'

'Sacrilege.' Edward wagged his finger.

Fenella sat up suddenly and pulled her shawl tight across her.

'You've got a ring too, Tristram !'

Tristram peered at his finger, as if surprised to see the heavy greenish stone.

'Ah, yes. Edward and I went shopping.' He made it sound as if they had nipped off to buy tin tacks in Woolworths.

'I see.' Fenella rose gracefully. 'Would you like a drink? You must be exhausted after an expedition like that.'

'Your ring suits you so well,' Tristram gushed.

'Or perhaps a cup of lemon tea. I have some superb Lapsang Souchong.'

'I see you wear your ring on your little finger.' Tristram tried to capture Fenella before she wafted from the room. 'I so love tear drops round the sapphire pool.'

'Perhaps you want to try it on?' Fenella stopped suddenly, finger extended, as if an idea had struck her.

'I would be honoured indeed.' Tristram took the ring and slid it easily onto his third finger.

Edward smiled at Fenella. 'Did you say Lapsang Souchong?'

Fenella, ignoring this, circled him intensely. 'You should try on Tristram's ring.'

Edward saw she was weaving some witch-like spell. *'Strega!'* he exclaimed, but obediently took the heavy stone.

'And now I'll be dressed in mourning!' Pouncing tigerishly, she pulled off Edward his black enamel, gold ornamented ring. Then fell back triumphant. They all three looked at each other.

Edward was delighted. He saw that Fenella had conquered. She was flushed, beautiful, panting slightly. 'Go on, Tristram. Bum off, old fellow. This lady and I want to talk.'

Fenella went into the kitchen and made the tea. When she reappeared, Tristram had left. Edward stood up politely, took the tray and said,

'Of course Tristram is a jester.'

Fenella didn't wish to gloat over her victory. 'Have you been painting lately?'

'Mourning suits you.'

Fenella considered the black and gold band. 'Death will too. I'll make a better death mask than you.' She allowed one of her longest pauses to elapse before adding, 'You tried the sapphire on him, of course.'

Edward took Fenella by the elbow. 'I've never been in to your bedroom.'

'I have a Martin Paradise over my bed.'

'Adam and Eve were the first of the bourgeoisie.'

'Except for their nudity.'

'Victorian Puritanism.'

Hand in hand they went into the small bedroom. It was

darkish with only one window shrouded in red silk curtains. Light from a street lamp struck across the bed. Fenella let her shawl drop and flung herself onto it. She posed there, with one arm behind her head and waited.

Edward stood by the bed and looked at her. He had been longing to ask her to remove her clothes for days. They were as far apart as ever from any physical contact. Fenella, who had worked herself up into a state of determined intellectual desire, closed her eyes. She felt as if she was buzzing there like a machine tethered on the bed, perhaps she would suddenly rebel against all this waiting about, cut engines, and fall into sleep. The idea quite appealed to her. But at last Edward moved. She felt the springs sink as he climbed onto the bed and leant over her face.

'Hell has always convinced me more,' he said, in a coldly critical voice.

Fenella opened her eyes. Still fully clothed, he was peering over her head at the engraving of Paradise.

'One can hardly countenance sex in heaven.'

Fenella was outraged. She clenched her fist and punched Edward in the face. Clutching his cheek with one hand, Edward swung back with the other. It was a purely reflex action which nevertheless caught Fenella's left breast.

She gasped but before he could apologize, if that was his intention, she was on him again, biting and scratching, punching and pulling his straight yellow hair. 'You beast! You monster! You cad!'

Edward, in his protective armour of a corduroy suit survived the onslaught passively for a little while. But then he received a particularly malignant bite on his nose. This was an indignity. Like a piston he shot out a steely arm and, in strong pincer grip, grasped Fenella's two flailing wrists. With his other hand he began to undress himself.

Fenella had lost all sense of dignity. Pinioned, half-sobbing, she tried at first to kick and since the necessary swivel of hips proved impossible she used her head like a hammer on Edward's shoulders. Her black snaky hair caught in his mouth and slashed across his teeth.

Edward gave up the attempt to take off his shirt. He lay

diagonally across Fenella's torso and while she was flattened pulled off his trousers.

'I hate you! I hate you!'

Edward wondered whether it was all a scheme to seduce him from admiration to passion. If so, it had succeeded. He tugged Fenella's head round by the hair and aligned his body on top of hers. Her legs came round him like white tentacles and her silly shrieked protests disappeared. Their two faces, white and staring, bobbed a few inches from each other. Edward was grunting an unconscious ugly sound. Fenella's sobbing turned into spasmodic heavings. The room seemed to grow dark.

When light returned they fell apart and lay silent. The bedclothes had fallen to the floor. Fenella, white face half covered with black hair, shivered, partly with shock, partly with cold. Yet on the whole, neither was disappointed by the experience. Fenella felt violently assaulted which fixed Edward more clearly in her mind as the demon conqueror.

Edward, flattered by Fenella's final submission, nevertheless felt that she had created the scene out of her mysterious strength of character. As a first venture into heterosexual love it had been less overwhelming than he expected, less different. He could still dominate; still remain uninvolved. He liked the way she didn't talk. He stroked her leg from hip to thigh and felt the fluff of her hair spring delicately under his fingers. He crouched over her and smoothed his hand round her shoulders, over her breasts, under her armpits, down her waist; rested for a moment in her navel and then continued pressing into her black curly hair and between her legs, down the inside of her thighs, held her knees briefly and ran down lightly to her thin white feet. 'Turn over.' He pushed gently. Her buttocks were the fleshiest part of her, heavy and full in his hands. A woman's buttocks. He lowered himself slowly across her and felt them depress softly under his chest like two cushions. It was too tempting to press the cushions apart and push down into her.

Afterwards, he turned her over again and parted the hair from her face. She looked at him passively, blue eyes wide open. Then she found her hand and touched his face.

Edward drew back slightly but nevertheless felt a tremendous surge of comradeship for her. She was girl, boy, man, woman.

'We'll get married tomorrow.' His voice was loud, authoritative. Fenella looked startled; she drew her legs together and felt for something to cover her body. Edward, seeing what she wanted, bent down energetically and pulled a blanket onto the bed. She folded it carefully under her chin.

Edward sat sideways on the bed. He waved a hand over her head.

'You're magnificent! We're getting married tomorrow.'

He reached for his trousers. Action taken, decision made, he felt gloriously freed for painting. As he left the room, Fenella stirred and whispered,

'I love you, Edward.'

He did not come back from the door but smiled, an enthusiastic but abstracted smile.

'Yes, Madonna.' But this appreciation hardly disguised his impatience to leave and in a moment Fenella heard his footsteps down the stairs.

'I love you. I love you. I love you.' She whispered as if to quieten herself, her ravished body.

*

Edward was standing under a very bright electric light bulb. It made his hair look silver grey and his skin a shining white. He was wearing a green short-sleeved aertex shirt which had been the uniform at his prep school. It had slashes of paint all down the tightly stretched front. Tristram crept into the studio and stared enviously. He had never seen such concentration. Edward was himself staring at his picture which was to be the monkeys and the courting couple, but was as yet only monkeys. As he held up a paint brush to measure the height of the cage, he looked exactly like Tristram's image of a painter. If he had taken up that pose himself, it would have been acting. Edward was so upright, so obsessed, so far from the ordinary world. Several minutes passed and then Tristram ran out of patience. He sighed heavily.

Edward swung round with a look of fury. Tristram cringed. Edward started towards him and then instead lunged at his table where a row of jam jars held his brushes. One. Two. Three. Four. He swept them off onto the floor where they crashed and rolled and shattered.

'I'm sorry. I ...' whined Tristram, who had become quite white himself.

'How dare you sneak in like a little worm?' Edward's veins were blue and snaky in his arms.

'Tish came to see me and I took her to Cherry ... she really wanted to see Fenella.'

Edward's scorn if anything increased. 'Spare me your social life.'

Tristram revived slightly, though his cringing-dog look didn't alter. At least the mention of Fenella didn't change Edward to sweetness and light.

'I was working. Working! A word that is peculiarly absent from your vocabulary!' Edward who had been hissing with anger began to shout. But something theatrical had entered his tone. He heard himself and stopped. Suddenly he was laughing. He threw a cloth over his painting and put an arm round Tristram.

'You don't know what you looked like. Did I really scare you that much?'

Tristram looked down at the glass-strewn floor.

'We'll find a broom then,' said Edward. 'What time is it?'

'Late.' Tristram was gradually recovering. He found a broom in the corner of the room and began to sweep in a graceful but ineffectual way. Edward took it from him and brushed briskly. 'There's some port under the sofa.'

Camaraderie seemed to be re-established. Tristram poured out large glasses of port and, smiling weakly, sat down on the sofa. Edward, who was covering the picture, turned swiftly.

'Oh. No. We'll go out in a moment.'

'It's late.'

'Not really. I feel like walking, talking. Or you talking. You talk to me.' He grasped Tristram's shoulders energetically and half shook him. 'What have you been doing?'

'Doing?'

'What? Where? Who?'

Tristram made a clown's face, 'I had lunch with you. And afterwards we bought three rings and went to Fenella's flat.' As Edward made no reaction to Fenella's name he paused and looked down at the pearl ring she had given him. It blinked girlishly. He would put it away somewhere before tomorrow.

'Yes. Yes. I know all that. But since? Since then?'

Tristram began again. 'Tish has come back. She seduced an attendant in the Uffizi from his duties, so her mother sounded the recall. I introduced her to Cherry.' He knew the confrontation would amuse Edward, but now he faltered.

'The little lamb and the luscious fruit. What absurdity. Tell me. Go on. But outside.' Edward flung open the door. An icy blast of midnight air blew in. Tristram drew back.

'It's cold.'

'Coward.'

'I want to go to bed.'

Edward laughed. 'I'll walk you home. You mustn't be pitiable, Tristram. We're young.'

Tristram hunched his shoulders, and then with sudden relief felt the port hit his stomach and rise warmly to his head. He took a breath and although the cold air met his teeth unpleasantly, he was able to cry out gaily,

'I'll race you. First to Sloane Square. One. Two. Three. Go!'

5

Edward had not installed a telephone in his studio. He did not wish his work to be interrupted by tiresome people. Besides, he enjoyed the ceremony of the call box; the walk, the wait while another put his case, the pips, the coin dropping slowly. He didn't like communication to be too easily available. Only trivial spirits lived by the telephone.

Fenella knew all this when the pips went in her ear early the next morning.

'Albert Bridge. 12 p.m.'

Clearly this was Edward making an assignment. Her sleepy brain reacted back into childhood, 'Gosh. Yes!'

Edward put down the phone immediately. He feared that after all the mystery of Fenella had been cracked at the same time as her virginity and he found the idea an uninspiring cliché. 'Gosh,' rang grotesquely in his ears. However, he had always been obsessively keen on advancing according to organized plans. In fact he had arranged the licence some time ago. Then it had been an objective act of the imagination. Now it was his marriage day. Perhaps he had misheard Fenella. A car as big and black as a hearse had passed making a vile noise just when she had spoken.

Fenella fluttered round her flat. No one who knew her publicly would ever have believed she could seem so young and flurried. She threw onto her bed all the clothes from her wardrobe; she picked up one garment, then another, held them against herself, looked in her mirror, dropped them all again. Finding none of them inspired her to a high enough plane, she found the *Oxford Book of English Verse* which she had won as a school essay prize. She placed it on the floor and going to her workbasket selected a long pin with a pearl head on it. She shut her eyes and stabbed at the book. The pages fell apart.

O tell her, brief is life but love is long,
And brief the sun of summer in the North,
And brief the moon of beauty in the South.

She sighed and then shivered. It was suddenly very cold in her nightdress. She looked out of the window and saw to her amazement large white snow flakes drifting past. She hadn't noticed it was cold enough for that. Her preoccupations over the last few days had all been inward. She had been too obsessed by the temperature of her emotions to notice the weather outside. But now she realized that snow was quite a natural phenomenon under the circumstances, for it was the week before Christmas. She was struck uneasily by the idea that her parents might be expecting her home. But she had heard nothing. Fenella tried hard on this day of all days to avoid thinking of her mother who had foolishly enslaved herself to an undeserving, unappreciative husband. Instead she chose a long red skirt from the pile of clothes and a tweed cape. Though hardly bridal, it had, she considered, a romantic air, suitable for a pair of lovers eloping to Gretna Green or the King's Road, Chelsea, via Albert Bridge. Down she went, into the street.

'Fenella. Fenella.'

'Oh heavens, Tish.'

'I tried to find you yesterday. There was this attendant in the Uffizi ... I'm so miserable. He looked after me like you did.'

'*I* did!' Fenella took in Tish's pink and cream face above her neatly buttoned coat and decided her misery was not insurmountable.

'He said I reminded him of that Titian nude. In bed with a dog.'

'There're two nudes with dogs. I'm getting married now.'

'The one where the dog's asleep. Not that other great fatty ...' Tish, who was not as idiotic as she sounded, stopped, astonished. 'What did you say?'

'Two nudes have dogs.'

'After that.'

'Edward and I are getting married.'

'What?'

'Now.' Fenella started to stride away, getting a good start on the amazed Tish. She bobbed along behind.

'That's wonderful. I mean, are you sure you mean married?'

'Come round tomorrow.' Fenella spoke over her shoulder.

Tish gave up the race. She stood and watched the tall, floating figure till it disappeared round a corner.

*

Maggie was cross with her son. You might have called it a lover's tiff. She felt spurned by him for another. 'Another' was generally divided between all those who had seen him the previous night, when she had been waiting for him to escort her to *Love's Lusts Lost*, a film she was particularly eager to see. In revenge she strode into his room at the unearthly time of ten and pulled all the bedclothes off his bed. This did not disturb him as much as she'd hoped, because he was still fully dressed. Since he was secure against chill draughts, she raised her voice.

'What slut were you with last night, I'd like to know?'

In fact this sort of demonstration never upset Tristram who liked to be reassured of the depth of her love. He turned onto his back and half-opened one eye, 'God! You look luscious!'

'Who? Who? Who?' Her voice sweetened against her will.

'Cherry. Tish.'

'I bought a cream gateau for our supper.'

'Fenella. Edward.'

'Soaked in Armagnac, decorated with angelica.'

Tristram rolled out of bed and crouched in front of his mother.

'Let's have it now. For breakfast!'

Maggie rose joyfully to the occasion. She gathered her pink frilly housecoat round her. 'With the strongest black coffee imaginable.'

'An early morning feast.'

'Not that early.'

The gateau had matured delightfully over night. They sat

59

formally in the elegant dining-room and ate it in great
mouthfuls.

'What do you see in Edward? Such a hard, cruel boy.'

Tristram waggled his finger. 'Jealousy. Jealousy.'

'And that girl. Such a cruel, hard girl.'

A blob of cream dripped to Maggie's chin. Tristram saw
it, but decided to say nothing. It gave an edge to her youthfully shining face, her bouncy hair.

'How would you like to attend a wedding?'

'I have a hat and a handkerchief wrapped ready with
lavender.'

'Between Edward and Fenella.'

'Edward and Fenella!'

'It might be a joke.'

'I should think so.'

'But worth a stroll to the Chelsea Town Hall.'

'It is snowing,' Maggie drew back a little.

'Like confetti. Charming.'

'But I'm not convinced.'

'Oh, but neither am I. That's the fun of it.'

Tristram licked his fingers and they both noticed with
equal surprise that the cake was gateau no more. Maggie
clapped her hand to her mouth.

'What a wasted opportunity. It could have been their wedding cake!'

'Fenella's too pure for things like that.'

*

The snow might look like confetti in the sky but it turned to
unwelcome mush on London's streets. Edward and Fenella
were irritated by it as they left the registry office. It con-
firmed the unsatisfactory nature of the whole experience.
Non-recognition had been their first set-back, for Edward,
sentinel on the bridge, peering through driving snow, had not
realized the voluminous lady approaching determinedly was
Fenella. And she had been so overcome by this that she had
passed his blank face, and continued on. Afterwards they
both turned and came together, but the damage was done.

They had walked silently to the registry office where they

were faced by pairs of young lovers with carnations in their buttonholes and powder blue hats. This was a conveyor belt of average human beings, something Edward had studied to avoid. His face became rigid with disapproval. It was left for Fenella to notice how the supporting phalanx who talked cheeringly round the bridal couples had also a role to play.

'Edward, we haven't any witnesses.'

'God is my witness.'

'We can't get', Fenella failed to pronounce the word 'married', 'unless we have witnesses.' A lady with a large cheerful smile appeared suddenly at their side.

'Aubrey? You're next. Have all your guests arrived?'

Edward came to life. An elderly man in a dark suit happened to be passing. He snatched his sleeve. 'Excuse me. I wonder if you could be my witness.'

The man looked stupidly, 'It's not my department.'

'A witness doesn't need a department.'

'I'm only passing through marriages.' Edward stared understandingly, but did not let go of his arm. 'I'm births and deaths.'

'Deaths.' Fenella watched uncomfortably. 'Oh, Edward.'

'Let's have a lavatory attendant then. Or a lift man.'

'I could simply write registrar under my name.' The man, seeing Fenella's miserable face, tried to be helpful. The smiling lady said, 'You need two. We usually use Ernie for people who've come without.'

'Who's Ernie?'

'He serves teas. But we write in caterer. We should think of starting now, if you haven't any guests . . .'

They went into the wedding-room; it was a big room with rows and rows of empty chairs. Edward and Fenella were placed in the middle of the front row. The smiling lady reappeared with Ernie who was rolling down his sleeves.

'Hello, hello, Ron,' said the births and deaths registrar to a man remarkably like him who was seated behind a desk. 'Don't worry I'm not looking for a job.'

'Witnesses to the left,' said Ron formally.

The smiling lady whispered to Fenella, 'That's so we know who they are.' Then she reached down below the desk and carefully pulled on a pale straw hat with red cherries bowing from the brim. She sat down beside Ron. The cherries tapped at her forehead.

Fenella suddenly felt near hysterical laughter. She nudged Edward. He looked at the cherries; they bobbled and danced.

'Do you Edward Tursoe Aubrey . . . ?' The cherries swung bravely.

They had done their best to save the occasion, Fenella thought as she came out of the hall. She looked down at her left hand where the mourning ring was still alone on her finger. Edward hadn't remembered to buy a wedding ring. He had taken off the black and gold band and replaced it. She rubbed its hard cold surface against her lips. Objects were so much more reliable than people.

Now again they were faced by the weather. Awful slushy muck around their feet. Romance was far away. Only one thing could increase Fenella's disillusion, and that was the sight of Tristram and his mother skipping along the pavement towards them.

'Oh, Edward !' she wailed.

Edward looked. The bobbing couple were still some way in the distance, their breakfast having required a siesta. There was time for evasive action.

'Taxi !'

They pushed each other into it hurriedly.

Down the road, Tristram and Maggie couldn't be sure. Had that been Edward and Fenella getting into a taxi? The snow and Fenella's swirling cape had obscured their view. They wandered arm in arm along a desolate King's Road, their interest in each other's reaction to such a bizarre paper-chase saving them from too great disappointment. For some time they stalwartly paraded in front of the Chelsea Registry Office, until finally the cold defeated the diminishing level of Armagnac in their bloodstream.

'Darling,' Maggie stopped and stamped her feet in best guardsman manner. 'This can't go on.'

'Joke over,' Tristram banged his hands fiercely together. 'But it might have been them.'

'Lunch?' suggested Maggie, closing the subject, for she

felt her son's whim, which was all she would call his obsession with Edward, amply indulged. Nevertheless their icy vigil had given her a special interest in Edward as something in which time and energy had been invested.

'The Ritz?' Tristram made one last throw.

*

Edward and Fenella sat behind their menus. The champagne was taking a long time to arrive. Eventually Edward's face reappeared.

'I shall have lobster soup and quail.'

Fenella, despite herself, looked sickened. Edward noticed it and also with disapproval that her black hair hung wetly round her face making dark patches on her blouse. She should be able to manage herself better than that.

Fenella wondered about the mechanics of an annulment. Edward tried to remember what had inspired him to this moment of emptiness.

'I shall just have a salad,' said Fenella.

'Just that? Just a salad?' Edward's coldness turned to hatred. He remembered he was a misogynist.

'I'm not very hungry.'

'With my quail I shall have baked stuffed aubergines and glazed carrots.'

Fenella thought that even Tristram would have been a welcome sight. She looked despairingly towards the open space of desert Ritz, and there, settling into a table ten yards away, were Edward's mother and father. As she stared harder, she wondered if her memory had deceived her, for Mr Aubrey looked much heavier than she remembered him in the summer and his wife seemed more imposing and even more elegant, with a fur hat and well-cut suit. For the first time she felt the dampness of her shoulders, and the draggled edge of her long skirt. She had dressed for the romance of snow on Albert Bridge, not a London restaurant. Nor her new parents-in-law. The very idea was amazing. She had not informed her own mother. The whole thing was a strange coincidence. Unless. She looked at Edward's severe face briefly. Unless he had arranged it.

'Your parents are sitting behind you.'

His expression changed totally. Although he hadn't planned a meeting, he wasn't really surprised, because it was his father who had introduced him to the charms of lunch at the Ritz. He turned round and waved cheerfully.

'Oh, look. Mother has a hat on. What a joke. Now where was it we saw that extraordinary woman with cherries over her brow?'

Fenella saw that he was affecting to have forgotten their marriage ceremony and declined to answer.

At last they were sighted. Mrs Aubrey blew a nebulous kiss at them and Mr Aubrey half-rose in his chair. But Edward wanted more. He dashed to their table. Fenella smiled her most mysterious smile and noted that they too had a champagne bottle on their table. Then Edward was back again.

'They say we must join them.'

'But of course.' Fenella rose with dignity, while Edward fussed with waiters and plates and bottles of champagne.

'So you're celebrating too.' Mrs Aubrey took Fenella's hand and pulled her down beside her. Fenella blushed scarlet. Desperately she looked for some clue from Edward. But his lack of sympathy had reversed now into remote admiration. He saw her with the appreciative eyes of his parents. Her black hair, almost dry now, curled richly round her face. She was a naiad, caught in the crumbling gilt of the Ritz. She would never hang onto him like some laundry bag on the back of a bathroom door.

'We could be drowning our sorrows.' Fenella decided discretion was the better part of valour.

'Not at your age.' Edward Aubrey senior lent forward, and Fenella noticed with more certainty that he looked fifteen years older than when she had last seen him.

Before, he had been attractive, in competition with his son, now he was merely old. Fenella felt distressed and puzzled. Why, if he'd been ill, had Edward said nothing?

'How are your studies?' Mr Aubrey asked.

'It's holidays,' said Fenella, who did not usually think in such restrictive terms.

'Perhaps you've been visiting that superior doctor?' Edward sat beside his father with the sort of attentive look that Fenella had earlier hoped for in vain.

'We came from him directly,' Mrs Aubrey fixed an unfocused look on the ornamental ceiling and then with sudden uncharacteristic vigour snatched her fur hat off her head. To Fenella and Edward's horror, they saw large tears forming in her eyes. Fenella's throat immediately closed up in sympathy, and Edward jumped up to find a place for the hat which his mother was waving hopelessly over the table.

'Yes.' Mr Aubrey, appearing to consider, produced a whimsical little smile which sat oddly on his new face. 'He didn't think I'd see much of next year.'

'Hence the champagne.' Mrs Aubrey gave a shrill laugh.

It was followed by a horrified silence. Fenella felt physically sick.

'Celebrating death. Celebrating death,' ran through her head. It was all she could do to stop herself saying it out loud.

Edward did not sit down. He looked very angry. He was thinking fiercely about his painting. It was not that the idea of his father's death did not appal him. He had known of his illness for some time and had seen in it no glories, only misery. But he feared the effect it might have on him. Whatever happened, he was not going to be diverted from his purpose in life, which was to paint. He stood looking over their heads and biting his lip.

Fenella thought, 'And this is my wedding day.' It seemed terrible and ironic. Like Edward, she did not consider this death of an elderly man anything to do with their Florentine password. Then she began to consider the idea of their marriage as a kind of rebirth. A phoenix from the ashes. She tried to see if this might have occurred to Edward, but his face looked flushed and uneasy. However, he did sit down.

'And why were you celebrating?' Mr Aubrey, with some return of his old manner, as if relieved by his revelation, banged their champagne bottle on the table.

'Because we were married today,' Edward spoke with gloomy dispassion. The whole affair seemed so irrelevant now that he saw no reason to withhold the information. So he was quite astonished by the effect it had on his father. Enthusiasm gave strength to his face and his voice.

'Jolly good. Jolly good. Married just like that. To the lovely Miss Frith-Peacock, I may presume.'

Edward looked and sounded as startled as he felt.

'I don't know any other girls.'

'Jolly good.'

This stranger's bonhomie grated horribly on Edward. He couldn't think why his father should suddenly become so stupid. The prospect of death should not have this ridiculous effect.

Fenella understood better. She saw that events had suddenly speeded up for Mr Aubrey, that the future could no longer exist as a delightful mystery to be dallied with and flirted over, but must be made present now. What more acceptable action could his son have taken, than to telescope the years and become married here and now? Again she saw a ray of hope. She glanced involuntarily at Mrs Aubrey. They caught each other's eyes. At least Fenella thought they had. But Mrs Aubrey's blue eyes were so blank and far-sighted that she could have been looking past her at the waiter. Then she said,

'Such a relief to be married.'

'What do you mean, mother?' Edward sounded inappropriately irritable, but really it was a relief for everyone to have someone using their normal tones.

'I married when I was eighteen and I had been desperate for three years. Quite desperate.'

An uncharacteristic idea occurred to Fenella. Was Mrs Aubrey glad to discover that Edward was no longer homosexual? Or did she even know about his relationship with Tristram? She recoiled from further thoughts.

Mrs Aubrey continued in a flat voice, 'Your father fell in love with my elder sister first because she'd married his best friend whose taste he so admired. Luckily I looked very similar.'

Now his wife seemed in control of herself again, Mr

Aubrey revived still further. As she had at intervals during the day, Fenella wondered if the earlier action, the forecast of death, was all imagination. But the best thing had happened, for they had all come alive now and Edward, freed once again from emotional pressure, was determined to argue the case for plastic canvas on Bakelite stretchers.

'But why plastic, why Bakelite particularly?' Mrs Aubrey pronounced each syllable with such significant distaste that Fenella began to smile. They seemed suddenly to have become a family party and the idea thrilled her. Her smile spread past their table to include the whole of the Ritz's ornamental dining-room. Suddenly everything seemed charming, light, gay; Fenella smiled.

*

'Oh, heavens, how perfect!' Maggie Brown glinted and gleamed. The champagne, which she had felt necessary to restore her after their snowy vigil, made her feel young and giggly. They had sat for at least half an hour at the pretty gilt tables just outside the Ritz dining-room. 'You are so wicked. Of course, you knew all along.'

'As a matter of fact, I didn't.' Tristram walked behind his mother. The huge dining-room made him feel vulnerable. He saw the Aubreys too, but for once he felt no excitement at the prospect of a confrontation. Instead he felt a ridiculous nostalgia for Cherry's gentle vacancy; his earlier desire to prod Edward and Fenella with a finger of fun had quite gone. 'It was just guesswork.'

'Our table's miles from them.' Maggie followed the waiter regretfully.

Tristram knew he couldn't eat. He lay back in his chair. 'That cake's filled me up.'

'Their wedding cake.'

'Too early.'

'For them.'

'I'm not hungry.' Tristram pulled himself up. He waved away the waiter. 'I'll cook for you.'

'But the waiters. How embarrassing. Oh, darling ... We

can't just skedaddle . . .' And Maggie waved, but she was not looking at the waiter.

*

Fenella wished that her large blue eyes were as shortsighted as they looked. The mistiness was all internal. She could see Tristram and his mother as clearly as she'd seen the Aubreys before. The smile disappeared into a calm lack of expression. She hoped non-recognition would be catching. Then Mrs Brown waved. Fenella turned her head sharply away. She looked at Edward, talking with that lively dogmatism she most admired. They had already reached coffee, if only they could be left alone a little longer to consolidate their gaiety. Sweat started in pearly drops on Fenella's forehead and nose.

'Are you feeling all right?' Mrs Aubrey looked more curious than concerned.

'Oh. Yes. Yes. I just felt faint for a moment.' Fenella saw a way out of the situation. 'Some fresh air. Perhaps.'

'What you need is a honeymoon.' Mr Aubrey's extraordinary joviality continued.

'Honeymoon?' Edward didn't try to suppress his horror; then he grimaced quite cheerfully. 'I don't think either of us believe the moon is made of honey.' But as he said it, he remembered his 'Lunatic' painting which had been inspired by Fenella's dance under the honey-coloured moon. 'We've had it already,' he said, meaning that magic night and with no thought of the exciting struggle on the bed. For sex always took second place to his imagination. Luckily no one took it vulgarly. His mother was recalling her own winter honeymoon in her father's country house deep in a Swedish forest. Even then the sadness of death had been present in the long dark days. She could not be surprised by her husband's death sentence.

Fenella, like Edward, was shocked by the idea of a honeymoon. For some reason it made her finally admit the cruelty of marrying without her own mother's knowledge. The selfishness.

'Oh dear,' she said mournfully.

'Never mind,' Mr Aubrey patted her hand sympathetically. Fenella was embarrassed by the gesture, for she was not the sort of person who attracted unrelated physical contact and he couldn't know the cause of her agitation. Besides, he was the one in need of consolation.

'Fresh air,' she said, as she had before, and jumped up from her seat.

*

Tristram prevailed.

'But angel, it's going to be so late by the time we get home.' He dragged Maggie along behind him, in a whining trail of protests. The waiters, undecided whether the Ritz was being insulted or Tristram thought himself insulted, scurried about in widening circles. Tristram, despite his preoccupation, was reminded of seagulls following a ship from the harbour till it reached the open sea. He wanted the open sea.

*

Fenella, also looking for the wide open spaces, hurried through the tables. She kept her too far-seeing eyes firmly to the ground. Only Maggie saw the inevitable collision and no one was paying any attention to her. They collided just beyond the dining-room by the pretty salon where Maggie and Tristram had drunk their champagne. They would have ignored anything short of actual physical contact. Fenella stepped back shakily.

'We're just going to leave,' she said, 'but I came ahead for some air.'

'It *is* hot,' said Maggie.

'We're on our way out.' Tristram took his mother's arm. 'You must apologize to Mr and Mrs Aubrey for us.'

'Oh, yes,' Fenella breathed, with a noticeable sigh of relief.

'It is hot,' said Maggie again.

'It's because it's so cold outside.' Fenella had become lightheaded with relief. She didn't know precisely why she didn't want the Browns to meet the Aubreys on her wedding day. It was a childish feeling like jumping the cracks in the pavement.

*

'You do look revived, Fenella.'

'Rosy.'

'As Aurora.' Edward was happy, loving, desirous. But Mr Aubrey's face had reverted to a puffy grey. It came close to Fenella and kissed her.

'We mustn't keep you.' Gunilla pulled her fur cloche onto her smooth head and looked ironically at her son's obvious impatience.

'I'm sorry,' said Fenella, as her father-in-law's face pulled back into focus. But he didn't answer. So there was nothing more to say as they went for a taxi.

*

Edward and Fenella started to run in the direction of her flat – for that, she had discovered, was the next stopping-point for their marriage. It had stopped snowing, but the pavements were still dangerously slippery. His military cloak rose and fell around his elbows and his ankles; her tweed cape flapped like wings around her shoulders; they looked huge and strange as they jumped the little puddles and lurched round the big ones. Christmas shoppers who crowded the pavements parted nervously and then looked after them and thought they were mad or drunk. It was true they had drunk a lot of champagne. After a few hundred yards, it became a race and they were panting and staggering in an ecstasy of exhaustion. It was an endurance test, painful, exciting. Fenella was on the point of slipping a thousand times and once or twice nearly gave in and let herself fall, for she pictured herself lying like a broken albatross for Edward to lift and revive. As she ran, she carried a picture of him rescuing her from the dark streets. For now it was nearly four o'clock and the lights were lit and Christmas trees shone from shop windows. They turned into Oxford Street, dazzling, even more crowded, noisy. Still, they ran on.

Edward was exhilarated, more than he had been for years. He knew he could fly if he held up his arms. At that moment he saw a red seventy-four bus crawling slowly in front of him. It was brightly lit and bursting with people. He felt a sudden desire to show off his god-like powers. With a great flying bound, he flung himself aboard.

But there behind was poor Fenella. Still earthbound. She saw him go and with a valiant effort threw out her hand to catch him or the rail. But the bus gave a sudden lurch and, missing by several inches, she fell in a bundle into the slimy gutter. Desperately she saw the scarlet bus gather speed and disappear round the corner, with Edward triumphantly aboard.

Fenella lay collapsed in the road and thought that this was just as she'd imagined. The albatross. But where was Edward, the comforter?

Edward stood on the boarding platform with his cloak flying in the wind. He half saw Fenella fall, but disregarded it at once. The run, the champagne, the snow, the events of the day had put him into a special world. The number seventy-four bus was like some Wagnerian chariot.

'Fares, please.'

The conductor, tired and bad-tempered in the week before Christmas, stood beside Edward. Normally he would have told him to 'Pass right down the bus', or even turned him off for jumping on when it was moving, but today he didn't have the energy.

'Fares, please,' he said again dismally, as Edward remained staring strangely into the luggage locker. With an effort he found some sort of focus. He put his hand into his pocket. But there was no money.

'I'll be back.' The conductor moved past him. Brought so rudely back to reality, Edward searched through his pockets, but it was true he had no money. He seldom rode on buses.

Found it now, have you?'

'I'm afraid I haven't.'

'I'm afraid you'll have to get off then.' The conductor began to work up to anger in preparation for a struggle.

But the bus had lost all its charm for Edward now. People with inquisitive faces were pressing round him.

'I'm getting off,' he cried. 'Don't worry!'

'Wait for the stop then.'

But Edward had stepped off as he spoke and, with excellent poetic justice, collapsed in the wet gutter which was strewn with sodden paper bags and squashy fruit.

*

Fenella wandered along the road. Once more the day had become farce and horror combined. She pictured the joy of her independent life, and security of her warm little flat, the cosy domesticity of an omelette for one. She might have overlooked Edward altogether, if he hadn't groaned just as she was passing. He had, in fact passed out for a moment as his head hit the curbstone and Fenella's dirty boots were more or less the first thing he saw.

She sat him up and brushed a plum and flattened grapes from his cloak. Despite these impedimenta his face was as beautiful and romantic as ever.

'I'd better get a taxi.'

'Oh. Ugh.' Edward groaned in agreement pathetically, for he saw that he could relax now and be looked after. Fenella didn't know it, but this wild expedition was beginning to follow a pattern very similar to Edward and Tristram's outings, in which the latter eventually turned nanny. But while Tristram had always enjoyed this temporary reversal of dominance, Fenella felt it distorting her nature. She had imagined him picking her out of the gutter.

6

1968

The flat was cold and neat; as if no one was living there. Fenella wandered barefooted out of her bedrooom and surveyed the unpromising February morning. Edward had slept at his studio again. The supper she had cooked for him still waited. Fenella hugged her breasts which were hard and tingling with cold. Her bed had not warmed up all night. Her limbs felt polished and stiff, like a marionette's. When Edward made love to her, they burned; she wondered if there was some comfortable warmth between such extremes. But Edward's passions could never be cosy, never conducted into regularity. Shivering slightly, she noticed a stamped envelope pushed under the door by one of her neighbours. She recognized her mother's writing. A guilty flush brightened her face.

My dearest Fenella,

Your friend Tristram (who I met by chance in the Tate – he was flirting with Blake) tells me that you were married to Edward a short time ago. Under normal circumstances, I would be unhappy that you kept it a secret from me. As it is, I can only be thankful. A bright start should not consort with a bad end. Your father and I have decided to part. Or to be more honest I have decided to leave him. I hadn't thought it would be necessary to make this kind of formal statement as I expected you would be here over Christmas. Of course you were otherwise occupied. The immediate purpose of this letter is to ask a favour. Can I come and stay with you? Does this sound bald? I expect it does but you're not silly enough to have any newly-wed's inhibitions and I need somewhere cheap in London. How strange to be starting a New Life at my age. Do phone during the day when Roger's out; he's using it all as an excuse to be particularly irritable.

Much love and congrats, Mummy.
(Loelia)

Fenella thought this a very odd letter. The flush died with the guilt. She accepted at once the news of the separation. In effect her parents' marriage hadn't existed for years. But it seemed Mummy (Loelia) had suddenly decided to be her contemporary instead of her mother, and this decision had made her utterly insensitive to her daughter's feelings. However inevitable, it was still infuriating that Tristram should be the one to tell her the news of their marriage. And what was he doing in the Tate? Not on his own initiative, certainly. Quite probably with Edward. Her mother was right about one thing. She and Edward were not conventional newly-weds. But that didn't mean a rejuvenated Loelia would be welcome. Why could she not have rebelled before her marriage, Fenella thought. And then was ashamed. Something must be done.

At least it gave her an impersonal excuse for going to find Edward at his studio.

*

Edward had painted till four a.m., slept four hours and then started again. At intervals he made very strong black coffee on his primus stove. He was haunted by the ironic and silly expressions on the faces of those monkeys in the zoo. He thought with disgust that in his picture they either looked like earnest professors or Disney cartoons. Irony implies self-mockery, which implies intelligence, or could it be merely a question of physiognomy? Perhaps if they were lighter grey in colour? Colour was as important to mood as shape. He stroked his palette reflectively with his brush.

Fenella tapped on the door. Edward who, when he was alone for some time and intently concentrated, heard all sorts of noises in his head, ignored it.

'Edward! Edward!' Fenella had moved from door to window.

Edward looked up and seeing her head framed in the wall made a mental note to find an appropriate piece of covering material. He then looked back at his challenging monkeys and forgot about her.

Fenella felt the despair of rejection battle with admiration.

The admiration, reinforced by the knowledge that he would be in no mood to discuss domestic arrangements, even if she did manage to get his attention, conquered. However, in order to establish her own drama, she shouted again at the top of her voice,

'My mother's left my father!'

As she watched a shadow of response pass over Edward's face, a voice whispered in her ear,

'I've got a ladder, lady.'

Fenella jumped violently and turned round to see a window-cleaner complete with ladder and bucket looking at her impassively. It was maddening how people with no dramas of their own butted into one's privacy. She gave him a withering look. But he didn't seem inclined to move.

'Want to get in, do you?'

'Certainly not.' What did the silly man think?

'This ladder's just the height.' He gestured at the window.

'That's my husband in there,' she explained with dignity.

The window-cleaner looked as if he was about to smile; lines appeared at the corner of his dark blue eyes and creases in his sun-burnt cheeks. Fenella was embarrassed to recognize his sudden attractive masculinity. She swung round and dashed off down the street. And although she heard the man calling after her, she would not look round.

Quite soon she slowed down again, for the problem of Loelia remained unsolved. If Edward wouldn't listen to her, then someone must be found who would. Someone with an ordinary practical mind who would respond with ordinary practical suggestions. Tish Skeffington-Smith. How right was the intuition that had made Tish her intimate. Tish had always been ordinary, but lately she had shown signs of becoming amazingly efficient and organized as well. Friends of friends of her parents had found her a job at a small but prosperous art gallery off Piccadilly, which showed twentieth-century oil paintings, but made its money out of nineteenth-century prints. Tish sat at a rather elegant desk, dressed in the sort of bright neat clothes that were outside Fenella's imagination. When asked what she actually did all day, her answer included a lot about the telephone and clients. Edward thought her even more unbearable now and no longer a joke. But Tish's capabilities surely extended to finding a home for her mother.

Unfortunately when she arrived at the gallery, the wide glass windows were blank except for a small notice. This was unforeseen betrayal. Worse, it left her with no choice but to take the road from Piccadilly to Knightsbridge, from the security of Tish as a confidante, to the sly excitement of Tristram. At least, she consoled herself, he would be interested.

But here again she was unlucky for she was met with the worst of all possibilities. Mrs Brown stood like Pluto at the door.

Maggie held out her arms with glee. Tristram had not yet returned from the night before and her attitude of waiting was beginning to sour. 'But my darling, come in! You're purple with cold. Just look at your nose!'

Fenella was always annoyed to be reminded of her appearance; she felt it reduced her. 'I've come to see Tristram.'

'Come in. Come in. You don't look as if you've had breakfast.'

Maggie no longer regarded Fenella as the enemy since she was married to Edward. In fact she was inclined to include her among the Weeping Women of the World after Tristram had dropped a few hints about Edward's unhusbandly treatment of her.

'I can't stay more than a moment.'

'No, of course not.' Maggie was soothing. 'And how is your husband's painting going?'

Fenella blushed at the sound of 'husband'. She seldom heard anyone use that astonishing word.

'Oh. He's working incredibly hard. He's doing a picture of two lovers in front of a monkey cage.' Despite her desire to end the tête-à-tête, she became enthusiastic. 'There's the cage and the concrete floor and behind the black hole where the monkeys live and in front the bright trees and a few passers-by ...' She tossed her head and waved her hands in the air. The description continued and became even more vivid. Maggie, who spent her life searching for enthusiasms, became infected too.

'How strange! How compelling! How clever! If only Tristram could borrow a little of that concentration.'

'Perhaps Edward's example might help,' suggested Fenella unselfishly.

'But Edward doesn't take him seriously.' Maggie looked at Fenella sadly, and Fenella looked back. Then Maggie was furious with herself, for this betrayal of her brilliant son.

'And what colour are the lovers' clothes?' She reverted to the painting hurriedly. 'Gay. I expect. Symbolizing hope and happiness. Young love. Newly-weds. A future.'

'I don't know.'

'You don't know! How can you not know? Not know the colours! A student of art like you.'

'I haven't seen the painting.' Fenella became sullen. Her flash of excitement died away, making her face look grey and ugly. Why hadn't she lied and told that stupid woman they weren't painted yet? She didn't merit the truth. And now she would draw all sorts of idiotic conclusions.

'You haven't seen the painting,' Maggie repeated. She was silenced. She remembered the foundations of her sympathy for Fenella. What a beast that man must be. Not even to let his own wife (if she was his wife – Maggie began to doubt it) see the picture. When she obviously worshipped him and his art. What a brute! Maggie put out a hand to Fenella.

But Fenella stood up stiffly. 'I must go now.'

'I wouldn't dream of stopping you.' Maggie let her go, because her mind was still revolving the idea of Edward. Disapproval at his self-centred determination mixed inevitably with admiration.

*

Tristram had just woken. He enjoyed this leisurely moment of the day. Lazily he looked at his watch and saw with a lessening of happiness that it was midday. Rude interrupters or at least unwelcome guilt could intrude at this hour, however near his own awakening. Edward, for example, would have done a navvy's work by now. It was annoying to be thinking about Edward so early in the day. He was just a friend.

Tristram flung up his arms and sighed. Naked, he saw. That meant he was with Cherry. He opened his eyes for the first time. Yes. There was the sweet girl, fast asleep in her dream of pot. She was so pale and thin, not really anyone's dream of a bedfellow. Not in daytime. It was incredible how faithful he stayed to her. The trouble was that her charming lack of life-style suited him perfectly. He drifted in and out of her bed. No questions asked. She was clever in a way and even talented, but her efforts were muffled in a blanket of sweet-smelling smoke. So very different from Maggie. Bothersome, compelling woman. Perhaps he should introduce her to the weed. Tristram began to drift into sleep again.

There was no lock on Cherry's door, either downstairs or up. Fenella mounted slowly, doubtfully, for although she knew about Cherry's flat from Tish, she had never visited before. She pushed open the bedroom door and looked carefully around. By now she was only slightly disappointed to see no Tristram, only great mounds of embroidered cushions and in one corner a thick Kelim carpet apparently draped over a low sofa. She wandered over and fingered the heavy patterns of yellow and mauve. The half-open shutters across the tall windows behind her cast streaks of lightness increasing the asymmetrical woven blocks. How she would love to create something like that!

Tristram opened his eyes to see a dark silhouette peering over him. He shifted on his mattress resignedly. That's just what you must expect after midday.

'Tristram!' The figure jerked upright with what seemed to Tristram a maliciously piercing shriek. So it was Fenella. He snuggled back into the rug.

'What can I do for you, my angel?'

'Oh, dear.' Fenella was embarrassed to find him in bed – naked in bed. She could see the tops of his smooth shoulders and a dark mole below his collarbone. She didn't want to be intimate like this with Tristram.

'Noon *levée*. Front stalls. That'll be five pounds.'

But she mustn't be silly. Tristram was different now; light and flirtatious still, but impersonal, like a voice on the radio.

She needed a friend. 'Oh, dear,' she said again and sat down heavily beside him.

'Mind Cherry!' But Tristram was too late. Fenella's long bones rudely interrupted Cherry's quiet slumbers. As Fenella jumped up again nervously, she slid from under the covers and flitting like a pale wraith across the room, she disappeared behind a sack-cloth curtain. She seemed so very insubstantial that although Fenella had often been curious about Tristram's girl friend, she watched now with unconcentrated interest.

'It's my mother,' she said, slumping down again. 'She's divorcing.'

Halfway through the story, Cherry reappeared, making for the door. Fenella paused. She raised her eyebrows towards Cherry. Tristram swung round.

'Have a good day at the office, dear!'

'I hate screen printing.' Her voice was low and accentless. She shut the door softly.

'Isn't this her place?' Fenella's curiosity was again aroused.

'She's very communal.'

'She doesn't look like that.'

They returned to the serious matter of what to do with Mrs Frith-Peacock.

'What we want,' Tristram began tentatively, 'is someone with a charming house in central London who wants a lodger – or better still, if she happens to be a charming someone with a charming house, who wants a friend.'

'Lady's companion to a rich widow,' Fenella mocked. 'My mother's an intelligent woman.'

'That is a drawback.' Tristram looked downcast.

He tried to cross his legs which had grown cold under the rug, but came up against Fenella's hip-bone. She moved quickly and he said, 'How about my mother? She has that whole charming house in Montpelier Square stuffed with beds and chairs and bathrooms and lavatories and electric kettles and all the sort of things women want. I once found five hot water bottles in a cupboard.'

'Your mother's house.' Fenella didn't react as Tristram feared. She was picturing her visit there that morning and instead of seeing her own humiliation, she saw a middle-aged lonely woman, who talked too much because she didn't have enough listeners. Her mother, in her new incarnation as Loelia, might have become silly enough to enjoy Maggie's company. Or at least enjoy taking the superior attitude which had served her well over the years with her husband. She had developed a very effective line in protective irony.

'But would your mother want...?'

'She'd be *absolument bouleversée*!' Tristram sat up enthusiastically. 'We must go to her now and break the happy news.'

'Oh, no.' Fenella drew back, partly from the idea of seeing Maggie and partly from Tristram's uncovered torso. He was softer-looking than Edward, his skin was pinker. 'I couldn't go. You must. I can't. I've got to work. I simply must do some work.'

Tristram smiled soothingly, 'You sound just like Edward!'

*

At last Edward had finished his painting of the monkeys and the lovers. He felt as if he'd been under a very bright light for a very long time, so that his pupil had diminished to a pinprick only capable of seeing the square of canvas. And now, all at once, the light had become normal and he could see around him. Immediately, desperately, he wanted human company and, reverting to the habit of years, he thought of Tristram. Only secondly he remembered Fenella and their marriage. But then he wanted to rush to her and talk and talk. '*Nunc est bibendum, nunc pede libero pulsanda tellus!*' The thought of drinking made him reconsider Tristram, for Fenella was too gloriously cool for drunken carousals.

With a sense of excited anticipation, he took a clean shirt and trousers from a hanger and rubbed his shoes with a paint rag till they shone. Then he chose a peacock-blue silk handkerchief from a large cardboard box on the floor and looked at his watch. It was ten o'clock at night. Just the time to begin a carousal.

*

Loelia Frith-Peacock and Maggie Brown sat in front of the television. Loelia was tall like her daughter, but her short hair didn't curl and her face was criss-crossed with lines of ironic dissatisfaction. She smiled a lot, mostly at the cruelty of life, but never laughed. This sceptical expression of hers, despite the lines, made her look surprisingly youthful, like some student with Nietzsche under her arm. Maggie also looked younger than her age, but in her case it was a question of colouring, energy and superficial gaiety. If Loelia was like a dissatisfied undergraduate, Maggie was like a child at a birthday party, slightly aggrieved because it wasn't hers, but nevertheless ready to enjoy herself.

Now they sat side by side in a weird harmony founded on their need for company. They had been together two weeks and although they had stopped making polite conversation, they still didn't know each other well enough to relax into silence. So they watched television. Loelia, who considered herself superior to anything television might offer and therefore had never owned a set, was secretly enchanted by Maggie's large colour set. She felt all the excitement of being young again and seeing her first film. They were watching an American gangster serial to which Maggie was much attached. They drank whisky.

When the doorbell rang, both looked cross at the interruption and then equally quickly became eager. As Maggie went to the door, Loelia fixed her face into a more suitable casualness.

'It's your son-in-law!' Maggie announced. For a moment Loelia was really nonplussed. She had only met Edward once, when Fenella had introduced them formally in her flat and she, like others around Fenella, seriously doubted the existence of the marriage.

'Edward,' elaborated Maggie.

'Oh, Edward.'

'He's come for Tristram, but he'll stay for a drink.' Maggie leant forward in stage whisper. 'He's finished his picture.'

'I'll get some more ice,' Loelia responded to the more conventional piece of information as if she questioned the validity of the other. Achievement was not part of her scheme of things.

Edward burst in. His presence immediately filled the small dimly lit drawing-room. He kissed Loelia gallantly.

'Whisky!' he announced, beaming with the joy of relaxation. 'With no water and no ice.' He took a stride or two up the middle of the room. 'Tristram, I presume, is otherwise engaged. We won't miss him. What are you watching? Is it good? Should I watch? I never do. But I don't despise it. Not on occasions.'

'Nothing special.' Maggie switched off the set without feeling it a sacrifice, for Edward's obvious pleasure in being where he was, his obvious feeling that where he was was the only place to be filled her with satisfaction.

Loelia wondered if he was aware of her relationship to Fenella and supposed not, although there had been that kiss.

Both women tried to remember if this absolute confidence was common to youth or particular to Edward.

'So you've really abandoned the countryside?' Edward remembered perfectly his meeting with Loelia. He had not taken her flight seriously but at the same time he'd been impressed by her reserved manner and thought her worthy of being Fenella's mother.

'... and my husband,' Loelia waved her hand in a casual manner, though the statement still shocked and delighted her. But Edward did not seem to have heard.

'It's very bad for the morale. The countryside in winter. A human being is not a squirrel. He needs company, conviviality, gaiety!' He looked round eagerly, his grey eyes bright like silver, his thin face working enthusiastically. He was really delighted to be with Maggie and Loelia. He couldn't imagine what they were doing together, unless they were waiting to welcome him.

Maggie began to talk about portrait painting, and although Edward saw she was fishing for compliments, wanting to be told how rich her skin would look in oils, how shining her eyes, how mysterious her mouth, he encouraged her to become more and more coyly excited.

Loelia smiled and said all portrait painters were syco-phants. 'Ah,' said Edward. 'What about Goya, Rem-brandt . . . ?' But she would only shake her head and say she was talking about the twentieth century. There was dis-agreement enough for the liveliest discussion.

The evening progressed. The whisky bottle was empty. At one point they all three moved into the kitchen where the ladies, at last aware of Edward's wolfish look, created him a meal of pâté and brown bread followed by an omelette ooz-ing jam. Afterwards he sat with a spoon and the jam jar. How starved he had been of sweet things.

Maggie and Loelia were having such a good time that neither felt inclined to bring up the subject of their off-spring. They wanted their own relationship with Edward. Not one channelled through their children's immature grasp of human nature. It seemed a perfectly innocent neglect.

Eventually it was two o'clock and Edward had talked him-self into a desire for the restful cocoon of sleep. He had neither wanted nor been able to sleep more than a few hours over the last weeks. He thought of Fenella's comfortable bed under that glorious Martin Paradise. How exquisitely tran-quil it seemed to him now.

'I must go to sleep,' he said decisively, and suddenly the two women were looking at an empty chair. 'It was a spec-tacular evening,' he called from the door, adding with a charming flourish of his hand, 'Farewell dear, deluding Women. The joy of joys!'

Maggie who could never hide her feelings was downcast; the word farewell had never appealed to her. But Loelia smiled at this betrayal, knowing as she did the faithlessness of men. His stay with them was probably only the curtain-raiser to his night's entertainment.

Nevertheless Loelia, like Maggie, dreamt of Edward that night. The vigour of his personality left so many waves behind.

*

Fenella was asleep. She lay like a mummy with her legs straight together and her arms by her sides. She had read

Troyat's biography of Tolstoy till midnight so she had gone to sleep with dreams of torment and genius.

Loelia was quite wrong to suspect Edward needed further entertainment; he had become like an animal seeking a warm burrow. He did not consider that Fenella might reject him unannounced at two-thirty in the morning after an absence which, though it might seem vague to him, was a clear-cut matter of eight days to her. He opened her flat door with a key he found in his pocket and walked as directly as he was able into the bedroom.

Fenella woke with the smell of whisky all around her. She screamed loudly. Edward, who had not put on the light, waved a soothing hand over her head. He supposed he had found the bed. As the cold hand brushed her face, Fenella screamed again. Paused. And then said quite calmly,

'Edward.'

Edward who had at last managed to struggle out of his cloak fell heavily across the bed.

Fenella woke up enough to see that this was a crisis. He had come to her trustingly, like a child – men became like children when drunk – and she must not fail him.

'Take off your clothes,' she said as unemotionally as possible, to convey a motherly care for his well-being rather than any devouring female animal's instinct for her mate. Nevertheless, despite the whisky, she would not have been adverse to *un petit ravissement*. It was hard to feel his flesh so near hers and so unaware. 'Here, let me help you.' She bent over Edward with carefully calculated concern. She would never be a Sonya.

But Edward had fallen asleep.

Fenella lay awake at his side. Again she told herself that this was a test and that their relationship as human beings was far more important than their relationship as lovers. Sleep was far more important than sex – well as important. She should be proud that he wanted to sleep beside her, that he felt able to relax in her presence. Perhaps only in her presence; for she knew how tense he was in his studio. Loving someone as extraordinary as Edward must demand sacrifices, for a painter's vocation was the most cruel for the most purely creative. All she, Fenella, could do was look, admire, criticize, anything she said or did was at least one remove from pure art. Beating her breast like a nun in the presence of God, she dulled her senses into sleep.

*

The next morning Edward woke quite early. He had no hangover and felt extremely well and energetic. He was glad to see Fenella lying beside him and admired her ivory pallor, her black hair dampened round her forehead, her long neck in the severe cotton nightdress. He considered making love to her, but his energy needed a more creative outlet. What he would have most liked was to gently draw back the bed-clothes, slip off her nightdress and look at her body, still as the marble effigy on a tomb. But that seemed cruel. Un-sportsmanlike too, for although he had hinted several times, she would not pose nude. She murmured deprecatingly about her thinness and, despite his undoubtedly increased enthusiasm, she had shrugged it into the air. As if he wasn't serious. No. He must use his energy some other way.

Sliding quietly out of bed, he threw on some clothes and hurried down into the street. It was a cold and dismal day but that didn't deter him. He bought the newspapers which he hadn't seen for a week, some croissants, French jams, new sliced bacon, oranges, a mango and a bunch of marigolds. Finally because he passed an antique shop he bought a milk jug painted with green ferns. All this took some time but when he returned to the flat it was still quiet. Enthusiasm mounting he carefully put a record on the gramophone and retired to the kitchen with his booty.

Fenella woke up very slowly. Waking was always a time of doubt and hesitancy for her. Sometimes she would lie awake for an hour or more before getting up, not happily, sensuously, like Tristram, but in a controlled stupor of wondering what it was all about.

But this morning there was music and the smell of bacon. They answered her questions simply, satisfactorily. She realized it was Edward and felt justified in her behaviour the night before. He was making her an offering.

In fact Edward was making himself an offering, as in everything he did. He had turned the kitchen table into a painting, everything in its place, nothing ugly. He smiled warmly at Fenella who sat opposite him. In her white night-dress looking like a Chagall lover, he thought. Beautiful! Beautiful!

'You mustn't get cold.' He rose and found her paisley shawl which he laid round her shoulders. He turned her into a Rossetti, rich-coloured, mysterious in every detail. She poured the rich-smelling coffee with the utmost grace.

'I expect you've finished your painting,' she said, all seeming clear in this light of morning.

'Yes,' Edward replied briefly, for he was taking a holiday and did not want to think about painting yet. At least he never stopped thinking painting but he didn't want to talk about it. 'I saw your mother yesterday,' he changed the subject, 'what a charming woman. So intelligent, so humorous, so relaxed, so civilized.'

Fenella looked extremely startled during this parade of compliments. 'Did you spend much time with her?'

'I went to find Tristram but there they were, the two of them watching television. Where is Tristram?'

'Didn't Maggie tell you?'

'We talked of course. But not about Tristram.'

'How unbelievable.' Fenella had worked out she was fourth best. Such low thoughts he drove her to!

Edward looked surprised at Fenella's tone of sarcasm which was quite unlike her usual haughty distance. Fenella saw his surprise. She wanted to ask if they had talked about her, but she realized that either way would be equally irritating, if they had or had not, therefore she became silent. And this self-imposed calm had an immediate good effect for she saw more clearly the beauty of the scene Edward had created for her and the hideous vulgarity it would be if she tore it apart by idiot ill-nature.

'Poor Loelia,' she said. 'Unhappy most of her life. It's such a stroke of fortune that she and Maggie correspond.'

Edward did not reply. His energy had left him; his breakfast had relaxed him. What to do with the day? He looked at Fenella still in that nun-like robe under the shawl with a hopeful questioning. But she remained upright and remote, determined not to be caught again. Edward remembered Tristram's easy availability. In those days he never had to ask in silly meaningless words. Edward's desire made him suddenly absurd, coy, like the schoolboy he had been for most of his sexual life.

'I shall get dressed.' Fenella gathered her shawl about her; she felt desirable again, queenly. Edward followed her slavishly into the bedroom where the curtains were still drawn. He lunged for her hand and snatching it from among the soft paisley, pulled her onto the bed. Fenella swooned there peacefully, but her large blue eyes fixed on Edward's pale irritable face. He felt irritable and yet determined. With a silly nervous giggle he climbed onto the bed.

*

Thinking over Edward's visit to her house, Maggie found it as odd as Fenella, that she had not spoken to him about Tristram. For she was seriously worried. That girl Cherry, who she had thought so innocuous, had turned out to be a lamentably bad influence. She knew that Tristram with all his talents was easily led and at the moment he seemed to be going in the direction of drink, sleep, unmentionable stimulants, unmentionable relationships and no work. Perhaps that poor Fenella – the prefix was habitual now – had been right and Edward would be a good influence. Pass on some of his power, his determination, his application ... Maggie became quite warm at the thought and, on the strength of such enthusiastic motherly concern, determined to visit him.

*

Edward had started a new picture. But it was not going well. He wanted to express the brute strength of a man's nude body and he was using himself as a model by looking in a long mirror fixed on the wall. He was gradually realizing that firstly, his long white limbs were not the right sort to exemplify the sort of unknowing force he wanted and therefore, secondly, he must find a model. His experiences at the life-class had put him against professional models. It was not just that he assumed they were all as unpleasant as Dorothy, but that he felt the need of an initial magnetism. Idiotic to link some meaningless general concept to his painting. Unfortunately, aside from himself, the only possible choice was Tristram and he was even further from brute strength than himself. Besides, he was so tiresome these days, with all his drug-taking and silly moony friends. He stopped and frowned first at his painting and then at his naked reflection in the mirror. He looked so intelligent and self-conscious.

There was a quick tap on the door. Edward was enough out of tune with his work to realize that it was late evening and an odd moment for a caller.

He unlocked and opened the door.

Maggie stared and gasped. Usually quick to react into words she could now only surmise wildly to herself. Edward nude! Bathing? Sleeping? Or had she interrupted an orgy?

Edward couldn't think why that normally effusive woman was gaping like a trout, eyes popping ridiculously. He had forgotten his nakedness, for spending much of the last few days that way it felt as natural as if he was fully clothed. He led her formally into the studio. Maggie was far too bemused to realize what an honour this was, owed entirely to his un-usual dissatisfaction with his painting. As he waved her politely ahead he came suddenly face to face with himself re-flected in the mirror and at last realized the cause of Maggie's behaviour. He grabbed the nearest disguise, which happened to be the sheet covering the Monkeys and Lovers canvas.

'I'm posing. Painting and posing.'

By this time Maggie had seen there was no orgy taking place and now also the unfinished painting. She recovered herself somewhat, though the sight of Edward's nude body even if now only on canvas, left her very hot and agitated.

'I'm afraid I've disturbed you.'

'My pleasure.' Edward, stately in white toga, indicated his chaise longue. 'Do sit down.'

'Thank you.' Maggie sat down nervously and found herself within a few inches of the painted lovers who were, quite indisputably, Edward and Fenella. 'Well, I recognize those two.'

Edward became furious. No one had seen the picture yet. He still wasn't quite sure if it was finished. And now this nosey woman came poking about. He gave a tug to the sheet under his armpits. He felt like throwing it back over the canvas; he was more concerned to hide that than his body.

'I came to talk about Tristram.' Maggie's nervousness increased with Edward's stern glance. 'If only he could be persuaded to do a painting like that.' She nodded sideways. Edward was numbed by the insult. Did this stupid lady really think that creation was simply a matter of persuasion, that in all respects but application Tristram's talent was comparable to his? Was this the way it looked to outsiders? Fury giving way to gloom, he sat down on the other end of the chaise longue and fixed Maggie with a look of deep disapproval.

Maggie didn't know what she was saying and therefore had fallen into the train of thought which came to her most naturally, the problem of Tristram. It was not adapted to her listener. But her eyes kept flitting nervously to Edward's broad but delicate shoulders, the blue veins inside his arms, even his long narrow ankles. He was so extraordinary, so young, so beautiful. So desirable. She thought of that hard white flesh, through which she could see the bones, pressing against her like some glorious jigsaw.

Maggie, whose *affaires* of late had been confined to single nights with oldish married men, friends of her solicitor or accountant, or for that matter her solicitor or accountant in person, lost her head. For a moment her voice continued to flutter on.

'Yes. Tristram could be a modern Turner. He has the imagination, the breadth of vision, the love of England, the love of colour, the mystic appreciation of life, the psychic feeling for inanimate objects.' Then her throat became blocked and she swayed convulsively towards Edward.

All at once Edward saw what she really wanted. Warm surgings of her lust washed over him. She was wearing a shirt opened at the neck and he could see the smudgy soft skin. It did not appear wrinkled, but nevertheless quite definitely old and, Edward thought with sudden excitement, interesting. It had never struck him before that something as purely matter as skin could be interesting, but now he saw that it was so. And that Fenella's young unmarked skin was dull compared to this old used skin. He put a hand out to the base of her neck. Just as he thought, like elastic that has been washed too often it was filled with changing pressures and frayed ends.

Maggie's desire reached such a pitch under Edward's cool examination that she could not hold herself back any more.

'Oh, Edward! Edward!'

The physical onslaught was a shock. Edward recoiled and then recovered himself. It was a new experience to be swept away on a tide of someone else's energy, particularly when he could keep his own critical eyes intact. Only a slightly hesitant victim, he submitted to Maggie in the interest of observation. Her manner he thought, before finally disappearing under the onslaught, was similar in technique though not in volume, to her son's and in direct contrast to the remoteness of Fenella's love-making.

*

Maggie came to, feeling ashamed and embarrassed. The word incest flitted through her mind before she was properly in command of herself. It was three o'clock in the morning. Thank God Edward had switched off the light. Finally. She had never known anyone so keen on light. She shuddered slightly. It was better not to imagine her dishevelled image in that long mirror. Besides, her head ached terribly and her back was twisted where she had slept across Edward's bony thighs. She crept off the chaise longue, terrified of waking him and dressed herself in what crumpled clothing she'd discarded. She couldn't regret such a night, that would be hypocrisy, but it must quickly become a black unrecognized dream. She shut the door of the studio behind her.

Edward woke briefly. Like Maggie, he felt guilty. It was an uncomfortable alien feeling. His objective reasons for accepting her did not seem quite so convincing after the event. In fact he was repulsed now. Disgust was a more acceptable alternative than guilt. To be seduced by a mature woman was just too exciting. Shivering, he groped for something to cover his nudity and came across the fallen dust sheet. Twisting and turning, he hid his cold limbs in its white folds. He fell asleep immediately. But some time later he woke in an icy sweat, for he had dreamt of being crucified and laid to rest in a white winding sheet. It was a relief to find himself alive in his studio with no great stone to keep out the dawn light.

7

Fenella didn't know what she'd do without Tish. The same Tish, who'd been so nervous and dependent in Florence, had become a rock of regular habits, cheerful manner and positive planning. She was still fairly unimaginative, certainly, but Fenella was beginning to think imagination a painful commodity. Only Edward seemed able to control it, and that was because he had a creative outlet. Had anyone ever died of frustrated imagination, Fenella wondered.

Only work helped. Fenella was in the last year of her three-year study of art. There was plenty of work she could do. In fact she often felt most comfortable shut up in her flat with her books and her pictures. But then she would become restless and this was when she realized the joys of Tish.

'Yes. Of course we'll have lunch and I must nip along and get some tights afterwards. I haven't a decent pair.'

This sort of remark delighted Fenella who wore socks under her long skirts and didn't possess even one pair of tights.

'And then there's a new exhibition I want to see. Plastic cows on felt grass.'

Fenella would laugh and hurry about the flat to find a hat for the occasion. She was looking like a beautiful witch these days, with her flowing hair and clothes topped by a tall, black hat.

Tish still hero-worshipped Fenella. She recognized her own talents but knew, unaided, they would never take her beyond the foothills of Olympus; while Fenella was naturally at the summit. Whenever Fenella telephoned her with an echo of sadness, she would drop whatever she was doing and find something to amuse. Her reward was that feeling of being pulled upwards, stretched in her speech and ideas, till she stopped being merely ordinary and joined for a fleeting hour or two the gods.

Edward was still outside her range. For one thing, there was no obvious way she could serve him and, for another, he did not hide his lack of interest in her. The marriage between Fenella and Edward, in which Tish almost alone sincerely believed, was another reason for her awe of the two of them. The privacy of their relationship, the way they lived basically apart but sometimes together seemed the height of sophisticated mystery. Fenella never talked about Edward to her and she never presumed to ask.

*

Edward was still having trouble with his picture of man, the naked ape. In the flat morning light it looked like a brown plastic doll instead of the collection of threatening muscle he wanted. Since the evening of Maggie's visit he had given up posing for himself and was attempting to paint it from his imagination. But this was worse than ever before and finally convinced him that he must hire a male model or give up the picture.

There was a tapping at his window. It was the same window that had once framed Fenella's face. Immediately afterwards he had nailed up a curtain made out of a heavy silk handkerchief so that he had to lift the flap to see his visitor.

It was an unknown man's face : brick red with inky blue eyes, long black sideburns and greasy black hair brushed from a side parting just above his ear straight across his forehead. Edward looked further and saw that, although it was March and very cold, this man only wore a pink singlet under a scruffy corduroy jacket. He therefore could see a huge reddish-coloured chest covered with thick curly hair and decorated by a small medallion on a thin chain.

'Your wife dropped her scarf.' It seemed an unconvincing calling line, but Edward didn't care. It seemed that here, *deus ex machina*, might be the answer to all his problems. He rushed to the door, flung it open and called imperiously,

'This way. Do come in please. That's only the window.'

The man duly left his post at the window and still quite composed appeared at the doorway. Here Edward saw that he was carrying a short tapering ladder and a bucket filled with various sorts of cloths. A window-cleaner. What an extraordinary stroke of fate, for he saw at once it was even more what his picture needed. His concept had been the lovable absurdity of a man developed like an ape and what could be more absurd than a superb muscular body devoted to the art of climbing up ladders, sloshing on water and rubbing it off. Magnificent. Perhaps behind this creature of iron he would paint the humiliating tools of his trade, a halo of buckets, ladders propped up to his great biceps. Edward flushed and waved a brush in the air.

The man said,

'I've been meaning to bring it for weeks. Your wife dropped it when she was shouting through the window.'

Again Edward didn't properly take in what he was saying. The mention of wife, a description he never applied to Fenella, put him off the scent. Besides, he was racking his brains for ways of keeping the man in the studio so he could persuade him to his plan. He took the proffered scarf which was dark plum-coloured and fingered it absently. As he did so he noticed the man's feet which were shod only in sandals and noted the perfection of their width and strength and little black hairs. Although he was probably six inches shorter than Edward, everything about him was built on a solidly mammoth scale.

'It was a good silk, I could see, so I thought she'd miss it.'

Edward saw an opening. He dashed over to the box where he kept his own collection of handkerchiefs.

'You like silk, do you. Perhaps you would accept one of these from me. As a present. A reward.'

The man came over and looked at the rich silk squares.

'Go on. You choose one.'

'O.K.' The man bent down and after carefully turning over the contents, chose one patterned with scarlet, green and blue paisley which Edward had never worn. 'This will do,' he said without changing the expression of his face, and shaking out the handkerchief, immediately knotted it round the thick tendons of his neck.

Edward was ravished. The man had dignity, simplicity. A painting of him would not after all be totally absurd.

'You're a bit er Romany – are you?'

The man looked wary. 'I'd best be off.'

'Oh, no. I mean,' Edward grabbed the man's arm in his panic and even then he felt with excitement the hardness of his muscles. 'I mean why don't we have a drink? I'm a painter, you see, and I work on my own time. Like you, of course.' He smiled foolishly. 'I'm afraid we'll have to go to the pub because I haven't anything here but it's no distance. Do say you will.'

The man shrugged, extricating himself from Edward's arm in the process, and they set off down the road.

Edward swirled his brandy and soda and thought that the window-cleaner's silence did not make him easily approachable. The matter probably came down to a question of money. Edward had never discussed money in his life.

'How's the window-cleaning business these days?'

'O.K.'

'You're glad there're not many places like mine, I expect. One window.'

The man didn't respond to Edward's smile. However, he accepted another Guinness.

'What's your name? Mine's Edward.'

'Austin.'

'Oh,' Edward was unsure whether this was surname or Christian name but felt he must take the plunge. 'Look, Austin, your business may be O.K. but I expect you could use some extra cash. As I said, I'm a painter and I need a model. Fifteen shillings an hour. How about it?'

'Nude?'

Edward became flustered. He had not thought yet how to approach that side of it. The man must have seen his painting on the easel.

'Well, yes. Actually.'

'A quid.'

'Of course. Yes. Yes. That will be fine.'

'Do you want me now?'

'Well. If you haven't any commitments.'

So the matter was settled. Austin, which on balance Edward decided to treat as his Christian name if a rather unusual one, turned out to be the perfect model. He arrived punctually, took off his clothes which he folded into a neat pile and stood rigidly in front of Edward for the two hours required of him. His body, naked, was more perfect than Edward could have hoped; the muscles were equally developed all over his trunk and limbs, bulging like some hero of a comic strip. Edward did not wonder how he had come by such a body, assuming in some vague way that under every working man's overall lurked a man of steel. Luckily, his preoccupation with translating steel into paint dulled any sexual excitement he might have felt. Besides, the super muscles unconsciously reminded him of rugger changing-rooms at school, a scene he had always considered more squalid than erotic. Nor, perhaps surprisingly, had he ever fantasized a rough tough lover. Fantasy was reserved for his paintbrush.

He had been afraid Austin might ask to see the painting and was prepared to find suitable excuses but he showed no interest at all, stared silently into space until the session was finished and when Edward handed him the money, as he did daily, he left immediately.

'Very good. See you tomorrow then.'

Meanwhile, the picture was progressing. It was bigger than life-size and since Edward had definitely decided to give Austin's figure a patchwork background of a window-cleaner's tools, there was a great deal of meticulous time-consuming work to be done outside the modelling sessions. But Edward had entered his obsessive mood and didn't notice the hours he spent on it day and night.

One evening at about seven, as he was standing back to decide on the shading of a rung of a ladder, there were voices outside the door and before he could go to it or cover his canvas, Fenella and Tish came in. For the last few days he had seen no one, so it was particularly difficult for him to wrench himself into society so abruptly. He was angry with himself for not locking the door.

'Oh,' said Fenella, stopping and staring. 'I know that man.'

'Heavens!' exclaimed Tish, who had been brought along for moral support. 'You couldn't.'

Edward found a sheet and threw it over the painting.

'We thought you might like to come out to supper or go to the cinema.'

Edward looked at Tish with cold amazement.

Fenella began to weave about the room; once she sat down on the chaise longue and then, rising again, continued on. She had been lonely, reading Swinburne when Tish had arrived; they had drunk sherry together and it had seemed a good idea to visit Edward. Now she saw the overture was a mistake and she tried valiantly to replace herself on the pedestal where Edward liked her most. Her manner became vaguer, almost *distraite*.

Then she saw something which stopped her in her perambulations.

'Oh, look. There's my scarf I lost!' She waved the plum silk scarf in gracious arcs above her head.

Edward, soothed by her Bernhardt movements, at last made sense of Austin's introduction through the window.

'Austin found it. My model.' Appreciating now that Fenella had been the goddess to arrange his arrival, he warmed to her. It was marvellous how, unknowingly or not, she was so often the inspiration behind his paintings.

'I must say I am hungry.'

'Oh, good!' Tish was nervous. That great nude man on the canvas made her more than ever frightened of Edward. She was glad he had covered it with a sheet.

'Does he pose for you often?' Fenella was frustrated by the presence of the sheet. She wanted to relate this model to the man she remembered. She did not think she'd liked him. Certainly his brutish red and blackness was a new departure for Edward whose paintings were normally so elegant, so unphysical. She was pleased to have discovered this new development in him, but not yet understanding.

'Every day.' Edward, cleaning his hands carefully with a special rag, looked at Fenella appreciatingly. She was standing calmly now in the middle of the room, her large blue eyes staring at some blank space in the wall. It was her attitude of introspection he admired most; oddly enough, it was the same quality which he found interesting in Austin, though in his case he believed it due to sublime stupidity rather than refined intelligence. They were both mysteries. Edward hung his black overall tidily on the wall. Not like that idiotic girl Fenella dragged about with her. Why was she coming to dinner at all? To spoil his enthusiastic ideas with her silly pretence at understanding. There was nothing secret about her. She was like one of those medical dolls with all the organs exposed under a transparent plastic skin. Tish jumped aside as Edward with a savage expression plunged at her feet. But it was only to choose a silk handkerchief.

Tish had a special reason for wanting to talk to Edward. Her mother had remarked, 'It would be nice with all your connections in the art world, to have a portrait of you, darling.' Tish had been excited and had first thought of how it would encourage Tristram's ego. But he had not found the idea appealing. 'Commissioned portrait painting is hack work. Journalism. An artist's worst enemy.' Tish had been cross and hurt. So then she had thought of Edward and wondered if she dared approach him. If only he had been on the phone, she could have rung him formally from her gallery – that would have been much easier. She considered asking him through Fenella, as it were Christ through the Virgin Mary, but their relationship was so unexplained that she feared this might be some complicated misjudgement. But now she'd seen that great hairy naked man, she began to feel afraid of posing for Edward and wished after all that she had told Fenella. It would have seemed more normal.

Fenella was looking particularly unapproachable. She was calm and upright as a marble bust behind their restaurant table. As usual when in Edward's company, they had ended up in a very expensive restaurant. Edward ordered oysters and spaghetti and steak; he had not eaten for two days and felt ravenous. The waiter circled impatiently as Fenella regarded the menu with unseeing eyes and Tish said she only wanted a salad. Fenella was reminded of her wedding lunch, although this time it was the waiter who glowered. Edward looked almost complacent. Soon after that lunch Mr and Mrs Aubrey had sailed away on a winter cruise. It had worried Fenella that Gunilla Aubrey, who had seemed inseparable from her home and garden, should consent to such a vulgar step, or that her husband, always so sensible of the value of the Best, should want it. But perhaps the shadow of death changed people at once, making their previous reality unbearable, a constant reminder of what had been; in a new world they could accept more easily their new position : he about to die, she about to be a widow.

'You ought to eat something.' Edward spoke reprovingly, but quite gently. And it was true that Fenella had become thinner; the heavy mourning ring slid about her finger and her skirts slid down from her waist so that instead of swinging round her ankles they brushed along the ground giving her the contradictory air of a regal waif.

'I'll have a glass of milk. And chips. And pudding.'

'Excellent.' Edward ordered and, ignoring the waiter's contempt, became enthusiastic because with wine in his glass and Fenella's appreciative face before him, he could not resist boasting about Austin. 'Did you see that body? That solid red meat! That lumpen proletariat development? It's incredible! A work of art in its own right. If only I can capture half that useless bulk.'

Fenella didn't answer because she was remembering the odd misunderstanding of her own meeting with Edward's model. The fright he'd given her as he'd whispered into her ear. Even if unknowingly – and he'd seemed to her a very knowing sort of person – he'd witnessed her humiliation.

'Is he a gypsy?' Tish sounded critical.

'I expect so.' Edward was evasive because he didn't want the man to have a background except that he gave him. He preferred him as a symbol.

'He has the remote look of a traveller,' Fenella, putting aside earlier memories, wondered cautiously about him.

'He has children,' said Edward unwillingly, 'but I'm not so sure about a wife.'

'Those people don't marry,' said Tish. 'We had some near our house in the country. They had women but not wives. They left the most terrible mess.' Mention of her home was leading Tish nearer to what she was trying to say. She turned pink and spoke loudly to Edward's mouth so that he retreated backwards into his chair. 'Mummy wants to commission you to paint me.' It came blurting out into a shocked silence. Indeed Fenella looked so startled that Tish turned even pinker, and decided that after all she'd made the most terrible howler in not telling Fenella first.

Edward recovered first. It had been a shock to hear the word commission linked to his art. But, he discovered, a pleasurable shock. Tish might be without point, but her parents were owners of a large house and even paintings, a Reynolds, a Stubbs, a Gainsborough, not exactly his sort of thing but more than respectable. Tish's face, before so flaccid, pink and empty, now clicked into focus. He saw that despite its present flurry, it was filled with strength and determination. Naturally he would not accept the commission. 'How charming of your parents! When they haven't even seen any of my work.'

Tish became confused, thinking he was not taking it seriously. 'They'll pay a proper price. A good price. I could find out from the gallery.'

This was a new approach. Money. Money handed over to him as he handed it to Austin. There was an amazing reality about it that he couldn't take in. But did that mean they would want to have the picture? Presumably it did. And that was inconceivable at this stage.

'I'm afraid it's out of the question.'

'Of course. I do see,' said Tish immediately, humbly.

Fenella looked relieved. Edward must not be bought in this presumptuous way. She gave Tish a fierce look, who retreated, shaken, behind a glass.

But Edward was excited by this new idea of earning money. He had never imagined himself doing that. He had always taken for granted that his signature on a cheque would pay for whatever object he wanted at the moment – more like magic than anything else, for he never looked at or even kept bank statements. He stared at Tish's face as if it was a pile of gold bullion. However, for the moment he said nothing more. Nevertheless it was noticeable that during the remainder of dinner, during which he proved that David

Hockney used perspective in just the same way as Giotto, he carefully included Tish in the conversation.

Fenella noticed, but because she knew more about the subject than Tish she was happy, even jubilant. She drank more than she usually did and became flushed and hot.

Afterwards Edward came back to her flat and stayed till morning.

*

Maggie and Loelia's honeymoon period was passing over. Their differences were becoming more noticeable. Ever since Maggie's night – or partial night – with Edward, she'd been particularly restless and easily irritated. She looked at herself often in her bedroom mirror and realized that she was very nearly old. If Tristram had been a more satisfactory son, she thought bitterly, she might have become reconciled to the idea, but he was being even more elusive than usual. Drugging himself stupid with that whore Cherry, no doubt.

Once more it was the evening of Maggie's favourite television serial. Once more Loelia sat at her side, watching with that patronizing faked interest of hers. Maggie gave her a vindictive glance. The truth was that it had given Maggie's conscience a very nasty twinge the first time she'd seen Fenella's mother after her little fling with her son-in-law.

The serial was not up to standard that evening. Maggie switched it off.

'Oh,' exclaimed Loelia with mild disapproval, for she distrusted abrupt actions.

'So puerile.' Maggie curled herself up in an armchair. 'Don't you miss having a man around, darling?'

'With pleasure.'

Maggie found one of Loelia's greatest drawbacks her inability to gossip. Surely she must be longing to pour out all the horrid malignities she had collected against her husband over the years. She listened attentively enough but commented only in a sharp word or two. In the end it became boring.

'I missed Johnny most late at night. In bed too. Just as a

comfort, I mean. The other can always be found.' She paused, thinking that she couldn't imagine Loelia a very comfortable person in bed. She was so eternally watchful. Like having *Private Eye* on the pillow – without the laughs. One was driven to crude questioning. 'Even though you've left him voluntarily, I expect you miss him in bed?'

'I never did see all the fuss about sex.'

Maggie felt rewarded for her perseverance. 'Sex is very much a matter of metabolism,' she said. It was not something she'd ever considered before, but she wished to encourage Loelia.

'Oh dear. I hope it's not hereditary.'

Maggie saw what she meant at once and became nervous and thrilled. 'You mean dear Fenella. What a beautiful girl.'

'She married young though, so I expect it's all right. Edward is such a handsome boy, don't you think? He's the sort of man who admired me before I married Roger. I dreamt of him, you know, after that evening he visited us here. I dreamt he was a snake and strangled Fenella. Don't you think that's rather funny?' Loelia gave one of her rare laughs.

Maggie didn't think it at all funny. She began to wish she hadn't probed Loelia, if such unpleasant things had to come out.

'Yes,' Loelia continued slowly, but with an uninterruptable deliberation, 'Edward is just the sort of man who admired me most when I was young. Before I went to Italy. In a way I went there because I knew they wanted to destroy my personality. And when I came back from Italy there was only Roger left, so I married him. I mean, whatever his faults, he was never strong, Roger, he could never destroy the essential me.' Loelia laughed again.

Two laughs in one evening, thought Maggie, trying through mockery to reduce the atmosphere of gloom Loelia was creating. 'Well, I suppose you regret it now,' she said. 'I mean your theory didn't work, did it?'

Loelia only looked sceptical as Maggie plunged on, 'Perhaps you should have married a strong man, like Fenella has, and dared the worst to happen.'

'But then there was the matter of sex.'

'Oh, yes,' agreed Maggie, who began to feel they were going round in circles. 'You don't like that.'

'I do. On its own. But strong men don't. They want to conquer, dominate, defeat, annihilate.'

Maggie was becoming annoyed by Loelia's flat self-assured voice. She had admitted sex had never been her thing, yet here she was setting herself up as an expert. Maggie began to take quick sips at her glass of whisky.

'When I met Edward, I saw at once he was that sort. He's so charming, so courteous, so deferential, so admiring to women, but underneath he hates them. Most men do, but strong men more than any. I should think he views the frenzied coupling of naked bodies with the most utter disdain. I expect he despises the act of sex like ...'

'Well, I can assure you he does not!' Maggie shouted. She jumped out of her chair and whirled round the room. Her glass fell from the arm of the chair and a piece of ice dropped onto the carpet. 'He's marvellous! Extraordinary! And I can tell you from my own personal experience!' The triumphant cry hovered between the two middle-aged ladies.

Loelia, with a face paler and more expressionless than ever, looked at the ice melting. Soon it would be only water and then it would be nothing, soaked into the thick pile of the carpet and by morning dried out of existence. She looked up sadly to where Maggie, flushed, bosom heaving, listened to the vibrations of her own announcement.

'I'd better go to bed,' she said gently.

Maggie's own excitement hindered her seeing the effect she was having on Loelia. This need to tell about Edward had been growing daily. She had always regulated – or not regulated – her life by its potential for drama. It was too late to break the habit now.

Loelia thought she would probably leave Maggie's house soon. Her stridency was becoming unbearable. Her talent for invention incredible. Could she not see how ridiculous was the idea of her tired old body consorting with Edward's youth and beauty? The most sceptical of all Loelia's expressions appeared on her face.

It never crossed Maggie's mind that Loelia would not believe her shocking piece of information. She presumed Loelia's desire to go to bed was merely a desperate escape from unaccustomed emotion. When she actually found herself alone in the room she continued perambulating for some time, furbishing her stark description of the event with more detail: 'He was so hard and bony that my thighs had dents like saucers where his knees had pressed, my stomach had holes from his elbows, my arms red welts from his fingers, my face scratched and bruised . . .' But eventually she missed an audience. She picked up her fallen glass and looked at it indecisively; she was tempted to visit Edward again. Yet the passion of remembering had slaked her appetite enough for her to recall the shame and guilt that followed. It was better to follow Loelia to bed. Satisfactorily tired, she swayed slowly up the stairs.

Loelia couldn't sleep. She put on her man's silk dressing-gown and went down again to the drawing-room where, in her disgust with Maggie's performance, she had left her book, Mrs Gaskell's *Wives and Daughters*. Sighing, she lowered herself to the chair Maggie usually appropriated. Only then she saw Tristram asleep on the sofa. Even in sleep, he lounged gracefully. She had succumbed to his charm long ago and it was a pleasure now to watch his elegant limbs draped over the red velvet, his fluttering breath stir his long curling hair – even if the breath was expelling a rather pungent odour.

'Let sleeping dogs lie, eh?'

While Loelia was admiring the delicate fingers drooping like white stamens off the end of the sofa, Tristram had opened his eyes. They looked at each other pleasantly. Both felt in the mood for a tranquil word or two. As long as it didn't involve too much effort.

'Maggie and I were talking about love.' Loelia gave the word an extra derisory beat, but it didn't fool Tristram who could see she was unusually stirred.

'I can't imagine Maggie's discourse on Lo—ve lasted long. On sex now . . .' He blinked in a drooping drunken way.

'Maggie's sex life is predominantly in her imagination,' she said confidingly, temporarily forgetting Maggie's relationship to Tristram.

He smiled encouragingly, 'A romancer. She's always been a romancer.'

'In one way it's understandable.'

'The long lonely years of widowhood, you mean.'

'She was so young at the beginning. Ten years younger than I was when I married.'

'Unbelievable,' murmured Tristram, meaning to flatter. He began to see that Loelia was circling some piece of information about his mother. About her sex life. His curiosity was instantly aroused.

'She's still very young in many ways,' Loelia went on, 'her enthusiasms, her jealousies, even her generosities are childish in their suddenness.'

'She still thinks she's the centre of the world.'

'Like a child.'

'That she's a beautiful princess and everyone loves her.'

'And wants to hold her and kiss her and . . .'

'Even the most unlikely people.'

'Edward,' supplied Loelia, who had begun to feel that Tristram knew all along.

'Edward,' repeated Tristram to the ceiling above, and although his expression didn't change, his legs stiffened like tin soldiers. Edward. Edward. What was Loelia implying? He had assumed that she had discovered some *jejeune affaire* of his mother's that, being Loelia, she didn't want to believe. But this could be horrible. 'She thinks Edward's dying of passion for her, does she?' He tried to keep the tone light.

'Swooning.'

'Unconsummated passion is the root of all energy,' said Tristram, hardly wanting to probe further.

'Maggie is not so attracted by the unconsummated,' said Loelia a little severely. 'Her imagination has led her into much deeper murkier waters – "Chaos of thought and passion all confused".'

'Consummated,' mumbled Tristram who found it difficult to unravel Loelia's quotation. It didn't seem the moment to show off the depth of her education.

'All in her imagination, of course. There they roll on the bed of lust :

> So he sighed and pined and ogled
> And his passions boiled and bubbled.'

Now that she had started talking in references, everything seemed so much easier. She pulled herself together firmly and, fixing Tristram with a pale stare, continued in an unconvincing apology. 'Rather ridiculous, I'm afraid. Dreams are so vivid and important to the dreamer and so pale and meaningless to the listener.'

This dream seemed anything but pale to Tristram. If Maggie had told Loelia she had slept with Edward, then she most certainly had done exactly that. Maggie never lied and despite Loelia's ironic understanding of her desire for passion, she had never had the imagination to invent.

This was a betrayal so great, so unthinkable that Tristram's usual protection of jeering cynicism was numbed. He lay flat on the sofa, and his face, paler than ever, gaped at Loelia across the room like a silver fish.

Loelia saw his change from beauty in repose to dull enervation, but put it down to the same tiredness she felt now that she had talked out Maggie's misguided confidences. 'I must to bed.'

Tristram, abandoned, pallid and prone, was considering what reaction he should have to the treachery of his mother and his oldest, best, only friend. But the longer he considered, the more lifeless, exhausted, incapable he felt. A spark of indignation roused him, as he thought of Fenella; it raised his eyelids for a moment or two but then sank again. It seemed that what he'd always instinctively felt was true : that nothing was worth anything, that nobody was worth anything, that nothing was worth doing in the world – when people, who you loved and were supposed to love you, could behave like this. Tristram put an arm over his face and, perversely consoled by this despairing philosophy, fell into a heavy sleep.

8

Edward decided to paint Tish. He had found, on reflection, that the excitement of a lump of money placed into his hands outweighed the vulgarity. Also, perhaps more admirably, he had thought what a queer picture the combination of Austin and Tish would make – that black mystery allied to that blonde doll. After he had finished her portrait – which would help him to know her plastic outline, he would ask her to sit for him. It did not strike him she might refuse.

Mrs Skeffington-Smith was delighted when she knew Fenella's husband was to be Tish's painter. Fenella was such a charming girl and had been so kind to her daughter in Florence. She was sure Edward, though rather younger than she'd expected, would be equally talented and agreeable.

'Darling, why don't I organize an arty dinner party here? Our pictures deserve a bit of informed appreciation.'

Tish, though not a show off, agreed this would be fun and between them they drew up a list. They decided that intimacy should be the keynote, so that everyone would really get to know each other.

The main guest of honour, apart from Edward, would be Sir Arthur Gore, the friend of Mrs Skeffington-Smith's friend, who owned the art gallery in which Tish worked. He was seventy and had been knighted the previous year for his services to philately. Fifteen years ago he had inherited a fortune made from bricks and soon after he had married Nadia, now Lady Gore. She was thirty years younger than him and had been working in an almost bankrupt art gallery. He married Nadia who was clever and sexy in a gaunt way and bought the gallery. He was not very interested in sex himself, having more or less done without it for so many years, but enjoyed possessing what others found desirable. However, if he bought the gallery in an effort to substitute art for love in his young wife's life, it was an error of judgement, for on the contrary it gave her the opportunity to discover attractive young men outside her house. Fortunately she was discreet with her lovers and as there were no more than half a dozen over fifteen years Sir Arthur kept himself in contented ignorance. Besides, philately had always been his real passion.

At the time of the dinner party, Nadia, Lady Gore, had been without a lover for a year. Although she was forty, her thin brown-skinned body had hardly altered since she was a girl and she still wore her chestnut hair waving neatly to her shoulders. People often remarked how she reminded them of Lauren Bacall and this amused her. She took the trouble to see a few of her early films and allowed them to influence her taste in clothes so that she often wore loose silk pyjama suits with padded shoulders. Her laconic manner was all her own and a great part of her attraction for Sir Arthur who had an aversion to bossy females. She was extremely efficient but never fussy.

The Skeffington-Smiths lived about forty miles from London. Nadia drove her husband because he preferred her at the wheel to a chauffeur. She wore very expensive pigskin gauntlets which completely covered her thin forearms. When they arrived she first looked up to the large rather ugly house and then very carefully stripped off her gloves and folded them neatly into the glove compartment.

Edward, who had also just arrived, watched her precise actions in the dusky evening light. It struck him with admiration that he had never seen a glove compartment properly used before. Edward and Fenella had been driven to the house by Fenella's mother in her Mini. Loelia had been surprised by the invitation, but gracious. She thought she had once met the Skeffington-Smiths.

Nadia helped her husband out of the car, folded the rug that covered his legs and then glanced curiously at her fellow guests. She knew the dinner was in honour of a young painter, but saw no one who fitted the description. Edward wore a white silk tuxedo which his father had brought from America in the thirties, and presented to him on his twenty-first birthday. The wide taffeta lapels fitted smoothly across his broad young shoulders and the double row of mother of pearl buttons curved closely to his narrow waist. He managed to look theatrical without being vulgar. With his height and yellow hair he looked like a matinée idol, some hero of romantic dreams, rather than an unknown artist.

Fenella had done her best to live up to Edward's image – especially buying for the occasion a new flowing robe – but at the last moment she had felt such terrible pangs of insecurity that she had fled to her pierrot suit, white pompons a trifle grey from her cupboard but red silk shining as bright as ever. Once encased in this magic armour, plus the multi-coloured striped socks, she felt much restored. She did not look very well, however. Her thinness had increased, for she found any quantity of food sickened her. Her complexion had become so chalky white that suddenly seeing herself staring bleakly above the scarlet material she had hurriedly placed a large blob of rouge on either cheekbone. The effect was to increase her already remarkable resemblance to Coco the clown. Loelia was shocked by her daughter's appearance which she identified as strange rather than unhealthy, but with her habitual policy of non-interference, said nothing.

Edward said nothing either, because he had always enjoyed Fenella's eccentricities. He found her thinness interesting and when they lay in bed made a game of counting her ribs and discovering previously submerged bones. Fenella said he treated her like a biological skeleton and perhaps he would like to hang her in his studio. She had a vivid picture of her naked form dangling on the end of a rope while Edward, brush in hand, gave her an occasional twirl to find a new angle. She did not confide this picture to him.

Tish appeared out of the house to welcome them. Having passed on the Gores to her mother who appeared behind her, she looked about anxiously.

'Oh, where's Tristram? Didn't you bring Tristram? He said he'd contact you for a lift.'

'How gossamer you are this evening! So fair! So pale! So Queen of the Willies!' Edward did not have much interest in the whereabouts of Tristram.

'A healthy Queen of the Willies.' Tish laughed deprecatingly, but nevertheless whirled her full white skirts above the bright green grass. 'Follow me.'

The drawing-room was oval and sky-blue. Sir Arthur Gore had been found a throne-like chair with a footstool. A thorn walking-stick with a silver knob was propped against the arm. Nadia encouraged him to enjoy a fixed position. Now she shook hands with Fenella.

'Lady Gore – Fenella Aubrey.'

Edward who was standing slightly behind them, as if queuing at a wedding, was very impressed by their meeting. They seemed to belong to a race apart; both tall and thin; both wearing trousers that flopped about their ankles. Edward didn't differentiate their ages, although Nadia was so much older than Fenella, but saw with objective clarity that Fenella was diminished by the juxtaposition. Her fantastic appearance seemed suddenly tawdry, while the other's crêpe pyjamas were strange and beautiful and fashionable all at once; Fenella's thinness seemed crimped and unhealthy while the other's was full of animal sinuosities; her white skin, black hair and blue eyes, usually so admired by Edward, seemed suddenly coarse beside the other's changing tones of tobacco : brownish skin, yellowish eyes, tawny streaked hair. Edward didn't identify what he was seeing as an older woman's answer to youth, as style, as a conscious projection of a fixed personality and as above all, the product of money, but he was impressed.

Fenella was feeling very ill. When Tish's father offered her a glass of champagne while asking for her appreciation of the newly painted cornices, she could only mumble incoherently, afraid if she opened her mouth too far she might be sick. Mr Skeffington-Smith, judging her no conversationalist, immediately delivered her up to Sir Arthur who was known to enjoy lecturing young girls. He made a space for her on the footstool at his feet and assumed, by her pompons, that she must be a flighty ignoramus.

'I don't expect the square inch of ivory has much appeal for your generation.'

Loelia noticed her daughter's strained expression with irritation. It was typical of Fenella's self-obsessed obstinacy, she thought, that on such a hedonistic evening she should be so whey-faced. A widowed Canadian doctor called Jamie Ferguson had been invited for her entertainment. Though smiling ironically at such an obvious pairing off, she actually liked his doctor's grey suit with its padded shoulders and his attentive bed-side manner. He had a respectably lined face for a man of his age – a year or two before retirement she judged – and rather more bushy grey hair than usual. Under his appreciation, she had a sense of what she looked like herself for the first time in years. It seemed that her unchanging slimness and pallor which, in the light of Roger's infidelities, had seemed a sign of sterility and age, might, served up as they were tonight in a long flowing dress, be a source of attraction in a dignified adult way.

'My husband and I are separated,' she informed Dr Ferguson, in a pleasant way. She turned her back firmly on her suffering daughter.

Mrs Skeffington-Smith was fussing about the non-appearance of Tristram. Everybody else had arrived and she hated to hold back dinner. Eating late made old people like Sir Arthur bad-tempered. Already the evening had fallen short of expectation when her neighbouring Duke and Duchess (with an interest in art) had at the last moment preferred a cricket match at Old Trafford to her hospitality. Their replacements, Phyllis and Marcus Tully, though quite successful as local painters go, did not go as far as a Duke and Duchess. And now this Tristram whom Tish had particularly invited not turning up at all. Five more minutes and she would start dinner.

Edward had become trapped by Phyllis Tully. She was dressed as a kind of Afro-Gretchen with frizzy hair and a low-cut blouse. She was talking a great deal about the bond between creative artists. Edward, perhaps luckily, did not take her point. He was trying hard not to be reminded of Maggie by the creased skin he could see below her décolletage. He thought that Tristram's mother had made him realize what a macabre phenomenon was the undefeated older woman. He much preferred Loelia's dying fall.

Nadia, who was nearby, enjoyed the look of disgust on

Edward's face. It was so youthfully sincere. Taking pity, she insinuated herself between him and Phyllis and pulled him away, whispering sympathetically, 'Age has its compensations. You see I can snatch you from her and no one thinks it rude.'

Edward was uncomprehending, though thankful for his deliverance. He could not conceive that this elegant creature grasping his arm and looking up into his eyes was actually several years older than Phyllis.

'Aren't you starving?' continued Nadia, in conscious contradiction to high-flown talk of art. Edward admitted that he was and, in simple interest, looked about him for Tristram.

'Do you know the man we're waiting for?'

'In a way. We were at school together. I believe he sees more of – Tish now.' Edward pronounced her name with some hesitation, for it was contrary to his concept of her in white gossamer. He was hoping he could paint her as the romantic heroine.

'Her real name is Felicity,' said Nadia understandingly. They both looked across the room. Tish's face wore exactly the same look of concentrated worry as her mother's.

'We'd better start without him,' she whispered fiercely.

The dining-room was grander than the drawing-room or perhaps it was the effect of darkness lit only by tall candelabras. There were some Venetian scenes on the walls but Edward couldn't be certain if they were Canalettos. Fenella, through a haze of nausea, saw that they were and managed a graceful compliment to her host as he took his place between her and Nadia. Nadia also recognized the paintings, but was too cross that Edward had been placed between his hostess and that dirndl-skirted freak to be cheerful about things.

Edward couldn't believe Phyllis was his neighbour; it was no consolation to him that but for the lure of cricket she would have been a Duchess. Listening to his hostess's lengthy explanations, he decided that dinner parties, even if given in one's honour, were frustrating experiences; like watching some inferior person holding the palette and painting the picture. On the basis of that simile it struck him that he might like being host at a dinner party. He tried to remember if Fenella could cook.

'You do cook, don't you, Fenella?' He found that by leaning behind Phyllis's freckled back and across the blank space that should have been Tristram, he could address Fenella quite easily.

Mrs Skeffington-Smith, frowning at this unconventionally free treatment of her dinner table, took such a fierce gulp at her wine that she spluttered. Sir Arthur, who was looking her way, decided with the peremptoriness of old age that the wine must be corked. He pushed aside his own glass. Meanwhile Edward's question had been too much for Fenella; it had suggested a mental picture of a frying pan filled with sizzling eggs. Clasping her hand to her mouth, she leapt from the table and ran for the door.

Sir Arthur, seeing his supposition so dramatically reinforced, looked exceedingly grave and said loudly to Mrs Skeffington-Smith,

'Amazingly sensitive, the liver.'

Mrs Skeffington-Smith was therefore diverted from the extraordinary scene at the door as Fenella swayed and grappled with a figure trying to enter as she tried to leave. After several seconds of apparently mortal combat they managed to shake free of each other and Fenella receded outwards, while her antagonist burst into the room.

'Tristram!' cried Tish, who was the right side of the table to see.

A medium-sized elation began in Mrs Skeffington-Smith who suddenly realized that she was giving a wild Bohemian party and that the Ducal absence was not a misfortune but a stroke of good luck.

'So glad you could make it!' she cried, swivelling in her chair.

Tristram didn't seem quite clear whether he had made it. He tottered towards them – very pale and very drunk – or very high. No one at the table was qualified to tell.

'W-was that F-f-f-Fenella?' Tristram stammered, and fell into the nearest chair which happened to be the one designated for him.

'Oh! Oh!' Phyllis, who had the chair on Edward's right, used this opportunity to snatch his arm in youthful fear and trembling. Throughout the interruption, Edward had remained remote and calm, preferring now to admire the pictures and the decorated ceiling.

'One must presume they looked up more a hundred years ago.' Ignoring Phyllis's clutch he addressed Mrs Skeffington-Smith with almost ducal *savoir faire*.

'Up? Up?' Mrs Skeffington-Smith was afraid Tristram might do something daring with her crystal glasses.

'To God, perhaps. Or merely higher things. Your ceiling is perfection.'

'Adam,' managed Mrs Skeffington-Smith, as she watched Tristram's hands flail about.

'When one considers the low undecorated ceilings of the modern house, the paucity of elevated thoughts is hardly surprising.'

Across the table Nadia nodded attentively to Mr Skeffington-Smith and wondered if Edward's languid manner which was becoming more pronounced as this unexpectedly dramatic evening progressed, meant that he was homosexual. His style, his occupation, his dress all suggested it and yet he possessed a certain stern masculinity and, of course, a wife. Nadia didn't take the fact of Fenella very seriously because she judged Fenella to be one of those clever *jolie laide* girls who often capture the heart and imagination of homosexuals without proving anything about their real sexual desires. However, she did find Edward attractive and her instinct about these things did not usually lead her down the pansy path.

'I see you have some fine burgundy there,' Sir Arthur shouted confidentially to his hostess. Having relinquished his white wine he was keen for a substitute.

'My husband's a wine buff, I'm afraid.' Mrs Skeffington-Smith missed Sir Arthur's implication, but was beginning to relax over the safety of her glasses, for Tristram had subsided into an unthreatening somnolence. 'Personally, I prefer cider.' She turned anxiously. 'I think I should see about that poor Mrs Aubrey ...'

'I'll go, Mummy.' Tish rose, glad to avoid Marcus.

'Burgundy's such a boon to arthritis,' persisted Sir Arthur longingly, but still unavailingly.

Tish could not find Fenella in the house and going out into the cool garden realized she had driven herself away in her mother's Mini. Tish's admiration for this sort of dramatic action overwhelmed any normal human sympathy. She saw it only as a gesture, possibly of defiance. She did not picture Fenella in pain or unhappiness.

*

Fenella lay on her bed in her flat. Tish was right in a way; it was her sense of the dramatic that had made her flee. Her nausea was simply due to pregnancy; her thinness due to her inability to eat, due to her nausea; her pallor due to her anxiety due to Edward. She had not told Edward that she was going to have a baby. She did not see how she could.

All her reading of romantic Victorian novels could not make him into a father. She could not even pronounce the word to herself, it seemed so far-fetched. Fenella sighed and pressed her concave stomach; it seemed impossible that something could be growing in there, but then there was this awful sickness.

She smiled slightly. Idly, almost happily, she wondered how her mother and Edward would return without the car. The drama of her exit must provoke Edward into a question. She tried to imagine the scene in which she could break the news.

'Why did you run away?'

'I felt sick.'

'Sick of what?'

Already it was turning away from her revelation; she would never say 'Sick because I'm going to have a baby.' She would say, 'Sick of other people.' And Edward would vehemently agree and tell her that he was about to spend a week alone in his studio painting, which meant, of course, that she herself had become 'other people'. Fenella sighed again and noticed how the breath hardly lifted her thin ribcage. A cage for a baby. The truth was she didn't really believe in its existence herself. The prospect of Edward becoming a total hermit concerned her far more.

In fact at that moment, Edward was nearer becoming a socialite. After the food had finished, the ladies had left the gentlemen to whom some excellent port was served. Under its influence, both Tristram and Sir Arthur came out of their individual comas and the latter became so animated on the subject of African stamps that Edward began to see he might not be Nadia's father as he'd vaguely assumed.

When they re-entered the drawing-room, Edward was surprised to see Fenella was not lying gracefully on a chaise longue where he imagined her flight would have ended. He looked about, too exhilarated for real anxiety, and his eye was caught by Nadia's conspiratorial smile. She came over.

'Like Jean-Louis Barrault in *Les Enfants du Paradis*. The pierrot flees. So dramatic. Those great blackened eyes, those thin hunched shoulders, those long clumsy feet.'

Edward saw that she had perfectly appreciated the romance of Fenella and felt soothed. Her problems had disappeared into the realms of fantasy. Or art.

'So few films have an equal content of matter and form,' he began eagerly. 'As if the visual fights against the active.'

'Oh. No. No.' Nadia contradicted him adamantly, but drew closer all the same. 'Even a painting must have a beginning, a middle and an end!'

Edward laughed excitedly; it was just the sort of concept he most liked discussing. He began to talk volubly, fixing Nadia with a brilliant stare so that she couldn't have avoided it even if she wanted to. In fact she drew him down beside her on the sofa and although she didn't listen to absolutely everything he said, she loved his energy and enthusiasm. Edward, not allowing her to speak, felt certain she was brilliantly clever.

Tish, who had been waylaid once more by the dreadful Marcus, looked longingly at Tristram who had taken up a quiet vigil on a footstool. He would rather die than talk about painting as if it were a packet of liquorice allsorts. As a matter of fact, just at the moment, it rather looked as if he was going to die.

'Excuse me a moment.' Tish hurried over. Tristram's head had fallen forward and his face turned ashen. She pulled him up and dragged him determinedly from the room. She feared he might be sick. Staggering backwards and forwards, they lurched through the hallway and out onto the wide stone steps leading to the garden. Tish thought the fresh air might do him good.

Mrs Skeffington-Smith saw them go and once more had to remind herself that this was her Bohemian party. In one direction, it seemed to be going very well. Lady Gore and Edward had clearly hit it off, which could be very helpful to Edward in his career. Look at the way they were talking, gesticulating, now striding about. They were similar physical types, Mrs Skeffington-Smith thought, enjoying her own discernment. It was not surprising they got on so well together.

Tish and Tristram had just reached Mrs Skeffington-Smith's largest herbaceous border, for Tristram had revived enough to request a stroll. However, they were not admiring the delphiniums. Tristram was trying to explain something about Edward.

'We'd always been colleagues, colleagues ... more than that ... musketeers ...' Giggle. Giggle. Tish grabbed Tristram as he tottered and tittered. He was like a drunken old lady, slight and giddy, mind and body, light as a feather. Tish felt she had become a dragoon stamping beside him. She wondered what had suddenly happened to reduce him so, or had it been a gradual process which had culminated in this evening's sudden drop.

Tristram was trying to explain. But his peculiar sense of humour muddled the message.

'Maggie was always like a mother to me ... a mother ... a mother ... heart throbbing as big as a house ... snatched away.' Giggle. Giggle.

Tish, whose relationship with Tristram had developed away from Mrs Brown, decided she must have remembered her name wrongly.

'Edward said ...' Tristram stopped walking and stared bleakly at his shoes which Tish noticed for the first time were a pair of scuffed tennis shoes. 'Edward said ...' He rubbed one shoe against the other and began muttering, 'It's not what he said ... It's what he did ... actions speak louder than words. Much louder.'

Tish started as his face suddenly disappeared from her view. But he had only sat down in order to take off his shoes. Despite the damp and gravelly path, she joined him valiantly. 'Edward and Lady Gore seem to be getting on awfully well.'

At once Tristram sprang to his feet, now bare, and hissed malevolently, 'Ah, but he loves, loves, loves older women, old bags, tattered hags, smelly rags, bosom sags, bottom drags ...' His hissing began to recede and he was running off into the darkness. The only light came from the windows of the distant house, but Tish could just make him out crouching and hobbling as fast as he could over the rough stones. Though he didn't slow up, his hissing became interspersed with 'Ouch!' 'Oooh!' 'Agh!' 'Ugh!' His knees bent as each foot touched the ground in an unconscious effort to lessen the painful impact so that he looked like some awful black bow-legged spider zigzagging down the path.

'Oh, dear.' Tish pulled herself together and, having the benefit of shoes, soon caught up with him. She was just considering her next move when his legs totally buckled and he collapsed like a game of spillikins at her feet. On the whole she was relieved by this development. It had a conventional simplicity about it; everyone knows young men pass out after too much to drink – her elder brother did it all the time. Conveniently overlooking the probability that drugs were more to blame than drink, she went in quite gaily to find her father. He would deal with the situation.

Edward was exhilarated. He had no wish for the evening to be over so he would take no interest in the discussions about how everyone should get away. It appeared Fenella had taken Loelia's car – well, one car was as good as another; he was not going to concern himself with which car. Whenever possible, he continued talking to Nadia about the Sien-nese influence on eighteenth-century landscape painting, but she seemed to be getting absurdly involved in the transport discussions. It was most annoying. He wandered out of the drawing-room into the hall (where he saw, with no surprise, Tristram slumped on a chair) and out into the driveway where he registered a plethora of cars. From there he strolled into the garden. It was a calm romantic evening. When spirits should roam in bosky bourns. Edward crossed the lawns reciting,

'What hath night to do with sleep', and as he saw a flash of light from the house,

'Was I deceived or did a sable cloud
Turn forth her silver lining on the night?'

Soon he came to some real bushy bosks and such was their feathery thickness that he couldn't resist shaking a bough so that the dark fronds brushed across his face. It was as he pulled aside one particularly loaded branch that he saw the motor bike. It gave him a most terrible fright for it looked so like a great black beast lurking there. However he recovered himself quickly and advanced, bravely shouting,

'Virtue may be assailed but never hurt,
Surprised by unjust force, but not enthralled.'

Meanwhile back at the house, the argument had now devolved on how Tristram had arrived there originally. He must have had some transport. With varying degrees of interest, they processed to the driveway. Sir Arthur Gore who had taken a particular interest in the problem waved his cane in front of him.

'Nothing. Nothing save the night,' he announced in sepulchral tones.

At that moment, as if summoned up by his magician's wand, a black roaring shape came bursting out of the evergreen at the end of the lawn and raced across from grass to gravel straight for where he stood.

'What have you done, darling?' said Nadia, as she saw her husband apparently disappearing under smoke and wheels and noise. But then the motor bike swerved past him and came to a dramatic halt.

'It's Edward!' cried Tish, with relief.

Her parents thought there was little cause for relief, but tried to enter the spirit of things which, considering the huge tyre marks on their lawn, was verging on sanctity.

'So that's what the boy came on!' said Mr Skeffington-Smith.

'Mystery solved.' Sir Arthur, apparently rather disappointed, made his farewells and got into his car.

'What a gorgeous monster.' Nadia stood beside the motor bike and stroked its flanks where they were visible under Edward's long thighs.

'That's settled then,' said Mrs Skeffington-Smith. 'Edward takes Tristram's bike. The Gores kindly take poor Tristram. So kind really. And Jamie takes Mrs Frith-Peacock. What a lot of excitement!'

However, as it turned out they returned somewhat differently. The Gores, after inspecting the torpid body of Tristram, decided they were not so kind after all – at least without the guardian presence of Edward. So Loelia (rather late in the day, Nadia thought) owned up that she and Tristram shared the same destination so if Dr Ferguson would be so generous . . . He would.

Edward had only ridden a motor bicycle once before. He had not previously been attracted by the loud noise and the physical effort needed. But this evening under the admiring eyes of Nadia, under the night sky, he stamped on the pedal and felt the surge of the engine roar through his body. Forgetting any conventional farewells, he took off at great speed down the drive. He was so taken up by the new vital experience as trees and bushes and then lamp posts and houses flashed by, that he didn't notice Nadia driving her car slowly by, nor Loelia's gay salute. He thought he should ask Austin at his next sitting whether he had ever possessed a motor bicycle. He swerved dangerously as the exciting image of Austin naked on a motor bicycle presented itself to him – Austin's great flexing muscles against this shiny beast. What a picture that would be! Or was it too banal? Common? Absurd? Too much a sex flick, skin flick? And yet there could be beauty in the erotic, the vulgar. One mustn't become purist, sterile, out of touch. Edward began an argument with himself and quite forgot he was riding a 500 c.c. motor bicycle. He clapped his hands on the handlebars and waved his head about. The bike swayed, jumped and took control. At the next sharp bend, it skidded right across the road, turned sideways and threw itself onto the ground.

Edward lay on his back and looked up at the stars. Luckily he and his charger had fallen onto a soft verge so he felt unhurt. But dazed. He noticed the air was cold now.

*

Loelia and Dr Ferguson heaved Tristram out of the car. They were both aware that this Christian action was only to please the other which complimented them nicely. Loelia was particularly relieved at the thought of how Maggie would drag him away eagerly for her maternal ministrations, for his pale slumped face gave her a guilty conscience. Perhaps she should not have revealed his mother's fantasies. She opened the door and called out. But no Maggie appeared.

'I'm afraid she must be out,' said Dr Ferguson. Loelia looked helpless, an attitude she despised in others.

Together they pushed and dragged the sagging body into the house and then with even more difficulty up the stairs and into his room. Again Loelia took it as a compliment that the doctor made no attempt to diagnose Tristram's condition but paid all his attention to herself.

Afterwards, she offered him some coffee and a drink. They sat in Maggie's drawing-room enthusiastically discussing the change from married status to single. By mutual consent they stayed in generalities, but the knowledge that each talked of his own experience gave the discussion a particular excitement.

*

Edward was driving slowly through the outskirts of London. His fall had reduced his physical and mental speed. He was considering where he should spend the night. Normally after such a hedonistic evening he would have chosen the comforts of Fenella's bed. But if her flight implied the need for solitude, as he presumed it did, then he must not trespass on her privacy. He was always very careful to respect her rights as an individual. A night in the studio would have the advantage of encouraging him to an earlier start in the morning. *En passant*, he wondered about the Gores' destination. Dreamily he imagined cream and gold with slithery materials covering the chairs and sofas. Nadia he thought of as a silky snake.

*

Edward lay on his chaise longue and looked sleepily at the motor bicycle. He had not had the heart to abandon it to the pavement outside but its presence was keeping him awake. The chrome handlebars seemed to glitter even in the darkness and it gave off quite a strong smell of petrol. The headlight stared at him like some terrible Cyclops. He had just decided to turn it out to its fate, when there was a rattle at his door handle. This was annoying for he had reached that flushed state of post drinking which calls for darkness and silence.

'Who's there?'

The door rattled again. Stumbling round the motor bicycle, he found the key and with some difficulty turned it in the lock.

'I didn't say who I was, because I thought you wouldn't let me in.'

'Who is it?'

'You could put on the light.'

'Oh, no.' Edward sat down despondently on the sofa. He had realized it was Maggie.

'It is nicer without. I've been dancing. Dancing ... My God! Aaaagh!' Maggie had come across the motor bicycle. Her shriek made Edward's head spin.

'It's Tristram's motor bicycle.'

'Tristram's!' Maggie sat down abruptly on the sofa beside Edward. She would rather his name had been kept out of it. 'But he doesn't have a motor bicycle.'

Edward, shuffling his feet evasively, felt a bottle on the floor. It seemed the only way. He filled two large goblets with red wine. Maggie decided to overlook the presence of

Tristram's bike with its great seeing eye. If only it didn't stare so. She had been giving her accountant dinner and afterwards they had gone to a gambling club where she had lost just enough to give herself the pleasure of his disapproval. She had also drunk enough for the evening to need a climax. She was prepared to create one if it didn't seem to be arising naturally.

Edward thought that if he said nothing she might disappear like some emanation of his over-heated brain.

'It's ludicrous of course in a woman of my age. But I've always hated anything that came between the romance of it. I expect girls these days manage better but then they've none of my generation's complicated feelings. I still can't pronounce the word, you know, without a conscious effort of will. Sex. Sex. Sex.'

Edward, though not attempting to understand her general train of thought, registered that the word rolled off her tongue like oil and also remembered with fear that he had accepted her advances last time, mostly to stop her talking.

'Nowadays, of course, it's all so much in the open. Advertisements, hoardings even !' Her voice rose indignantly. 'But I can't like it all the same. It seems to show such a coldness of heart. I've always been too warmhearted, too warmhearted. That's why this happens. A too romantic warmhearted nature. Ludicrous really. Childish. Childlike. I expect it isn't true, but one can't help worrying.'

Edward saw she was working herself up into some misery, and made an effort to understand the problem. The additional wine seemed to be fuddling his head without making it any the less painful.

'I know it's a danger of course. Even at my age. Indeed some people say it's the most dangerous age of all. But I wouldn't take it seriously, except that I'm usually so very very regular. So much part of my system to be so regular.'

A quite dreadful inkling of Maggie's subject matter began to reach Edward. It was like an awful trickle of poison in his ear. She was using words that represented a nauseating female world that he obsessively avoided. How could he worship women if he knew the sort of disgusting peculiarities she was suggesting? He got up from the chaise longue and touched like a talisman the hard clean masculinity of the motor bike. His action as he stroked the smooth petrol tank reminded him of Lady Gore; he could never imagine such an animal babbling coming from her.

'The terrifying thing is that my own mother conceived her last child, her sixth child, well over the age of forty, much older than me, so that one simply can't rule out the possibility.'

Edward felt a sudden desire to pick up a cushion and stifle Maggie. He turned pale and gripped his fingers round the edge of the sofa. Maggie, seeing this evidence of emotion, was pleased and felt more ready to compromise.

'On the other hand I have to admit it does seem, generally speaking, rather an unlikely event. I mean the natural reaction would be shock, don't you think?'

'Yes,' said Edward bleakly, who still hoped she might go away. Whatever happened, he wasn't going to join in her conversation. Without exactly realizing what he was doing, he slowly swung his leg over the motor bike and pulled himself upright. He at once felt more dominant and looked at Maggie's puffy face with some sympathy. How humiliating it must be to grow old.

Maggie drew back onto the chaise longue. Edward's refusal to participate was sabotaging her constant need for a scene. She felt herself ebbing away under the combination of his hard stare and that villainous animal he bestrode. She felt her eyes begin to lose vision and float wetly in their sockets.

*

Fenella could not sleep. Lately, though feeling dreadful when she went to bed, she had not fallen to sleep but had gradually revived so that by two or three in the morning she felt better and more energetic than she had all day. Usually she read or, if Edward was with her, wandered round the flat, played music. Tonight none of these things satisfied her thirst for action; she felt so sociable. Remembering her mother's car parked below – it seemed impossible that the

Skeffington-Smith dinner had only been a few hours ago — she wound her paisley shawl over her nightdress and let herself out of the flat.

*

Edward and Maggie had reached an impasse. They looked at each other across the dim room. Maggie could not speak; and Edward would not. He knew his will was stronger than hers and soon she would go unless – horrible thought – she crumbled under him so completely that she wouldn't even find the will to leave.

Fenella opened the door quietly. At first she could see very little except a strange glittering object in the middle of the studio. Then she saw Edward's pale head raised oddly. She didn't see the hunched figure of Maggie at all.

'Edward !'

Edward who was not looking at the door only partly heard her voice. He had so effectively blocked Maggie's dialogue from his ears that they were still not functioning properly. He did not turn his head. Fenella went over to the sofa and sat down.

Maggie was paralysed with horror. It was inconceivable that Fenella could overlook her presence. When there was only a few feet between them. Her mind became a total blank, and she could think of nothing to save the situation.

Fenella felt much happier. She was finding it easier now to see in the darkness and saw that Edward was mounted on a motor bicycle. It was just the sort of mad thing she would expect him to be doing in his studio in the middle of the night. She was so pleased she had left the confines of her flat and come to join him in his wild fantasies.

Edward stared. There were now two figures in front of him. Unless his exhaustion and the wine had produced double vision. The idea momentarily interested him but could not be validly sustained, for the figures were such particularly different shapes. One was short and round and the other romantically long and flowing. Etiolated. So that's who it was. He welcomed her with simple delight.

'Fenella !'

The other shape heaved convulsively. Edward look at her scornfully. Why couldn't she have the grace to vanish in a puff of smoke. There was nothing Maggie wanted more. What explanation could she possibly find for her presence there at three in the morning?

'Why ever are you sitting on that thing?' Fenella spoke warmly, happily. She had not missed Edward's welcoming tone of voice.

'It's a motor bike.'

'I can see that,' Fenella laughed gaily which caused a quickly repressed shudder in Maggie. If only she dared creep from the room, but if she moved Fenella would certainly see her.

'You took the car,' Edward patted the handlebars, 'so I had to come back from the Skeffington-Smiths somehow.'

'Oh, them!' Fenella waved her hand dismissively. 'But where did you find the motor bike?'

'It's Tristram's.'

'Tristram's! But he doesn't have a motor bike.'

At last Maggie saw her opportunity. It seemed impossible to her that Fenella hadn't yet noticed her presence.

'I've come to collect it!' she cried leaping to her feet. She stood between them shouting and waving her hands.

Fenella gazed with bewilderment. 'Maggie Brown?'

'She's just going,' said Edward firmly. 'I was giving a demonstration.'

'A demonstration?'

'A tutorial.'

'She's not going to ride it? Is she?' said Fenella, thoroughly bewildered.

'I'm not going to ride it!' shrieked Maggie.

'I just thought you might enjoy it more,' said Edward maliciously. 'Still, it's not far to wheel it to Knightsbridge.'

'No,' said Maggie faintly with a terrible feeling that she was going to pay a high price for her excuse.

'I'll get it out for you then.' Edward got off the heavy machine and began to wheel it from the room. Maggie hopped behind, terrified of being left with Fenella.

'Here you are then.' Edward put the bike carefully onto

the edge of the road and handed it to Maggie. Fenella wandered along behind. It really was a quite remarkable sight. The little round woman and the great shining machine.

'But I can't actually wheel it,' Maggie hissed in a terrified whisper to Edward.

'Off you go then,' said Edward loudly and cheerfully. Fenella crossed the ends of her shawl across her bosom and came to stand beside him. Together they watched Maggie struggling off into the night.

'Are you sure she can manage it?' said Fenella doubtfully, as for a moment it looked as if the whole bike was going to tip over on top of Maggie and crush her underneath.

'Oh, yes,' Edward smiled reassuringly. 'These old ladies are tough as old boots. Anyway mother love will spur her on.' He turned to go back into the studio. Fenella followed more slowly.

'But why did she pick it up now? It seems an odd time . . .'

'She was just passing.'

'In the middle of the night?'

'Lots of people do. You do. You have.'

'But that's different.'

'Yes.' Edward went over to the chaise longue and picked up the glass of wine which Maggie had been drinking from and offered it to Fenella. She recoiled with a look of disgust.

'Oh, no thank you. I couldn't.' Edward looked at her pinched face with annoyance. Suddenly the camaraderie which had been established over the motor bicycle episode had evaporated. Fenella remembered why she had come to Edward. What she must tell him. And Edward remembered that she was a woman as Maggie was a woman and that he was exhausted and she was disturbing his night's sleep. And that all he wanted was to be left alone so that he would be fit to paint with the morning light.

Fenella went to the chaise longue and took up Maggie's old position. Edward remained standing.

'What did you come to pick up?' he said coldly.

'I came to tell you something,' Fenella shivered, and became conscious that she was only dressed in a nightdress and shawl. Although aware of Edward's unreceptive attitude, she felt that the darkness and the extraordinary circumstances might make her news more digestible than at a more normal time. Certainly the darkness made it easier for her to speak.

'We're going to have a baby.'

Edward switched on the light. It was rather the act of a conjuror who expects the scene to change at the flick of his finger. Fenella bent her head and put her hand over her eyes. Then she looked up at Edward sadly.

Edward thought she had never appeared less beautiful. Her skin was dull and ghastly white, her nose was long and bony, her jaw and mouth were rigidly bound, her eyes were surrounded by ugly brown smudges. In fact she was altogether ugly. Edward looked away.

'I couldn't think how to tell you. I know it's not the sort of thing you think about.' Fenella saw all her worst dreams of this conversation realized. At the same time she took obscure comfort from the conviction that this dead face of his was turned to her pregnancy and not to herself. She would not therefore let herself doubt his essential love. She had told Edward that she was pregnant and now he would have to find an attitude to face that fact. She would not press it home any more. If he wanted, he could overlook it as long as he was able. She had never expected him to become involved. The idea of an abortion did not occur to either of them.

'How was the dinner after I escaped?' she said lightly. She put her feet up onto the chaise longue and rested her face in her hand. 'I thought our hostess suffered from a touch of the Lady Catherine de Burghs.'

Edward seemed to meditate. Her tone of voice was strikingly changed but he could not immediately change his own attitude.

'The pictures I could appreciate which is, I suspect, more than they could.'

Edward enjoyed her waspishness. He felt it clever and unsentimental, the reverse of what she had seemed before. He turned to look at her again. Fenella smiled slightly. Draped across the chaise longue in the gracious sweep of a Recamier, her ankles were smoothed out, her pallor disguised by soft shadows. Edward noticed the paisley shawl for the first time and remembered the evening she had thrown it wide for him. His desire for sleep was leavened by the image.

'I should enjoy it more if we entertained.'

Fenella felt an odd breathlessness as she heard his 'we', as if some dreadful danger had been successfully negotiated.

'Of course we should entertain. I love cooking jugged hare!'

'Jugged hare?' Edward looked suspicious, as if he suspected she was making fun of him. But Fenella had only spoken wildly, happily. She had told him about the baby and he was still talking to her, better than that they were making plans for the future. 'Oh yes! Jugged hare is sensational. Swimming in red wine and bay leaves. From the garden.' Fenella dropped her face on her hand and felt a flush of excitement coat her cheeks. 'Jugged hare is absolutely my speciality!' Then a terrible thing happened : a vision of the bloody uncooked lumps of meat floated before her eyes. Before she could stop herself she was retching and heaving convulsively. Her head hanging off the chaise longue gaped and shuddered above Edward's wooden floor. In pain and misery Fenella shut her eyes. Because she had eaten so little only hot slithers of bitter-tasting liquid were forced out of her mouth, but she could find no consolation from this. She knew Edward's dreadful aversion to all things he considered unpleasantly feminine. And here she was, a pregnant woman being sick at his feet. She prayed desperately that she might faint. Or die.

Edward looked at Fenella with a curious fascination. His initial reaction had been of horror but now the sight had captured his imagination. Anatomically, the way her back and shoulders pushed up her neck which in turn threw forward her mouth which resulted in those orange worms trickling across the floor was unlike anything he had ever seen. He would not have chosen to see it, but now he found himself too interested to turn away. As the paisley shawl slid off her shoulders, he leant forward and carefully placed it on the end of the chaise longue so that it would not get dirtied. Now he could see even more clearly Fenella's moving anatomy under her thin white nightdress. It gave him the same distasteful yet exciting sense of discovery that the awareness of the smudgy age of Maggie's skin had brought. He put his hand on one thin shoulder blade.

Fenella jumped ridiculously. She had stopped being sick now and had fallen into a kind of coma. She had presumed Edward would have somehow disappeared. His hand on her back gave her a tremendous surprise.

Edward took her white strained face in his hands. Her large blue eyes, instead of receding under the tears she had shed, seemed to have become more protuberant. Her mouth was astonishingly pale. Edward rubbed his finger over her lips and watched with interest as they turned a faint pink colour. Fenella remained tense. She couldn't believe that Edward was being sympathetic. Her mouth tasted dreadful and she could smell that horrid liquid on the floor. If she only could make her legs move she could find something to mop it up with.

'Are you often sick?' Edward asked, in a perfectly matter of fact tone of voice.

Any flicker of hope Fenella might have had died at his question. So he was going to act the part of a stranger. Not the father of her baby. She was sick because she was pregnant. He had made it impossible for her to say that.

'There were boys at school who had very weak stomachs,' Edward continued. 'In fact I did myself, until I was about sixteen.'

'Yes,' Fenella said wearily. 'I'd better clean it up.'

'Here. Let me help.' Eagerly, rather as if he had become a schoolboy again, Edward dashed to the corner of his studio and produced an assortment of his silk handkerchiefs. 'Do you feel better now?'

'Yes, thank you.'

'I expect it's lack of sleep.'

'I expect so.' Fenella got down on her hands and knees and started wiping the floor. Edward felt again that distasteful excitement as she crawled slowly round his feet. He would like to ride her like a motor bicycle. The urge became too strong to resist. He swung his leg over her flanks.

Fenella collapsed as his weight rested on her back. She couldn't tell if it was a joke.

'Oh Edward,' she said weakly. Edward pushed her backwards on the floor and began to kiss her. The brightly coloured handkerchiefs fell across her long black hair and her white nightdress. A bitter sickly smell rose around them from the floor.

9

The motor bike stood unregarded on the kerbside. By some miracle Maggie had managed to push it all the way to her doorstep. She could hardly believe it herself when she saw it the next morning from her bedroom window. Its size and shining chrome were even more majestic by daylight. Vaguely, Maggie wondered where Tristram had found the money to buy it. Tristram had not yet appeared. Nor had Loelia. Maggie felt wistful and unwanted as she wandered down to the kitchen in her dressing-gown. However, she was not as *distraite* as she might have been, for the scene in Edward's studio had mercifully disappeared into alcoholic mists.

A police car drew up outside the house. Two young policemen got out and bent to examine the motor bike. Satisfied, they went to ring Maggie's doorbell.

Loelia turned in her bed at the sound of the bell. She had not been asleep for some time, merely luxuriating in memories of the night before. Warm admiration, was how she put it to herself. Dr Ferguson was not foolish; had not paid her meaningless compliments which would have made her suspect him to be a man like most; he had been dignified, reserved, only paying her the compliments of objective appreciation. As he left, he had placed a deliberate kiss on her cheek. Loelia loosened the bedclothes round her and ran her hands down the side of her body. Suddenly she was more glad than she had ever been about anything that her figure was still good. She jumped out of bed and ran to the long mirror.

'I'm sorry to disturb you so early, ma'am.'

'Mrs Brown,' said Maggie nicely. The policeman's apology, she realized, was a reference to her dressing-gown. If they had warned her she would have put on something more becoming. One policeman was checking some notes he held.

'So you must be Tristram Brown's mother.'

'Yes,' agreed Maggie a trifle coldly, for she didn't see why it should be so obvious.

'Is your son at home?'

'Young men are not often early risers.'

One of the policemen glanced shiftily at his watch. It was after ten. The other continued blandly, 'So we can expect to find him in his bed.'

'Oh yes. Sleeping beauty.' And Maggie, apparently taking his words literally, led the way to the stairs. 'Come up, please,' she cried as the two policemen hung back.

'Won't he want to dress?' said one.

'Heavens no!' In fact Maggie thought she was being clever for, with a mother's partiality, she felt certain that Tristram's exquisite innocence as he lay asleep could not fail to move all hearts.

So it was that Tristram opened his bleary and not very beautiful eyes to the unedifying sight of two severe male faces. One spoke with unpleasant deliberation,

'I must warn you that anything you say will be taken down and may be used in evidence against you.'

*

Edward was painting Austin. He was placing onto his chest each curly black hair with delicate precision. Every now and again he looked up and saw for a moment Austin's unfocused gaze. He had meant to bring up the subject of the motor bike, but felt unwilling to instigate the human contact necessary for the matter.

'I won't be able to come in tomorrow.'

'Why ever not?' Edward hated interruptions.

'I'm seeing my kids.' Austin's voice was unemotional as always.

'So early?'

'I have to get there.'

'Where?'

'They're away.'

Edward carefully wiped his brush and put it down. 'How do you get there?'

'Hitch.'

'Can you ride a bike?' Austin looked out of the window where his own bicycle stood on the pavement.

'Not that far.'

'I meant a motor bike.'

'I haven't got one.'

'Would you like to borrow one?'

'No reason why not.'

'I'll fix it then.' Satisfied, Edward picked up his brush again. He thought that Tish should be placed above and behind the motor bicycle as if she was Austin's imaginings, in a thought bubble. He might even paint a bubble round her. She was that sort of girl.

Austin said, 'What sort of bike is it?'

Edward was surprised. Austin had never showed any interest in anything before. 'Big and black.'

'What c.c.?'

'Oh. Masses, I should guess. Very fast.'

'Pillion seat?'

'I expect so. Why ever?'

'For my girls.' Austin became indifferent again. 'When do I get it?'

Edward decided the morning's session was finished. His precision was confused by new ideas. He wrote on a piece of paper. 'Take this. I've written the address. Ask for Tristram. He'll give you the bicycle.'

'O.K.'

'Bring it back here. Afterwards.'

'Very good.'

Edward walked restlessly about his studio. He was very conscious of wasting half an hour. Tish was due for a sitting in the afternoon. What he wanted now was an invigorating argument. He felt temporarily imprisoned with his work. He decided he must buy a car. He remembered there was a large car showroom two streets away. He had often walked past it and thought how like an updated zoo were the gleaming Jaguars behind the confining sheets of glass. He had always hurried past with the foolish feeling that one might come crashing out. Now he would liberate one himself.

*

Fenella sat looking at the telephone. The shiny black surface was still a little dimmed where she'd pressed it close to her ear – silly really, sad news was more bearable filtered by distance. It was unfair of Edward not to be on the telephone. Unfair and typical. And, of course, perfectly right. He had to be served like an eighteenth-century lord with a personal information service. Instead of being shocked as ordinary mortals were by undigested news, he would have a slave to mould it to his tastes. This irrelevant cynicism, Fenella recognized, was a shaming reaction to the news, but she felt so low, so drained that she couldn't even rise to tragedy. She frowned as a particularly grating noise in the street below made her imagine the energy needed to cross London to Edward's studio. She wandered over to the window and imagined as she looked down that she was a princess shut up in an ivory tower. It seemed a delightful idea.

A large crimson car was making all the noise. It had just drawn up below her. The crimson, she thought with distaste, was the colour of blood.

Edward revved up once more and then sprang out gaily. His joy of possessing had now spread into the material world. Although not thinking in these terms himself, he had an exciting sense of growing up.

Fenella sank back into her armchair. She listened to Edward's long strides up the staircase.

'I'm celebrating!' he cried, throwing himself towards her. 'Look out of the window.' Fenella thought he was like a child and that all heroes were children. *Boy's Own*.

'Your mother phoned me from Izmir,' she said hopelessly.

'Izmir. Ah, you mean Smyrna. I've always favoured Greek over Turk. Civilization over barbarity.' Edward was delighted to be already discussing.

'The boat made a special stop.'

'To see Ephesus.'

'No. Round about Gallipoli your father died.'

'Gallipoli?' Edward stood quite still. 'At Gallipoli?'

'Off the coast. They went into Izmir, Smyrna, and took him off and now your mother's flying home with the body.'

'They should have put him into the sea.' Edward stared

fiercely. 'He would have liked that. With all the other Englishmen. He fought in the war, you know.'

'The First World War?'

'No.' Edward swung about. 'What does it matter anyway. He's dead. I bought a car.'

'Yes.'

'It's red.'

'I saw. What shall we do about the funeral? And your mother?'

'I don't know. I don't know.' Angrily, sulkily, Edward moved towards the door. 'What does one usually do? My mother's very efficient about that sort of thing.'

Fenella put her hand to her head. Large tears magnified her eyes. Edward stopped and stared. He went to the window. Then he began to hiccough in a dreadful rasping way. Fenella immediately stopped crying herself and rushed over to him. She put her arms about his bony heaving chest. After a bit they sat down on the floor and she smiled tenderly.

Soon Edward recovered. He felt very hungry and healthy. He remembered his new car with guilt and pleasure. He decided to exchange it for a less ridiculous model. 'When does my mother arrive? I'll meet her at the airport.'

*

Edward was important. In the days that followed his father's death, this was what made most impression on him. There were endless meetings with old men in suits and watch chains in a part of London he'd imagined demolished with Dickens. He was treated with deference; secretaries showed him to doors and brought him tea or coffee. It was a new sensation which he enjoyed.

However, after ten days he began to be irritated, for he had done no work. Death was a contagion which must not be allowed to kill his work. He and Fenella were staying with his mother in her gloomy London house. Fenella and Gunilla were very careful and gentle with each other. The advent of life and the advent of death seemed to have put them in the same quiet melancholy.

Edward had not been to his studio at all. He wondered

now about Austin whom he had never contacted. He said to Fenella, who lay on a sofa half-reading, half-dreaming – he found her tranquillity almost unbearable – 'I'm going to see Tristram.'

'Tristram? Where has he been? He didn't even come to the funeral.' Fenella didn't feel as disapproving as she sounded. Her nausea was beginning to pass and now she felt washed in some soothing syrup so that she never seemed to be fully awake. When she tried to write an essay – for she should be working up to her final exams – her sentences spun themselves into more and more circles till she quite lost her train of thought. And yet she couldn't make herself feel it mattered. All she wanted was a pile of Victorian novels, each with the maximum number of pages. She lifted up her book again; at the moment it was Mrs Gaskell's *Wives and Daughters*. Loelia had passed it onto her. She had already forgotten her conversation with Edward.

'No one was at the funeral.'

'Oh.' Fenella tried to remember. 'Wasn't Tish?'

'It's hardly surprising Tristram wasn't. Your own mother wasn't.'

'Loelia's so occupied.' Fenella looked vague. She wasn't sure why she knew her mother was busy. She hardly ever saw her. Perhaps that was the reason.

'Perhaps she has a lover.'

'Give my love to Tristram.'

'Good-bye.'

Edward still did not admit to Fenella's pregnancy; this, despite her change of character which she even exaggerated in an unconscious striving for recognition. Edward rose above such petty motivation. She had, of course, informed him clearly of her pregnancy that one strange night. But then so had Maggie – in that awful mumbo jumbo that had made him stop his ears.

It was good to be on his way to work via Tristram. He walked briskly down the street to his Jaguar and enjoyed once more the sable exterior lined with tan which had replaced the too shocking red. It was odd how surprised everyone had been when he had acquired a car; it had so quickly become an essential part of his life – a link between himself and the world, almost a second house where he kept what objects he considered essential for living – a canvas, a rug, a shooting stick, a packet of biscuits, a change of socks, gumboots and various silk handkerchiefs. To him the car represented freedom. That the Jaguar's image was generally associated with bourgeois businessmen did not interest him at all; he had freed his from that glass-fronted zoo.

*

Loelia Frith-Peacock was entertaining Dr Ferguson to a cup of tea and a plate of biscuits. Neither tea nor biscuits were particularly nice, because she had for too long sought pleasure in the ironies of failure rather than in the joy of success. If she had produced jasmine tea and real cream cakes (they were bought and discarded in the kitchen) she could not have smiled despairingly, but would have to preen and shine. She did not dare that yet. However well this new relationship was developing. If only Dr Ferguson did not prove himself too stupidly blunt. He might not realize the delicacy of her soul.

Edward knocked with his car keys on the window. Driving his car made him capable of doing brash things like banging on a window. Anyway he imagined Tristram inside the white shrouding, lying prone in negligent idleness. He knocked again vigorously and the window pane, old and frail, shattered into the room.

Dr Ferguson dropped his Crawford's plain and leapt to the fireplace. Loelia sighed with admiration as he bent and then stood erect again. She knew there was something absurd about a man with a poker, but it was so long since she had been made to feel like a young princess. He took up position in front of her and with a gallant flourish of his not very warlike implement (it was delicate and burnished, untouched by fire) cried vigorously :

'Whoever you are, come out right away !'

There was a pause while Loelia noted that in times of stress his Canadian accent seemed to predominate; and that too she liked, for it made him more manly, more remote from the home counties. Then a very English voice drawled, 'I'm out already.'

'Oh dear.' With reluctance Loelia was forced to recognize the voice of her son-in-law. 'It's Edward.'

'Ah. The painter.' With a severe expression Dr Ferguson returned the poker to the fireplace. 'There's still no reason for him to break a window.'

'Do come and open the door,' said Edward plaintively. 'I'm beginning to feel conspicuous. If a policeman comes by I'll be arrested.'

Loelia raised her eyebrows at Dr Ferguson and rose from her seat, 'You won't be the first one.'

'What?' Edward moved from the window to the door. It had been a very odd sensation feeling the glass give way under his fingers. A window had always seemed inviolable, protected by its nature, by the law, by what it represented; an important part of an Englishman's castle; and yet this glass had disintegrated at his fingertips. It fascinated him. He felt it meant more than appeared on the surface.

'I hardly touched it,' he declared emphatically as he entered the drawing-room.

'Then there must be a fault in the glass,' Dr Ferguson responded drily. Loelia relished his pragmatic solidity.

Edward dashed his hand through his hair. He was more than ever excited, 'A fault! Yes, of course, a fault!' He bounded over to the part of the carpet which was strewn with glass and started picking up the bigger pieces. The moral implication in the idea of a fault delighted him. 'Can you see a fault? Will I find it? What does it look like?'

Dr Ferguson smiled good-humouredly at Loelia. 'An unnaturally straight break would be some indication.'

'A fault. A flaw. A house with a fault.' Edward scrabbled among the glass, holding up first one piece and then another. Sometimes raising it hopefully for Dr Ferguson's inspection who always shook his head. 'Look,' he cried at one moment. 'It's like the centre drop of a chandelier.'

'Except that it cuts.'

'Ouch.' Sure enough Edward had pierced his finger and red blood dripped onto the carpet.

Loelia, who had not worried over Maggie's window, felt pangs of guilt at the black spots staining the pale carpet. She persuaded Edward to sit in a chair and hold his hand in the air.

'Will the blood really drain backwards like a Biro?' The car ride, the broken window, the blood had all put Edward into the best of moods. 'Now I understand why a broken mirror is considered unlucky.'

'I suppose this house isn't very lucky at the moment.' Loelia felt herself settling back into her usual self and was depressed. Dr Ferguson, too, had become safe and middle-aged again. She glanced at the little poker to recapture, before it was lost forever, that moment of shared danger.

Only Edward, finger pointed at the ceiling, continued invigorated. 'Unlucky here? How? A moral flaw?'

'Maggie wouldn't let anyone tell you. Because of your father, I suppose.' Loelia looked doubtful. 'Tristram's in prison.'

Edward felt a magic sense of rightness. He immediately pictured Tristram in a small barred room stretched on a low slatted bench. Tristram had always suffered from too much freedom; it had pressed on his too small share of talent and humiliated him. How he would profit from imprisonment! Then he became more sensible. 'Why Tristram? He never does anything.'

'He stole a motor bicycle. That motor bicycle you rode.'

'That was stolen?' A further experience. Edward thought that the excitement he had experienced astride the machine might have been an intimation of its illegality. 'Perhaps I could be had for aiding and abetting.'

'They're not very interested in that side any more.'

'I'm afraid your friend's in very serious trouble.' Dr Ferguson revolved a piece of biscuit solemnly. Loelia couldn't resist an ironic smile – although of course he was right, it *was* horribly serious. And yet it was hard to believe that anything Tristram did could be important enough to set the great wheels of British justice turning. Edward shared this view.

'But he never does anything,' he said as he had at the beginning.

'His room was filled with cannabis. Chock-a-block.' Loelia's smile crept in again. 'They think he's a pusher, the centre of a ring. He could get years. If it was just possession, he might have had a chance. But he had it in his drawer. Bales of it. Not hidden at all. They even suspected Maggie.'

'And you, Loelia,' boomed Dr Ferguson protectively.

'Not any more. But they couldn't believe anyone could take the risk of having so much just for his own use.'

'Tristram's so stupid,' Edward said dispassionately. His earlier ebullience had been flattened by the weight of the news. 'What about the motor bicycle?'

'It belonged to a painter working next door. He collected it. He wasn't very cross really. Oh. Look!' Loelia pointed. A hand was coming through the window.

'Everything all right here?'

'It's a policeman,' Loelia sighed. 'I expect the house is still under surveillance.'

'Quite all right, thank you, officer.' Dr Ferguson resumed his role as protector. 'Just an accident. We'll block it up in a moment.'

'I should do that, sir. It's not a good idea to leave a hole like that right on the street.'

'This reminds me of Gilbert and Sullivan,' said Edward. 'Would you mind if I have a biscuit and a cup of tea?'

'I'm afraid it'll be cold.'

'Good night then,' said the policeman stroking a bushy black beard. 'I won't be far away.'

Edward decided it was time to go. Loelia looked up surprised as he started briskly for the door. Her face, pale and excited, seemed suddenly young. Edward saw it and stopped.

'You are so brilliant this evening, Loelia. So ... *jeune*. Has something happened? Should I drop to my knee and kiss your hand?'

Loelia was embarrassed and pleased and, annoyingly, reminded of her daughter, of whom they had not yet spoken.

'I was going to make another cup of tea.'

'Don't bother for me. I swigged down that cold stuff. I believe it's the dark blue that suits you so.' Edward stood back appreciatively, as if he was looking at a painting. He decided she had style and one day he would like to paint her.

'How is Fenella?' cried Loelia. This reminded Edward of Tristram.

'Is Tristram in prison now?' he asked severely.

'You two certainly believe in *non sequitur*'s,' Dr Ferguson's indulgent tone had an undercurrent of irritation. Loelia heard it at once and was on her guard.

'Tristram would like you to visit him, I'm sure,' she said formally. 'Maggie too.'

'Maggie!' Edward swivelled nervously. As usual he had forgotten Maggie's relationship to Tristram. 'She isn't here, is she?'

'She's seeing the lawyer. Don't worry. I'll explain about the window.'

Edward was sorry he had left the results of an action of his in Maggie's house. She would gloat over it, clasp it to her ageing bosom, feel the glassy fragments directed towards her heart.

Dr Ferguson rose from his chair and extended his hand to Edward. In his opinion *jeunesse dorée* had dominated the scene long enough. 'I expect we'll see you again.'

'I'd like you to have seen my car.' Edward allowed himself to be guided to the door. Again he was picturing Tristram in prison, but this time he saw that he would not be able to cope with it; for confinement above all needs discipline. His studio was a prison. How Tristram would have enjoyed flying along in his Jaguar. Such a toy! On a reflex of enthusiasm he kissed Loelia very warmly on both cheeks.

'Oh.' She swayed back.

'Good-bye.' Dr Ferguson shut the door firmly after him. But Loelia, going to the holed window, saw him step into the Jaguar. 'How extraordinary. He always seems so much the aesthete.'

'Painters can be materialistic like anyone else.' Dr Ferguson put a hand on each of her shoulders.

*

Edward found a note and a letter waiting for him in his studio. He had thought it such a private place that he was surprised anyone should see it a suitable channel for communication. The note was of course from Austin, pencil-written in uneven capitals. 'No motor bicycle there, Austin'. Succinct as in life. Or perhaps angry.

Edward, wondering, took the other elegant letter to his chaise longue. He was excited to discover Nadia Gore's signature at the end. She was writing firstly to condole with him over the death of his father; she understood something of what he must be feeling because for years now she had been preparing for the death of her husband. 'He is some years older than your father was.' Also she would like to see him again for she felt herself capable of 'encouraging his talent'. She hoped this didn't sound presumptuous, for it was meant in all humility. Edward was flattered. It did not cross his mind that Lady Gore had never seen any of his paintings. Friendship in the name of his talent was too seductive a prospect for any mean questioning. Her reference to her husband made him seem already dead to Edward or at very least some remote parental equation. He wished for a moment that he had a telephone so that he could ring her immediately and be inspired by those clever tones. But after all a hand-delivered letter would be so much more effective – a painted scrawl, an obeisance to her command. Edward tore a piece of cartridge paper from his pad and found a smallish brush.

*

Tish was wondering when Edward would feel able to start painting again. She had only sat for him three times, but she had found a gap in her life when the sittings stopped. Twice she went round to Fenella and talked with her and Gunilla about baking bread, an ambition they shared, but Edward appeared distracted and did not listen to her remarks. Her only consolation was reliving those three sessions when she had had all his attention. She had sat on a gilded Searcy's chair in that white dress she had worn at that dinner party when Tristram (poor Tristram) had passed out. Edward had insisted on the dress, repeating that she looked like the Queen of the Willies; it seemed he was planning to put dark tree trunks behind her and silver stars tangled among the branches. It was a low-cut gossamery dress, provocative in an unfashionable naïve way. It felt strange to wear it in the hard morning light and even stranger to let a man stare at her hour after hour. And Edward did stare. She knew a painter must look at his subject but she had never imagined what it felt like to submit. Although Edward hardly spoke she found herself talking compulsively, as if at a cocktail party or on an analyst's couch. That's what the whole experience was most like, psychoanalysis; she came away from each session feeling exhilarated, more aware of her body and mind. How she longed for him to start again. For the third time she called on Fenella and Gunilla. Third time lucky. Fenella said,

'Edward went to the studio today.'

'Oh, really?' Tish was so thrilled that she pretended negligence and then wondered why.

'He's been very restless.'

'I could go round.'

*

Edward had delivered his letter to Nadia. He set up the two canvases he'd abandoned and already the idea of Nadia made him feel dissatisfied with a vulgarity in Tish's pose. He had taken her arrival in the studio entirely for granted and watched impatiently while she changed and brushed her hair. 'Brush it up into an aureole.'

Tish became nervous and tried to explain, 'But it's only fluffy when I wash it or I get caught in the rain.'

'Wet it then.'

And now she was perched on the gilt chair while he looked at her.

'Slightly to your left,' he commanded.

'Like this?' Tish was humble.

Today his effect on her was not entirely therapeutic. His look seemed more personal, more inquiring. As if he had not forgotten himself in his study of her.

'Have you thought of an exhibition, Edward? You seemed

to get on awfully well with Lady Gore. She's the power, you know, in the gallery.'

An unpleasant thought struck Edward. Perhaps Nadia's 'encouraging his talent' meant a mundane thing like an exhibition, instead of the personal inspiration he'd assumed. It was a depressing thought which could have compensations. Taking his brush very carefully, he twitched the corner of Tish's mouth so that the smile changed from being merely charming to complacently aristocratic. She was a stupid girl; he'd always thought so. 'Hold on a moment.' He picked up a canvas from the wall and stood it beside Tish. It was the nude painting of Austin. He placed it carefully so that the two figures, real and unreal, appeared to hold hands. If anything Austin looked more alive than Tish.

'I want to paint your feet,' he said scornfully. And then waited impassively as Tish hastily stripped tights and shoes. As he had suspected, she had short-toed, stuffy, broad, workmanlike feet. He thought of Fenella's arched insteps nostalgically; in the past he had admired them as much as her face. Lately they had become flattened. It was a sad thing to see a swan turn into a duck. Tish flexed her toes. But here was a duck already, pretending to be a swan ... Edward looked at the two figures in front of him again. How he longed to start on his double portrait. If only Austin had not disappeared. Tish and Austin. He must see them together.

'Have you seen Tristram yet?' said Tish who was still uneasy. Edward's concentration was definitely not on his painting.

'No. But I shall go to the trial.'

'Is that soon?'

'I've no idea. No doubt someone will tell me.'

'Will you give evidence?'

'Why should they ask?'

'Well.' Edward looked so majestic. More like a judge than a friend. 'You might give him a good character.'

'How could I do that? To Tristram?'

'He is serious about painting. You could say he was experimenting to extend his visual imagination.' Tish had thought about this and it seemed a good idea to her.

'No.'

'Why ever not?'

'I'm not prostituting my art. I wish Austin would come.'

Tish saw his mind was on something else all the time. 'You mean the window-cleaner? I saw a window-cleaner as I came along.'

Edward dashed out of the door. It swung behind him. Tish felt silly sitting alone on the gilt chair. Her white dress she noticed was turning grey at the edges. The back of her painting was facing her as usual. Edward had never let her see it; guiltily she crept forward.

'Boo!' Tish thought she would faint. She bent double and let the blood rush to her head.

'You shouldn't frighten . . .'

'You shouldn't peep and peer.'

'I'm sorry, Edward. Honestly . . .'

'I forgive you. I found Austin.' Edward pranced and glowed with excitement. 'He's very cross at the moment, but he'll cheer up when I've crossed his palm with silver.'

'Afternoon, miss.' Austin was so wonderfully perfectly unchanged. Although it had only been two weeks since Edward had seen him last, he'd feared terribly that the face would have changed, lost that challenging surliness, become smoothed and ordinary, vocal, sociable. He rejoiced in his bleak black face and staring blue eyes.

'He said the motor bicycle wasn't there. I said he could use it. It was most annoying for him.'

'I'm so sorry,' Tish became automatically sympathetic. She was frightened that Austin would take off his clothes and despised herself for it. Surely in this day and age, man's nudity was nothing remarkable. Anyway she could see his all in the painting. 'Perhaps I should . . .'

But Austin did not take off his clothes. He was filled with righteous anger and not in the least susceptible to Edward's charm. It was true, however, that he had come at the prospect of payment. Money was more important than any emotional attitude.

'Honestly, I am sorry,' said Edward. He smiled. 'You see the motor bicycle was stolen.'

Now Austin became even more agitated. A stolen motor bicycle was not a semantic frill, as it was with Edward. It meant the police, prison, poverty. He picked up his bucket which he had set down on the floor and prepared to go.

'And then my father died,' said Edward gently. 'So you see, it wasn't really my fault. Please don't be angry.'

Tish looked unhappy. It was as if Edward was using his father's death to lure back this window-cleaner. She wanted to leave even more, but couldn't think how to take off her dress modestly. Although Austin stood like a block with those oddly unseeing blue eyes, she was embarrassingly aware of that virile hairy body. 'I ought to go,' she said again.

Edward was aware of the heavily charged atmosphere. He noticed that Austin had never once looked at Tish. 'You are staying, then?'

'For the money.' Austin put down his bucket again. 'I'm sorry about the death.'

'That's all right. He knew it was going to happen. He had cancer.' Edward wondered why he did not take his clothes off and then noticed. Tish. Tish felt spurned by his glance and, going into the corner, pulled her trousers on under her dress and then, back turned, slipped off the dress. No one took any notice until she was ready.

'Good-bye, miss,' said Austin.

'Will it be tomorrow over lunch, Edward? I should work.'

'Darling Tish! How I use you.' Edward swooped forward and held the door for her. He bent down and kissed her with gallant appreciation. He smoothed a hand over her hair. 'Wash it before you come. Remember you're my fairy. My queen.'

Austin watched stolidly. And Tish produced a rather wan little smile.

'Adieu, darling.'

Austin took off his clothes and folded them as neatly as ever. After a quarter of an hour of silence he said, 'Was it your mate who stole the motor bicycle?'

'I suppose so.' Edward was struggling to paint his piercing yet somehow blind blue eyes. Then he remembered his vision of Austin on a motor bike. 'I promised you one.'

'Not stolen.'

'I want to paint you on one.'

'Did your mate get caught?'

'I suppose so. How much would a secondhand bike cost?'

'Out on bail?'

'No. I could buy you one. To keep, I mean.'

'Don't you care about your mate?'

'What?' Edward was shocked. Austin was not employed to give him moral guidance. He was a window-cleaner, a raw working-class chap with no better feelings. 'Do you want more money?'

'Wouldn't mind,' replied Austin unemotionally. 'And I'll take that bike.'

Edward began to paint again, but was annoyed still that his symbol had spoken. He thought that now he would have to put more than a ladder and pail into his background. In fact, it had occurred to him since the episode of Maggie's broken window that a street full of windows glittering provocatively like ice would be an exciting alternative. Austin had the brutish look of someone who could push in a row as easily as press a door bell. Yet he spent his days, soft cloth in hand, rubbing them as gently as a row of babies' bottoms. Edward realized it was this contradiction in his personality which had attracted him in the first place. Perhaps this new moralistic side of his nature was a further interesting discovery, that little silver cross round his neck more than an ornament. A window-cleaner had such opportunities for judging other people's lives. How could he get that 'God is everywhere' into his picture?

There was silence for some time. Edward was concentrating on the canvas. The studio began to get very warm. It was now July. The early afternoon sun poured down through the wide glass roof. Sweat started on Edward's pale forehead but he didn't notice it.

'Can we open a window?'

Edward started violently. Austin had become sculpture for him again. His black hair always shone with oil so he had not noticed the sweat; his complexion was always rubicund so he had not noticed it darken. He looked at the small square in the wall.

'It doesn't.'

Austin pointed upwards.

'There must be a skylight. All that glass.'

Edward looked up also. 'If you can open it. There's no cord.'

Of course Austin was a professional. He swung himself up by the two great black beams that crossed the ceiling. Edward felt a mixture of excitement and revulsion at the sight. He hadn't bothered to put on any clothes and his nude hairy body swinging above his head was exceedingly like a monkey's. Remembering his visit with Fenella to the zoo, Edward could even put a name to it, 'Hylobates Lar'. The absurdity of this lessened both excitement and revulsion. 'Can you manage?'

A loud crack answered him and a section of the roof about two feet by two feet shot into the air. Austin jumped down again.

'Heavens. How will I ever shut it?'

'The rain won't get in.'

'Burglars might.'

'What for?' Austin settled back into his pose.

But again Edward couldn't settle down to painting. 'How did you get those biceps?' Although Austin's nude acrobatics hadn't appeared at all provocative, indeed quite the contrary, even so he had been made uncomfortably aware of the intimacies of his body. Besides, despite the open window the room was very hot.

'In the circus.'

'Trapeze,' suggested Edward.

'Wall of Death.'

'That. On motor bicycles. I see.'

'I began as the Strong Arm Man,' explained Austin indifferently.

'And progressed to the Wall of Death.'

'Till they chucked me.'

'Not because you failed?'

'No. Not my work. There was never anything wrong with my work. It was my morals they didn't like.'

This was the longest sentence Austin had ever spoken. Edward thought it must cover deep emotion. He waited curiously.

'The trapeze artiste took a fancy to me. She was married to the boss.'

'I do see.'

'But I wasn't having anything to do with her. And the boss didn't like that. She was twenty years younger than him and he liked to see her have fun. But I had my missus then. And the kids.'

'Oh, yes. Of course,' said Edward, as Austin fell silent. The bleakness of his morals was frightening. Like suddenly coming face to face with a granite rock. He could see why the circus manager had sacked him. 'It really is hot.' He rubbed his forehead and nose with one of his silk handkerchiefs. 'Too hot to concentrate. Let's call it a day.'

'Rightio, chief.' Austin responded with alacrity, as if the telling of his story had released some special spring of energy. His dark shiny body disappeared quickly into the cuffed blue jeans and purple shirt. 'Tomorrow, then.' He tied the bright handkerchief Edward had given him round his neck and turned to the door.

He had such a hot-looking body and there was a pungent smell about him Edward had never noticed before. He doubted whether his clothes were ever washed. And indeed who was to do them, if he had no wife? Visits to the local launderette perhaps. It was the sort of dreary image Edward least liked to entertain.

'Very good. See you tomorrow.'

*

Fenella wandered slowly along the dusty London street. She thought sadly and nostalgically about the summer Tristram, she and Edward had spent with Edward's parents in the country. Now Mr Aubrey was dead; Mrs Aubrey mourning; Tristram in prison and herself no longer beautiful. Only Edward was the same or more so. Suddenly she longed for the countryside. But her childhood home where she would normally have gone was divided and spoilt. Her mother needed all her selfishness to fight for her independence in London, and she could hardly flee to her father.

London was so dusty and unreal in the summer. It became coated in the dreary aimless rush of too many tourists. It became a place without personality. Fenella wandered along. She was only four months pregnant, but seemed more. She had no particular destination, having set out only from a desire to leave the stuffy house for a while. She was beginning to realize her intimacy with Gunilla was not altogether a healthy thing. She did not try to cheer the bereaved widow, who indeed did not seem to wish it, but sank down with her. She had used to think herself something more substantial. What had happened for the change? Why did she feel so drained of stirring blood? Fenella's head dropped lower.

'Evenin', missus.'

Fenella looked up vaguely. A deep blush covered her face as she recognized Edward's window-cleaner. Again, as she had that first time on the street, she felt immediately overpowered by his violent masculinity. And today it was even more intense. That heat which, apart from that sudden now vanished flush, had drained and exhausted her made him seem even more alive – his black hair shinier, his blue eyes bluer, his complexion redder; his barely covered chest glistened with sweat and exuded a strong smell. Fenella swayed forward.

'Here, hold on. That's it.'

Fenella felt the hard muscles of his forearm under her fingers. It was like holding the bar of a trapeze – solid wood but swinging slightly.

'Look. There's a wall here. Sit down. Put your head between your knees.'

'It's nothing,' gasped Fenella. She felt him bending over her and the smell becoming more intense. 'Air. Just a bit of air.'

'My missus always came over funny. At the beginning like. Especially in the heat.'

Not recognizing his reference to her pregnancy, Fenella feebly tried to push him aside. 'Oh please.' At last he stood back. She shut her eyes and took a few careful breaths. Immediately she began to revive. 'I feel much better. So silly.'

'Going to see your boss, I expect.'

'Boss?' Fenella opened her eyes.

'I just came from him. The room was hot too. He looked a bit queer.'

'I'm better now. Really.'

'He'll find you something to drink.'

'Yes. Thank you.'

'I'll go on then.'

Fenella wondered why he didn't. She was quite pleased to discover she was near Edward's studio. She could say she had just been passing. She stood up and there was the window-cleaner still hovering. She didn't feel he was a threat any more, now that her mind was on Edward. He had been kind to her.

'You clean windows, don't you?'

'That's the thing.'

'If you're not too busy any time, I'd be awfully grateful if you could come and do my flat. The windows are filthy. They haven't been done for an age. Since I moved in.'

Austin took a step back. 'A couple of weeks I'll be freer.'

'Flat four. 33 Ladysmith Road. Thank you so very much. For everything, I mean.'

'Very good, ma'am.'

Fenella trod swiftly down the street. With the help of the window-cleaner, she had taken the decision to move back into her own flat. She would tell Edward so at once.

*

The first day of Tristram's trial was extremely hot. Even those most determined to go to court, like Fenella, felt it horribly constraining to leave the sunlit air for a windowless courtroom. The Old Bailey, too, was so huge along the street, towered so close over the pavement, that it depressed one even to look at it. And then they had to queue – at least

Fenella did, and Tish and Loelia who were all together – but Maggie was allowed in immediately as a relative. They met in the courtroom. No one mentioned what everyone noticed, that it was Number 13. They were all very surprised by the modern look of the room; shiny yellow wood everywhere, new green carpeting, not very big and no more impressive than the foyer of a modern hotel.

'Here comes Tristram.' Fenella thought he'd never appeared so heroic. On this midsummer's day, his face was white as snow. He wore a white open-necked shirt and a black sweater. Pinned to his bosom was a button with a picture of a baby gorilla on it. Fenella felt like crying, he looked so noble.

The jury came in and they were red-faced and sweating and terrifyingly ordinary. Fenella didn't think they were at all capable of estimating Tristram's kind of innocence. They looked more capable of weighing up best back bacon. Democracy, she decided, was not planned to help the individual. Then they were bidden to stand for the judge – and he was old and bent and a little sweaty too under his wig. Conversely, Fenella was cheered by the sight, for it showed he was not an unfeeling man of steel.

And yet it was horrible to see so clearly. She had expected the scene would be put in front of them, like a play, safely distanced from the audience by a stage and instead they were on the stage themselves. The visitors' gallery, which had sounded so remote and official from the outside, was almost filled by their party. Where was Edward?

Some of the jury were objected to and dismissed. Two women were sent away by the defence and a West Indian by the prosecution.

'I'm glad he's gone,' whispered Maggie, who did not really wish to understand anything but the beauty and dignity of her son. She, like Tristram, was dressed in black with a white blouse. With her high-brushed reddish hair and carefully executed make-up she looked like an actress playing the role of a barrister. Only the wig was missing.

'Where's Edward?' whispered Tish. 'Surely he's coming.'
Edward appeared at half-past twelve. It was very odd to

see someone from the world outside. Already after two hours they seemed to have been locked up forever with the slow dirge-like voices of the law.

Edward was dressed in white flannel from top to toe. Maggie, who had been dreading and longing for his arrival, flinched nervously as he bounded across her legs to the remaining empty chair. 'What a ghoulish place!' he said quite loudly, so that an usher swung his black gown disapprovingly. 'It's like being back at University. Ugly pomposity.'

Edward had hoped to be uplifted by the dignity of the law, but instead felt threatened by mediocrity.

'Is it as dreary as this all the time?' Edward bent to Fenella. Her calmness seemed frozen. He found it impossible to surrender to the stupefaction which makes court life bearable. He shifted restlessly on his seat, enjoyed for a moment the prominence of the judge's nose and then turned to Tristram. That was a relief anyway. He didn't look in the slightest bit affected by all the sordid display. Edward smiled at him warmly.

Tristram's expression did not alter. Then he looked down at his hands.

A plain clothes policeman on the witness stand said, 'On March 7th at twelve five a.m. I saw the accused carrying a plastic bag marked WOW! enter a pizza house in Shaftesbury Avenue.'

The judge stirred. 'This seems like a good moment to take a break.'

Fenella wondered if he was making a joke; most people in the court were smiling but that was probably with relief at imminent escape.

Loelia's Dr Ferguson joined them for lunch; he had been waiting on the pavement. He quite agreed with Edward that the decoration of the Old Bailey would shame a Ho Jo.

'But that's the modern addition. Just built.' Tish was always fair. 'There is the old marble and painted bit too.'

'Frescoes like Russian imperialism.' Edward refused to be placated.

Fenella stared at her plate and then took a quick look at Maggie. This guide book approach to the morning's experience must surely disgust her – unless she was completely anaesthetized by her role of tragic mother.

Fenella said, 'It's marvellous about bail. I'm so glad for both of you.'

'He says all the travelling will be such a bore,' said Maggie gloomily. She couldn't help remembering that Fenella had last seen her wheeling a motor bicycle from Edward's studio at four in the morning.

'I suppose you'll have to watch over him?'

'How can I control him? You know Tristram. He'll just go on as he's always done. Go back to that Cherry girl, I wouldn't be surprised.'

'But that would be madness. I mean wasn't she arrested too?'

'Fined ten pounds. In and out. No one except Tristram would have two drawers full of the stuff. It was worth thousands of pounds, they said. Whose money was that?'

'I am sorry,' said Fenella feebly. 'Have some more potatoes.'

'No, thank you.'

Loelia suddenly joined in. 'But you should, Fenella, dear.'

'What?'

'Have some more potatoes. In your condition. You're like a skeleton!'

'So fierce!' Edward laughed and abandoned his architectural review. 'Thin women are much more elegant. Fat is the same on everyone; bones are always individual.'

'Fenella has a duty to her baby.' Loelia smiled at Dr Ferguson.

'You will come to see Tristram tonight, won't you, Edward?' Maggie's appeal interrupted them suddenly, pathetically. Her spongy appearance made Edward's statement seem like a personal attack. Fenella's assumption of the maternal role left her only Tristram to lay at Edward's feet.

'Certainly not,' said Edward. 'Tristram would hate it. We would have nothing to talk about. I don't believe in drugs. He looked very fine this morning and I don't wish to see him again.'

*

As it turned out Tristram took bail but was hardly out long enough for any real visits. The second morning of his trial he managed to evade Maggie and arrive at the courts an hour late. The judge revoked bail. Tristram smiled and laid his head on the front of the dock. He kept it there all morning. He was dreaming quite comfortably of his night with Cherry, and it was not till very late in the day that the effect of the cannabis he had taken began to wear off.

Nor did anyone, apart from Maggie, return to Court Thirteen. She became unexpectedly gay and optimistic about the outcome. She had lined up his housemaster from Eton to evidence his excellent character and said that she was looking forward to going into the witness box herself. Even when it was decided not to call her, she remained cheerful, apparently needing no more support than that given by her legal advisers. In fact at last Maggie had a cause. A reason for dressing, a reason for getting up in the morning. Tristram was safely locked away and only allowed out at the times she could be with him. She did not imagine how it might end.

*

Fenella and Tish were having tea in Fenella's flat when Maggie called. It was still very hot but for once the sun was not shining. Fenella said, 'I wish it would rain.'

Tish, who had just come from Edward's studio, exclaimed, 'Oh, no!'

'But the air's stifling.'

'It started once as I was sitting for Edward. It clatters on the glass roof. It's horrid really.'

'Still being painted?'

Tish flushed. 'It takes an awful long time. All the detail, I mean. And actually Edward wants to do another after this.'

'Have some more cake?' Fenella had started eating again and although it was a comfort to her, it did not seem to increase her girth. Only the baby sat like a round plum across her waist. She particularly liked a chocolate-covered gateau in the shape of a hedgehog; it had prickles made of almonds and eyes made of raisins. It was very rich and expensive and extraordinarily like a hedgehog.

Fenella was eating the head when she let Maggie in at the door. She always started at the head and worked backwards.

'Gosh! Mrs Brown!' Tish jumped up and offered her a chair. Maggie had been crying; great pale rivers cut channels between her orange cheeks; at the source they were polluted by mascara.

'They gave him eighteen months. They gave him eighteen months. They gave him eighteen months. They gave him eighteen months.'

'Are you sure you didn't misunderstand?' said Tish hopefully.

'I told my solicitor the jury had misunderstood. But he said it wasn't the fault of the jury. They had to find him guilty. But the judge had decided to make an example of him. Too many middle-class children were getting away with it. My solicitor said we were very unlucky in getting a communist judge. He says we should never have called that foolish master from Eton. I said that all along, because he said that Tristram had always been artistically inclined and everyone in the court sniggered because it only meant one thing to them. The judge was prejudiced against him, he kept stopping him and interrupting him and saying he was to speak loudly and it was paying disrespect to the jury, to ... it was disrespectful to the members of the jury ... members of the jury ...'

'Please let me get you a cup of tea,' Fenella, still with hedgehog head in hand, leant hopelessly over Maggie. Maggie looked up and then absentmindedly took the cake. 'Thank you. Thank you.' She began to eat and cry at the same time.

'Oh Christ,' said Tish. 'What do we do?'

'Get her home, I suppose.'

'How ghastly. Poor Tristram. Poor Tristram.'

Fenella frowned suspiciously. Tish wasn't going to start that dreadful repetition too. 'The thing is to be calm.'

'Why?' said Maggie dourly, and then as if repenting, needing comfort, added, 'I will have some more of this gateau though.'

'Do please,' said Fenella, chopping at the tail.

'Tristram said you wouldn't like a wedding cake,' said Maggie, beginning to cry again. 'That you'd think it immoral.'

'I love cake.'

'So we ate it. We had such fun.'

'I'm glad. Really.'

'But you could have had it.'

'Never mind. Please. I had a wedding lunch.'

'Oh. Yes. But Tristam took me away.'

'Perhaps she should have a drink,' said Tish.

10

The Gores' country house appeared out of the dry warmth of an early August evening like a doll's house. It was built of red bricks. With a pair of bow windows, scrubbed stone steps leading to a neatly arched door and a sloping grey slate roof topped with a great many chimneys – one of which smoked in a cotton wool twist.

'How amusing.' Edward peered through the windscreen of his car. The sinking sun turned his pale hair from silver to reddish gold. Fenella shivered. She wished he had come alone. The nursery book orderliness gave her an unpleasant feeling, for she could not reconcile it with the snake-like Lady Gore and her decaying husband. 'Like the gingerbread house,' she murmured, 'witchlike.'

'How amusing,' said Edward again. 'We must tell Lady Gore. Nadia.'

Fenella was not sure which she was to him. It didn't help that neither was Edward. They had met twice since the Skeffington-Smith dinner; once for a drink at her house and once at his studio but on both occasions she had been curiously cool with him. She had admired his pictures but sensibly, critically, not ardently as he had hoped. So that he wondered if the encouragement she'd promised depended on some action of his. She had watched him continually.

It was Nadia herself who answered their ring at the brass door bell. She drew them in warmly, led them to the drawing-room and pressed drinks into their hands.

'You must be exhausted,' she kept saying, with her eyes flashing to Fenella's grey tight face and then downwards for a moment to her swollen tummy. And yet it was a small swelling still, round like a bubble.

'Not now we're here,' Fenella responded brightly.

'In this room!' exclaimed Edward, waving his hand at the

tall marble fireplace, at the bright vermilion walls, at the paintings everywhere.

'The colour.' Nadia smiled gaily. 'I call it my Ottoline Morrell room. You know she had a passion for the primaries. I often wonder whether it wasn't her unconscious effort to obliterate all those second-rate artists who hung about her.'

'Second-rate.' Edward was scandalized. 'You can't dismiss . . .'

'Mark Gertler for example. You won't dare pretend he could paint. Those terrible black outlines and those awful prune colours. In fact they all had a positive obsession for prune and dirty banana and noxious green. Hideous, if one's honest. I know it's the fashion now to adore them and of course as an investment they're a certainty, but don't let's pretend they could paint.'

'But their composition. Their perspective; their use of lines . . .'

'I never said they couldn't draw. They could draw all right. But if only they'd stayed away from paint. It's no accident, you know, that in a time of soaring art prices, they've taken nearly forty years to reach any value at all. Even the best of them. Frankly, only an unhealthy drab person could appreciate those unhealthy drab paintings.'

'Gertler isn't drab. Whatever else you can say . . .'

Fenella sat on an azure-blue silk sofa looking at her glass of sherry. She herself was wearing a long greyish-green dress and she felt as if Nadia's tirade was aimed at her. Drab and dreary. It was absurd really, for Nadia herself, despite the summer heat, was dressed mostly in black; black trousers, black silk shirt and a narrow black snakeskin belt. Yet she looked immensely sure of herself, chic, supple, and clever. Fenella, who had always considered Lady Ottoline Morrell a vituperative cold woman, wondered whether Lady Gore shared more with her than a delight in primary colours.

Edward was already in an ecstasy of argument. Nadia was the price she must pay for his happiness. So, with a start, she thought of Sir Arthur Gore, their host. She looked up frowning to Nadia who, as if reading her thoughts, took their empty glasses from them.

'I mustn't keep you from Arthur any more. He's been looking forward to re-meeting you both. But his deafness makes him an embarrassment in the drawing-room.'

Edward and Fenella followed Nadia up wide stairs and along blue carpeted corridors. She knocked at a door and when there was no answer opened it briskly and beckoned them forward. 'He's probably shut his eyes.'

The room was big and lined from top to bottom with books, as if it were a library. Although there was still light in the sky, the curtains were already drawn and the only light in the room came from a fire and a standard lamp near it. There was a strong medicinal smell.

'Arthur. Your visitors have arrived. Arthur.' Nadia addressed loudly a high-winged chair which stood by the fire with its back turned towards them. 'Wake up Arthur. You haven't even had dinner yet.' Smiling to Edward, she went over then and shook her husband's shoulder quite vigorously, till there were responsive snorts and grunts.

Fenella watched unhappily. Before, at Tish's dinner party, she had felt safe in assuming Sir Arthur a complacent old bore, but now seeing his wife's prattling patronage, she felt shocked. After all, whatever the age difference they were still man and wife. But she was treating him like an insensate animal. Unless it was that the situation itself was distorting. This brilliant woman married to that smudged old man. Fenella watched disgusted as his wrinkled hand grasped for his silver-topped cane and pushed himself up.

'Dinner, is it?'

'Not yet, dear. I was bringing our visitors.' Nadia bent over him solicitously.

Fenella moved backwards. She knew she must shake that soft old hand and the thought disgusted her; she didn't want the purity of her unborn child to be touched by the unnatural, the obscene union between this beastlike old man and this beautiful young woman. Nervously, she edged to the door.

'Aaaaahh!'

'I beg your pardon, miss.'

'Oh, Snepple. Is that you?' Nadia strode across the room

to them. 'Did he give you a fright? He's so quiet. Aren't you Snepple? Snepple's looked after Arthur for forty years. They don't really know they're two people. Do sit down Mrs Aubrey. You look quite pale.'

Fenella looked at the skeletal old man in his valet's dark suit. 'I'm so silly,' she said faintly. She felt her whole body thudding with terror. Surreptitiously, she slipped her hand across her tummy. For a moment she almost thought she could feel the baby thud too. It had never moved yet and more and more she longed for some evidence of new life.

Now she managed a wan smile. At least her hysterical outburst had avoided the necessity of shaking hands with Sir Arthur.

'Perhaps you'd like to lie down. After the drive. The heat.'

'Are we dressing for dinner?' Sir Arthur, who had been forgotten, asked suddenly, sternly.

Nadia turned to Edward. 'I hope you'll be flattered. You're our only guests this weekend.'

Fenella lay on her four-poster bed and watched the sky darken. Edward prowled about the room. He studied the rugs, the pictures, the books, as if he wanted to learn a secret from them. He was like a cat or a child, Fenella thought, turning himself round and round to make himself at home. She herself felt horribly homesick with that dry emptiness in her stomach and lonely desolation in her head. It could only be helped by a mound of hot water bottles pressed up around her but she could hardly ask Edward to find her that and she was too proud to ask Lady Gore.

'I could paint here!' Edward spoke fiercely into the silence. Fenella's heart sank even further.

'I find it creepy,' she said in a hopeless effort to communicate. 'That old dying man and – Lady Gore.'

'Nadia,' said Edward determinedly, but nevertheless he was interested. He had always a taste for sinister premonitions. 'How do you mean creepy?'

'Unnatural.'

Edward liked that too. He loved the supernatural. He had used to consider Fenella the most supernatural person he knew. 'The atmosphere of the house?' He came and sat on the bed. He bounced up and down on the springy eiderdown. 'Perhaps that's why I could paint. Inspiration is close to the supernatural.'

Fenella found his bouncing movement rocked her in a curiously soothing rhythm. She felt better than she had since they arrived at the house. 'I don't think I'll come to dinner,' she shut her eyes. 'I'm sure they won't miss me.' Although they were the only guests staying in the house, it seemed there would be twelve for dinner.

'No,' said Edward absentmindedly. Going through a door into the adjoining bathroom he turned on the taps into the bath. The rushing sound of water completed the process which the rocking had begun and Fenella fell soundly asleep.

Edward thought a little about Fenella as he went downstairs without her. He thought it very tactful of her to lie upstairs in the four-poster bed. It complemented his own ambitious energy. He liked the image of a young painter whose pregnant wife lay resting in their bedroom. With surprise, Edward realized that he had thought of Fenella as pregnant and found it acceptable. He smiled. A row of Virgin and Childs stretched in front of him. In his opinion none had succeeded in painting a baby interestingly since the sixteenth century – except possibly Goya. But then he made his babies look like small grown-ups. This was where the Christ baby had it over cupids or ordinary mortals, because he could be conceived with the wisdom of the ages in his face. The wisdom of the ages – Edward enjoyed the phrase and the theory. With a final twitch to his velvet bow tie, he hurried into the drawing-room; Nadia would find it a fascinating subject for discussion.

*

Fenella woke up sharply with a sense of dread. She put out a hand to turn on her bedside light and struck her knuckles on the wooden post of the four-poster bed. Then she realized where she was. It did not dismiss her dread. The night was cool now and absolutely quiet. Someone must have been in to draw the curtain, for there was not a suggestion of moon or stars. She had no idea what time it was and she did not pos-

sess a watch but she was sure it was after midnight, that she
really had slept through the whole evening, the whole dinner
party. Because everything felt so strange and uncomfortable,
she even wondered madly if Nadia had drugged her sherry.
Since her pregnancy she never slept so deeply for such a
length of time – even at night. It had left her quiveringly
awake, excited, curious. Who was still downstairs in the
drawing-room?

Fenella slipped gently out of bed and wound her paisley
shawl about her. She would glide like a ghost down the softly
carpeted stairs and peer into the great brightly painted
rooms. No one would notice her, so pale, so drained of force
and energy. Without that kernel of life inside her, she would
be nothing but a dried-up shell. She left her room, trod quietly to the head of the stairs and there hesitated for a moment,
pressing her tummy against the shiny banisters. If only the
baby would move. If only it would move. She put her thin
white hand on the rail and watched it slide slowly down in
front of her. The heavy black and gold mourning ring which
Edward had given her rolled from side to side of her finger.
Only the large bones of her knuckle stopped it falling off.

Edward had talked and drunk for five hours. Now he was
exhausted. He sprawled in the sofa listening to a record of a
Shostakovich cello concerto which Nadia had just put on the
gramophone. They were alone. The guests had all left. Sir
Arthur had gone up to his room long ago. Nadia stood by the
mantelpiece. She had exchanged her black trouser suit for a
shimmering silver grey. All evening she had darted like
quicksilver among her guests, never still, never settling with
anyone. Now, suddenly, she came and sat beside Edward.
She crossed her legs and her silver slippers hung from her
slim toes. She turned her particular expectant look onto
Edward.

'Has it been dreadfully boring for you?'

'Boring?'

'All those people. Who aren't very important.'

'Aren't they?'

'Not compared to you.'

Edward was silent. Her expression had been saying this

since their first meeting. 'I thought they were interesting. Enough.'

'But then people generally aren't very important to you. Are they? More like objects. And as objects you can admire them. Hang them round your neck.'

'Or from the ceiling.' Edward hardly knew that he spoke out loud. He felt so sleepy, so nearly asleep.

'What?'

'Chandeliers. They hang from the ceiling. I once found a beautiful glass chandelier. In Italy. In Florence. It glittered.'

'Where did you hang it?'

'I haven't hung it yet. I will though. One day. I don't quite know where it's gone to. I haven't seen it for ages.'

'Oh,' said Nadia losing interest. The chandelier had seemed important to Edward for a moment.

'Do you like this music?'

'Yes.'

'You should listen to music.'

'Yes.'

'Music and painting are complementary.'

'Yes,' Edward agreed again. 'Unlike painting and writing.'

'You should try painting to music.'

Edward felt under the command of a will stronger than his own. Nadia was part admirer, part guru : without surprise he felt her body insinuate itself along the length of his body. She put her warm hand on his hard wide forehead and whispered into his ear, 'I like to discover the inside of a man's brain. If I wasn't an art dealer, I would be a phrenologist.'

Edward smiled slightly, for even in his hazy state he could see she was being absurd. 'You're talking nonsense.'

'Why not?' Nadia lay close to him and moved her lips over his head. 'Such a strong delicate skull.'

Edward moved his head forward to hers and they kissed slowly.

Fenella began to wake up more as she descended the stairs and then she felt the danger. Ghosts and spies found nothing to make them happy. But it was too late to stop herself. All was quiet in the hallways and few lights burned. She crept along to the drawing-room. The door was half open and yet, for some guilty reason, she looked through the hinges, instead of the open space. Even so she saw Edward and Nadia perfectly clearly. They lay like a statue of lovers entwined on the sofa. They hardly seemed to move; their clothing was not at all disarranged but lay in graceful folds of silver and white along their limbs. They looked beautiful. It was this that struck Fenella with the deepest misery. There was nothing she could object to in the scene; nothing distasteful, vulgar; only her presence as the wronged spying wife reduced it. She stood still, thinking this, revolted by herself until she wondered if she could ever move. Then Edward slightly lifted his head; enough for her to see his staring grey eyes.

Fenella screamed. She ran back across the hall and started up the stairs. Halfway up, her paisley shawl unwound and straggled down her legs. Just as she reached the top it caught round her ankle and took her legs from beneath her. She fell like a dummy down to the bottom of the stairs.

Edward and Nadia came out from the drawing-room in time to see her bumping down. Nadia ran forward to try to stop her hitting the floor, but Edward stood back. Nadia caught her as she hit the last step. She held her in her arms.

Fenella, who was perfectly conscious, said, 'You didn't even think about me. I didn't even exist for you.' She meant it for Edward, but it was Nadia who heard. Then she said, 'I'm sorry, I'm sorry.'

Nadia commanded Edward, 'Snepple. Go and find Snepple. Quick. Don't just stand there. He's trained to carry bodies.'

'She's not a body,' Edward said.

'I don't mean a dead body. Quick Edward. Can't you see what's happening?'

'I'm not dead,' said Fenella weakly. For suddenly in an almost happy release she felt as if the whole central part of her was drifting out.

Edward gave a cry. 'She's bleeding. Look. Look at that blood.'

'For God's sake Edward come and hold her yourself and I'll get Snepple. And ring the hospital. Can't you see she's losing her baby.'

Edward took Fenella's head in his arms and watched the trickle of blood. Fenella felt much happier than she had for a long time. This curiously drifting loss made her feel light and almost giggly instead of that dreadful heaviness which had been pinning her down for the last weeks. She smiled at Edward almost gaily. 'Don't look so macabre, Edward. Honestly, I'll quite like going to hospital.'

*

Nadia put Edward into the ambulance with Fenella. The blood flowed secretly now and all he could see was her pale concentrated face. Every now and again she murmured,

'It hurts. It hurts.'

Edward who had never suffered pain of any sort was interested in this constant reiteration. She seemed to accept the pain, while he would have been angered by its imposition. He thought this might be a basic difference in their characters.

At the hospital, which was built of stone and looked reassuringly like a country house, Fenella was taken away on a stretcher.

Edward was shown into a small waiting-room. On one wall hung a fairly large and garish painting. At first it struck him as nothing more than that. He stood and stared at it, for he did not wish to commit himself to a chair. Not in such a place. The painting showed an alpine scene; after half an hour of close attention he knew it better than any masterpiece he'd studied in Italy or England. He suspected it would influence his style of painting more than any of them. Before he had a standard of greatness to aspire to, now he knew the base level to which a painter could fall. He was revolted, yet mesmerized, by the snow-clad peaks, the turquoise sky with white streaky clouds, the brightly painted wooden houses with verandas, the green lowlands grazed by fat dappled cows with bells around their necks, the dirndl-skirted maiden who attended them. She especially captured Edward's eye; and most of all her golden plaited hair. Over and over again he traced their intricate coils until he realized at last that they meant as much to him as the plaited coils of

Botticelli's Venus. With dawning horror, he realized that he no longer knew why one was great art and the other rubbish. This flat, badly executed painting held him as enthralled as any Botticelli. Did this mean then that he was basically a philistine, only capable of good judgement when there was only the good to judge? Was he nothing more than a pathetic imitator? A callow aesthete, infinitely impressionable but at heart empty?

Edward stood rigid at this dreadful thought. Opposite him those idiotic mountains reared their meaningless peaks against the laughing azure sky. If only he could laugh. If only he could stop looking.

'... So I'm afraid you'll have to think it all for the best. We'll keep her in for tonight but there's no reason why you shouldn't take her out tomorrow.'

With tremendous will power Edward wrenched his eye to the doctor. He had obviously been talking for some time. 'I'm sorry.'

'Yes. Of course. But it had been dead probably at least a month. So it had to go sometime. Really it's best. And your wife will be quite all right. Shocked, of course, but nothing damaged internally. Quite all right. Ready to start another in a month or two, no doubt. Nature's marvellously efficient, you know.'

Edward turned back to the painting. Was that Nature there? Is that what it was about? Brutal as per peaks, peaceful as per sky, bountiful as per green grass under cows. If only he could resolve the agony of not seeing its badness any more.

The doctor, who under his anonymous white coat was quite a young man, saw where he was looking. 'You like our painting?'

'Who chose it?' asked Edward, playing for time.

'A committee does all the buying. People who fancy themselves artistically inclined.'

'I see.'

'Well, I must be off,' and as Edward still stared at the picture, he smiled jovially. 'Pretty terrible, isn't it? They say the sight of the snow cools the brain but it gives me the willies.'

'Pretty terrible.' Edward drew a breath. Of course it was.

He looked at the fresh simple face of the doctor. 'Pretty terrible,' he'd said. 'Gives me the willies.' He could have hugged him. His sanity was safe after all.

The doctor, returning to his older persona, pointed his stethoscope at the door. 'You might as well go home now. Use the rest of the night sensibly. She's out cold now, so there's no point in waiting or I'd offer you a bed. Come back at noon tomorrow.'

'Thank you doctor,' Edward smiled with heartfelt gratitude. He could face the picture defiantly now. Watch it reduce in front of his eyes.

'She'll have to rest for a few days. No moving about. But that's better done out of hospital.'

'Of course.' Edward followed the doctor out of the room. Just before leaving he gave the picture a last venomous look. Although with the doctor's help he had eventually defeated its power, it had been a very nasty experience.

*

Nadia had gone to bed when Edward returned. Since it was four o'clock in the morning, he might have taken pity on her state. But the warmth of the night, the stars, the brilliant harvest moon, drew him out into the garden and once there, it was too tempting to throw a handful of pebbles at her window. Besides, he wanted very much to tell her about the Alpine Scene. He wished to reduce it still further by the logic of conversation. The only problem was that he didn't know which was Nadia's bedroom and although he suspected no amount of pebbles could penetrate Sir Arthur's deaf and aged sleep, he did not relish the idea of confronting a bristling Snepple.

He wandered round the outside of the pretty red brick house and soon decided that, by all reasonable logic, Nadia should have one of the large bow-fronted bedrooms.

The curtains were drawn back in a moment.

'Hello. Are you locked out?'

Edward was nonplussed by this practical approach. It didn't fit in with his own excited secrecy. 'No. That is, I don't know. I haven't tried the door.'

'Ah.' Nadia withdrew.

Edward, feeling silly and defeated, went and sat down on the front steps. He hadn't seen his pebbles as a schoolboy's summoning to a midnight feast, but he saw now that it was how they would appear to Nadia. Not Romeo at all, rather Ferdie of the Fourth. Nor, he noticed, was it midnight any more or even black night. For the stones of the house were taking a faint pinkish tinge and the stars losing their brightness. Soon it would be dawn.

'Edward. Edward.' Nadia appeared behind him. She wore a wide-lapelled dressing-gown, made out of some shiny material. It swung around her ankles. Edward would not look further upwards. He felt foolish and it was an unusual uncomfortable feeling.

'How was Fenella?' Nadia said, coming to sit on the steps beside him.

'All right. So the doctor said.' He answered sulkily, looking stolidly between his knees.

'And the baby?'

'The baby?' Edward was surprised into peering up. For the first time he took in what the doctor had told him. 'It was dead. It had been dead for ages. The doctor said it had to go.'

'I'm sorry,' Nadia spoke gently, paused a moment and then added, 'so you needn't feel guilty about her falling down the stairs. It would have happened anyway.'

'I wasn't guilty.'

'I see.'

'I wanted to talk,' Edward got up crossly and glared down at Nadia. The talk of the doctor had brought back the nastiness of the Alpine Scene and he desperately wanted to talk about it.

'But we are talking,' Nadia sounded puzzled. And then looking at Edward's angry childish face saw that he did not count this exchange of information, this talking of people as conversation. 'Let's walk!' she cried, springing to her feet. 'Through the trees over there. We'll watch the sun come up and you can tell me whatever you want. I promise I'll be the perfect listener.' Her pale feet scattering the pebbles of the driveway she ran without hesitation towards the lawn and the distant group of beeches. With her small head balanced on her long neck, her flowing dressing-gown and her flowing hair she reminded Edward of one of the three Graces. It was clever of her to be that just at this moment. He followed her urgently across the lawn.

Together they wandered through the ever-lightening dark. 'Is there beauty *per se*? . . . Is there perfect art? . . . Is there a standard? . . . Is there perfection?'

For over an hour he talked, while all around them the garden came alive and prepared for another summer's day. First the birds began gossiping and squabbling in the branches above their heads; then the insects started to buzz quietly in the dewy grass around their feet; and finally the sun rose very gently over the horizon, lighting up the beeches to a brighter bronze, making the distant house shine as pink as any self-respecting doll could wish, and glancing past the dark tree trunks to make their pale faces glint like phosphorus.

Then Nadia drew Edward down into the still dampish grass and undressed him there. His clothes made a bed for them and her dressing-gown a coverlet. So absorbed was Edward in his thoughts that Nadia's body, her supple seduction, made little impression on him. It was a continuation of their conversation. She didn't want to take anything from him.

*

Fenella cried silently in the hospital bed. She wished the doctor hadn't told her that the baby was already dead. It made a travesty of the last weeks. Perhaps it had been dead all along. Her only comfort had been that baby inside her, and now it had never existed. The doctor had been extraordinary, almost cheerful; trying to tell her that losing it was a good thing, that she should be pleased. He talked about clearing the decks and starting again. She had looked at his nice pink face and wondered how he could say things to her like that. Could he not see that she was now completely without hope? Could he not tell that Edward would never father another child from her. That she was now as useless as a split paper bag. Through which the strawberries had fallen. A squashed red mess. 'No! No! No! My baby! My baby!' Fenella began to scream and the nurse who hadn't realized she was awake came over to give her a sedative.

Fenella was brought back to the Gores' house; a day later than the doctor had originally suggested, because she seemed weaker than he'd expected. She couldn't or wouldn't (he thought privately) stop crying. But by teatime on Monday she had recovered some sort of listless calm and an ambulance was brought to carry her back to the house. She could not travel further for several days – perhaps even as much as a week – but Nadia was pressing in her offers of hospitality. She arranged everything. While Edward watched.

Edward himself began to feel restless. Days passing without work, however filled with drama, always made him restless and dissatisfied. His canvas and paints were in the back of his car, but some respect he felt for Nadia as hostess stopped him bringing them out. Perhaps it was her age. Gradually he had become aware of the age difference between them; that her youthful manner, her youthful body belonged to a woman nearly old enough to be his mother. But instead of revolting him, as it had in Maggie's case, it reassured him. It gave her independence; a past that he did not know about and a present in which he could not take part. She did not need him to survive.

On Tuesday morning she took him upstairs and showed him a room which had been entirely cleared of furniture, carpets and decorations:

'Your studio!' Edward accepted her efficiency eagerly. The room faced south, it was painted white, it had a high ceiling, a large table and one armchair. Beyond the windows spread the summer landscape of golden cornfields and behind lay a supporting web of kitchen, dining-room, bedrooms, bathrooms. Even people, when required.

'I'll be in London for the next few days,' Nadia said, as he stared, 'but I shall expect great things when I return.' She smiled but both were serious.

'I'll get my stuff from the car,' Edward said.

'Arthur won't appear while I'm away.' Nadia followed him as he bounded down the stairs, standing back for a moment as he jumped the last two steps to avoid the dark patch that resisted all attempts at removal. 'Would you like lunch on a tray with Fenella? And dinner downstairs?'

'Fine!' cried Edward over his shoulder. 'I don't want to be a nuisance.'

So Nadia left.

Fenella lay like a corpse in the four-poster bed. She couldn't yet think about her situation. However, she found the energy to be surprised when Edward first came into the room and sat on her bed. He had been moved to another room so there was no need for him to see her at all. She was so convinced that the loss of the baby had severed any remaining link between them, that it was as if a stranger had come to her. She looked at him oddly, almost coldly, and tried to understand why he was there. Perhaps, she thought, he would come once and then not again. But on the contrary he got into the habit of appearing every two hours or so, talking or merely sitting for a little and then retreating again. His manner was calmer and more ordinarily cheerful than she had ever seen; his painting, it seemed, was going well and although it had been a horrid wrench to realize that he must leave Austin's picture till he returned to London, he was fully occupied in painting a background of elm trees to Tish, Queen of the fairies.

One of the few remarks Fenella made was to comment on this choice of tree:

'But doesn't the knowledge of that dreadful elm disease make them a bit ghoulish?'

Edward became excited.

'I hadn't thought of it. Not consciously, that is. But, of course, how fascinating. How perfect. The beautiful young aristocratic girl dressed all in white against a background of seemingly perfect trees but in fact carrying that hidden decay. I might even have a branch half withered, dangling, to show where the rot has started.'

'The rot in what? Tish isn't rotting. Tish is the healthiest person I know.' Fenella saw her own white thin arm and thought of Tish's round golden one.

'What she represents, Fenella.' Edward was impatient as he always was when an idea caught hold of him. 'Our great English upper classes. Doomed to decay. Nothing can save them. Eaten away from within by their own conceit.'

'Poor Tish,' said Fenella, 'I hope she doesn't realize.'

'Good.' Edward jumped up. 'Good.' In a moment he was out of the room.

Fenella watched him go and thought that this conversation had on the surface been indistinguishable from so many in the past. She had given him a pinprick of inspiration and he had galloped away. And then she realized that Edward's attitude to her had not changed, except that he no longer paid homage to her beauty which in her present state would have strained even his independent imagination. All these months, these days, that horrible, unthinkable evening, which had changed her whole life, had not affected him in any way. This was the worst realization yet. Tears started to roll down her cheeks. She could no longer stop the total humiliation of her position overwhelming her. Staying in Lady Gore's house, or Nadia, as she was now forced to call her, looked after by her servants, organized by her, almost kept alive by her. It was Nadia who had caught her at the stairs. It was Nadia who had telephoned for an ambulance. It was Nadia who had seen that she was carefully carried to it. And now it was Nadia who supervised her recuperation. Nadia, who had lain like a silver angel in Edward's arms. And probably did so still. It was impossible. Insupportable. She couldn't bear it. She must leave at once. The idea thrilled her as if she was an escaping prisoner. Who did she know in the outside world who would help her? Of course, her mother. It seemed extraordinary that no one had thought of ringing her before. Hurriedly, shaking with weakness and excitement she pulled aside the bedclothes and put her feet to the soft carpet. She must escape before Nadia returned. Today was Thursday or was it Friday? She must be back soon. She would telephone her mother at once.

*

Loelia wandered in and out of Maggie's house, avoiding Maggie as much as she could. She had not felt so alive since before she went to Italy, when she was still a young girl, sixteen or seventeen. Dr Ferguson, as she still called him to herself, liking the solid sound of it, had asked her to return with him to Canada; had asked her to marry him when her divorce came through. Her excitement was only incomplete, because she could not quite throw off those years of expecting only the worst and receiving only the worst. With new hope came the terrible fear that something should happen to upset this sudden astonishing chance of happiness. Surely she deserved it after all these years? And yet her terror restrained her happiness and stopped her telling anyone about it yet. It would be a surprise for everyone. The day before she left arm in arm with Dr Ferguson. Or even on the day itself. In a week's time. If only nothing happened. She thought the something might come from Maggie.

*

Fenella dragged herself down to the vermilion drawing-room. Several times the telephone disappeared into a blur, but eventually she managed to dial Maggie's number. It was such a relief to hear her mother's voice that she babbled out a jumble of facts and images. She did not notice Loelia's blank silence.

'So you must come at once and pick me up. At once. To-day. I'm not allowed to sit up but I could stretch out on the back seat.'

Loelia said how sorry she was and began to talk about Maggie. It was easier than talking about herself. She could hide her desperation under ridicule, 'I know it sounds unbelievable, Fenella darling, but she really does believe she's *enceinte*. She stays in bed half the day complaining of morning sickness and when she does get up hardly bothers to dress. Or puts on some dreadful shapeless tent. So you see to bring a person to the house in your state would hardly be tactful.'

'I'm afraid I don't understand,' Fenella's hand shook so much that she could hardly hear. Besides an unpleasant crackling had begun inside the receiver. Or was it inside her head? 'Why does Maggie thinking she's a saint stop me from coming to stay? You've got to hurry or Nadia will be back.'

'*Enceinte*. Oh dear!' Loelia gave a snorting giggle which she knew was inappropriate, but couldn't suppress, 'I didn't realize my accent was quite so unrecognizable.' And she thought to herself how she must brush it up for French Canada. 'Pregnant!' she cried more strongly. 'She thinks she's pregnant! She's not, of course. All in her imagination. Menopausal.'

'Mummy,' whined Fenella quietly. 'Mummy.'

Loelia rushed on, 'She even persuaded Dr Ferguson, you do remember Jamie Ferguson, don't you? To examine her. And there's absolutely no question of a baby. But that makes it all the worse, doesn't it?'

'Dr Ferguson.' Fenella sat down on the floor. She remembered a solid man bending close to her mother. Suddenly, despite the warmth of the day, she felt cold. Her whole body began to shake.

'Yes. Yes.' Loelia swept on. 'It's probably all to do with poor Tristram. So dreadful to have a son in prison. But one needn't worry too much. There will be an appeal and there's absolutely no chance of him staying there.'

'In prison.'

'Well. Just at the moment.' There was a pause. 'Fenella. Fenella.' Loelia grew agitated as the silence persisted. 'Are you still there? Are you all right? I'm dreadfully sorry for you. Really I am. Dreadfully sorry about the baby. But life is a sad thing. People are suffering all over the place. And you see I have to live my life too. And you're old enough now to look after yourself. I have to go. He asked me to. But he won't ask me again. No one will. I have to go. We'd love you to visit us in Canada. You do understand, don't you, Fenella? I stayed to look after you all those years and now I have to go, don't I? Fenella! Fenella! Oh dear!' Loelia began to sob. It was a strange unaccustomed feeling. She had not cried for over twenty years. Since Fenella's birth when the doctor had held back the gas and air. But she didn't think of that. Why was everything so unfair? Why could she not be happy for a moment? Fenella had always seemed so strong, so sure. Sometimes she had even felt she despised her own mother. So why should she choose this moment to crumple like a pocket handkerchief. She hadn't even invited her to her wedding. She held the receiver to her mouth again. 'I'm very sorry, Fenella, and I hope you can hear me but I'm afraid I've got to go and I can't pick you up.'

Nadia was very concerned when she found Fenella on the drawing-room floor, barely conscious, barely covered.

'But my dear, the doctor advised rest till at least Sunday.'

'What day is it?' Fenella asked dully.

'Friday. And I brought a friend to keep you company. We'll help you upstairs.'

The friend turned out to be Tish. Tish in the pink of health and energy. She was dressed in a white embroidered smock which swung bell-like above her sunburnt calves. A slide shaped like a butterfly fastened back her yellow curls.

Fenella's eyes fixed on this butterfly. It made her feel nostalgic for scenes of a summer's garden, for lavender bushes fluttering with red admirals, for snap-dragons crawling with bees, for daisyfull grass curling under bare toes, for the numbing warmth of the afternoon sun. Tish's butterfly reminded her that all this was just through the open door and yet she could no more conceive of venturing out into it than that plastic butterfly could fly off Tish's hair. Both prisoners. All prisoners. A tear slid down her cheek.

Tish didn't know what to do with herself. She felt so horribly vulgar beside the fragility of Fenella. She was like some oversized doll won at a fun fair's shooting range, 'Press me and I squeak'. She wished she had covered her legs in stockings, worn anything but this silly girlish frock, left off that dancing butterfly. She didn't even dare touch Fenella. Speak to her. Humbly, she picked up the receiver which Fenella had left on the floor and put it back on the hook. And yet although she felt so crudely inferior, the feeling was based on the sense of her own strength. So that as they started slowly up to Fenella's bedroom, she darted guilty looks at her, took in her appearance more thoroughly and then was shocked and almost disapproving of what she saw. How could

Fenella, the queen, the goddess, let herself get into such a state? Of course it must be shattering to lose a baby but then she was only about halfway with it. Her hair had obviously not been combed for days, her nightdress was crumpled and dirty, her face was unwashed. Where was the phenomenal will power Tish had always admired? She had brought herself down to the level of ordinary mortals. She put an arm round Fenella's shoulders. She smoothed back her hair.

'Poor, poor Fenella. So awful for you. But honestly you'll feel better soon. Nadia says the doctor says . . .'

At the top of the stairs they halted for a moment while Fenella leaned against the banister to rest. Simultaneously two doors either end of the passage sprang open. Out of one appeared Edward, youthful and joyful; out of the other appeared more slowly, Sir Arthur, old and careful.

'The workers!' cried Nadia, looking gaily from one to the other.

'I'm sorry,' said Fenella dully.

'Let me take you to your room.' Tish took her arm and repressed a shudder as she felt her bones under the unpadded skin.

Edward and Sir Arthur met at the top of the stairs. Nadia put an arm in either of theirs and led them down. She forestalled her husband who wanted to produce a philatelic grumble with a running commentary on the horrors of London in a heatwave, ending with a flourish.

'But here all is progress, creation and recovery. Even Fenella found her way downstairs. So good to see her will reasserting itself.'

*

During the course of the weekend, Tish posed for Edward. The continuing sunlight poured through the open window, bringing with it the smell of new-mown grass and even a faint scent from the rose garden. At the end of each session Tish felt as usual both exhausted and exhilarated. Edward's concentration on her seemed to draw all her strength. He broke down her personality and took it for himself. The only trouble was that since he would not let her see the portrait, she did not know how he had put her together again. Who was she? Now, when she left his company, she did not know. It was this vacuum out of his presence which made her decide quite suddenly, over dinner on Saturday evening, through the candles over the plates, that she had fallen in love with him. She quite saw it was probably the same sort of emotion a patient felt for her psychiatrist, but all the same it had taken hold of her. This love. There was nothing she could do about it. She did not exist outside his presence. She was his. It wouldn't change anything, of course. She wouldn't try and snatch him from poor Fenella who looked so vulnerable now that one avoided seeing. She would just recognize her love to herself and that would have to be enough. However, it did have one effect, for seeing Edward with loving eyes, she could not help noticing the special relationship between him and Lady Gore.

Nadia laughed for him, told stories for him, held back her silky hair for him. On walks round the gardens, round the edge of the waving cornfields she was always beside him or just in front, as if she couldn't bear to miss a word from his mouth, an expression off his face. Tish noticed, because she felt that way herself and she was jealous. She could only take second place when Nadia kept so close.

Then on Sunday before dinner they went for a drink to a neighbouring Colonel. And Tish came to a new understanding and was relieved, for Nadia produced Edward with all the fanfares due to a genius. There was talk of portraits, of galleries and always of Edward's painting. Tish saw that Nadia's special interest was that of a patroness. That she cared about him in the same way as she cared about her gallery. Lightheaded with relief, Tish now realized she had seen that liquid-eyed absorption before – when they were planning a new exhibition. Nadia only wanted to help Edward. She was, after all, twenty years older than him. She could have been his mother. Neither she nor poor Fenella should be jealous.

Poor Fenella spent most of the weekend in her bedroom. She was quite tranquil, washed and brushed, which led those downstairs to presume her improved. Her face had a dead unlit quality about it, which made her easy to forget. She was glad they left her alone and sat in her small armchair by the open window preparing herself for life without Edward. She told herself she had only known him three years, but that didn't seem to mean very much. Then she thought about her conversation with Loelia and remembered the extraordinary remarks about Maggie which she'd hardly taken in at the time. Maggie thinking herself pregnant. And what else was it before that? Maggie imagining Edward had made love to her. Imagining. Fenella remembered that night after the Gores' dinner party when she had found them together. When Maggie had wheeled away the motor bicycle. And she had summoned up the courage to tell him about her own pregnancy. And she had been sick and Edward had made love to her. What had Maggie been doing in his studio? But then Dr Ferguson had said she was not pregnant, so the other must also be false? Or must it? Fenella wondered whether it really mattered.

On Monday morning, everybody set out for London. Sir Arthur and Snepple, who were spending a day in town, driven by Nadia; Tish and Fenella driven by Edward in his now dusty Jaguar. All seemed in order. The visitors book had been inscribed; the servants thanked and tipped; the rooms checked for stray belongings.

'It was gorgeous!' cried Tish, leaning her head out of the Jaguar's window. 'London will seem drear.'

'As long as we get there before the storm.' Nadia placed her gloved hands neatly on the driving wheel.

The sun had at last allowed itself to be hidden by a misty shroud, but the air seemed warmer than ever.

'I hope there is a storm!' said Tish to Edward, as they started off. Fenella who lay along the back seat recognized the emotion in her voice. It was the way Tish had used to talk to her. When she was in awe of Edward and he would not notice her. Fenella watched the thick sky and tree tops passing by and looked forward to her flat in London. After an hour she saw the topmost leaves begin to wave violently and at the same time she heard Tish cry out.

'Here it comes! What fun!' And all at once it was as if the

car was being sprayed by machine-gun fire. The noise on the roof was overwhelming.

'It's hail!' shouted Tish.

'Glass bullets,' Edward said.

'Don't be so morbid.'

'It's beautiful. Watch. Over there. The sun. And then a rainbow.'

Fenella had already seen it. From her lowered position it rose over the car like a triumphant arch. But only for a second and then it too was blackened by the hailstorm and destroyed. They were left in a grey and flat wake. The hail had turned to rain.

'Oh dear,' Tish said. 'I haven't got an umbrella.'

'Not much good against bullets,' Fenella's quiet voice, flattened by the noise of the rain, didn't reach the front seat. 'Even if they are made of glass.'

*

London was wet when they arrived but the storm had already passed over. A faint sun was beginning to make the pavements glisten. The dusty dried-up smell that Fenella so hated had been at least momentarily subdued.

'Good-bye Edward,' she said, when they reached her flat.

'But you're still so wan. Why so pale and wan?' He took her arm to help her up the stairs. Tish watched them from the car. When they reached the top he kissed her gently. 'You will recover now you're in your own castle.'

'Yes,' Fenella said. 'I will.' And then, unavoidably, 'But I'm sorry for Maggie.'

'Maggie?' Edward was bewildered. 'You mean Tristram?'

'It doesn't matter.'

'He'll be out soon.'

'Maggie thinks she's going to have a baby.'

'You should lie down.'

'I do. All the time.'

'Don't be dismal. Dear Fenella. *La strega.*'

'No. Of course not.' Fenella turned away from his smiling face. 'Good-bye.'

But now Edward seemed reluctant to let her go. Although

he would not recognize her meaning their conversation had restored her personality. 'You're such a gallant person. So admirable. Beautiful. Sad too. Nadia said sadness becomes you. *La Dame aux Camélias* or *Sans Merci*. I'd like to paint you all in black. Or white. Don't be cold. Not to me.'

'I want to lie down, Edward. When I feel stronger I shall get a job. I was offered a picture research job.'

'Picture research.' Edward withdrew towards the stairs. 'I see. A tower of strength. Nadia advised me to buy myself a house. We were talking about money.'

'You have a lot of that now.'

'A house would be quite a challenge.'

'I'm going to lie down now.'

'Under the Paradise.' Edward tried to kiss her again, but Fenella avoided him and going inside her flat, shut the door with a brusque click.

Edward felt rebuffed. He stood disconsolately on the darkish landing. Then he remembered Tish still waiting in the car and it struck him that she might be persuaded to sit for him before going to the gallery. He bounded down the stairs two at a time.

Fenella, leaning against the inside of the door, heard him go and despite everything found herself admiring his enthusiasm. It was she who had failed him, not the other way round. She and Tristram. And probably Maggie in a way too. And Gunilla and his father. The list unwound behind him like a trailing wake.

11

The fierce hailstorm brought summer to an abrupt and premature end. September was mild but never hot and brilliant like August. No one missed it. Only Edward noticed the diminishing of the light level in his studio. He looked upwards and said disapprovingly to Austin who was sitting for him,

'It's like being in a telescope. All that glass between me and the light.'

'It's grimy. That's your trouble. Grime of years. I'll have a go at it one of these days. Quite a job.'

'Perhaps you'd close that window at the same time. No. No. Not this minute.' Edward held up a brush hastily as Austin seemed about to spring for the beams. 'In the winter, I mean. That storm we had last month sluiced rain onto the floor.'

'I could just as well do it now.'

'No. Thank you.' Edward was reluctant to see Austin turn into an ape again. He had completed his first portrait and had brought him the promised motor bike which was now part of this second painting. Sometimes he touched Austin, putting his body into the right pattern with the shining handlebars and corrugated wheels and he was more than ever aware of his strength. Posed, fixed into his chosen posture, he could watch and put it onto canvas; moving, put into action, it was still too much for him. He looked away when Austin walked across the studio to get his clothes, when he bent and lunged to pull them on. He feared that relationship with Austin. With Tristram it had been a game in which he had been the leader but he suspected that Austin would not understand about playing games. Besides, his attitude was sternly unprovocative. Lately, it had become almost censorious. Something about Fenella.

*

Austin had come to clean Fenella's windows. He had been saving it up as a pleasure at the end of a day of bad-tempered housewives and mean shopkeepers. He whistled up at her window from the street – he had never trusted doorbells – and waited, swishing his chamois leather from hand to hand, for her madonna's face.

Fenella looked down and shouted,

'Oh, it's you. Do come up. I'll buzz.'

Leaving his ladder propped against the wall, Austin bounded up the stairs, bucket banging unnoticed against his back.

'Oh,' he said, 'Mrs Aubrey.' He was miserably disappointed. Instead of the blossoming, burgeoning, black curly-haired, white-skinned, mother madonna he'd expected, here instead was a wan thin creature, waist as thin as his thigh, bound in a hard leather belt.

Fenella understood his expression, though she didn't see why he looked so crestfallen. ' "Season of mist and mellow fruitfulness," ' she said smiling ironically.

Austin missed her reference, but understood her tone of voice. The smile particularly shocked him. It was inappropriate at such a time.

'I'm sorry, missus,' he said seriously.

Fenella shrugged and led him into the flat. 'Which windows are you going to do first? There're not many to choose from.'

'I'll need water for my bucket.'

'The kitchen's over there.'

Fenella was wearing trousers. She had never worn trousers before, because she knew they gave her a flat ungainly look but now she wore them constantly with a belt. She went over and sat in her armchair. She had just come in from a library where she was working. She had abandoned her degree for a picture research job which had a reassuring monotony about it. She didn't really want to see Austin. It reminded her of Edward and upset her. Although he had tried to see her several times she had always refused. It was her only show of strength.

Austin started cleaning the sitting-room windows. He

rubbed vigorously. So much so that eventually even Fenella's attention was aroused,

'Be careful or you'll go right through them.'

'I never have missus.'

'Never. Ever? How surprising.'

'It's a knack really.' He came back towards Fenella. 'I've finished these two. Where next?'

'The bathroom hasn't got a window so there's only the kitchen.'

'No bedroom?'

'I forgot that. How funny.'

Fenella got up and followed him. She found that now she wanted to talk. 'I expect you're still sitting for Edward?'

'I stand mostly. Although now he's got me all tangled up with a motor bicycle.'

'A motor bicycle. How eccentric.' While Austin worked, Fenella wandered round the bedroom, touching her hairbrush, her box of pins, the picture of Paradise on the wall. 'Do you like motor bicycles?'

'I used to be on the Wall of Death, missus.'

'So they were your job. But you didn't like them, I don't suppose?'

'No, missus. Except as transport. I can get places quicker and do more jobs.'

'Now, you mean. He's given it to you then?'

'That's right, missus. It'll be the kitchen next then.'

Once more Fenella followed after him, 'I think I'll make some tea. I expect you're thirsty.'

'Always ready for a cup of tea.'

'I don't expect Edward gives you one.'

'Bitter coffee, missus.'

'Nor on the Wall of Death.' Fenella filled the kettle with water. 'Do you call all women missus? It's so lugubrious and middle-aged.'

'I'm sorry, lovey.'

'There! That's so much nicer. Do call me lovey.' Fenella was delighted. She hadn't felt as nearly happy for ages. She couldn't think how she'd ever felt embarrassed by this man. He was so simple. Full of goodwill. His masculinity which had so overpowered her before now seemed translated into friendly almost fatherly concern.

'I'm afraid I've only got China tea.'

'Not to worry. Plenty of sugar.' They sat either side of Fenella's small table. The bucket stood at their feet neatly draped with the various cloths.

'It's a long way from a wall of death to window-cleaning.'

'I've got to support my kids.'

'Their mother is . . .?'

'Dead,' said Austin. 'Two years now.'

'Oh dear. Such a short time ago.'

'Cancer. She knew all about it though we tried to hide it. The kids knew too. Sharp little things. You can't hide a thing from children. They knew their mother was going away before she did. Though, as I said, she knew too at the end. They were only tiny then. Three and five but I've managed all right. I'm proud of that. I gave them a real home.'

'That's when you took up window-cleaning, I expect?'

'That was before. When she was still here. The doctor said she shouldn't have had children, but that's something you can't tell a married woman. That's what marriage is about. She knew I felt that. She knew I wanted children. They're everything to me, those kids. Two girls. Beautifully behaved. Good as gold. Long hair they've got. I insist on that, though it's much more trouble to keep clean. Real little girls have to have long hair, my missus used to say. So I've always kept it long. They look lovely together, they never go long apart. Babies are what it's all about.' Austin stopped abruptly. He looked at Fenella with abject apologetic eyes.

Fenella roused herself. Austin's litany of love for his children had had a curiously soothing effect on her so that she had fallen into a kind of dream. She certainly hadn't related any of his remarks to herself.

'Have some more tea, do. It might have got a bit more colour by now.'

'That's nice,' Austin recovered from his embarrassment and wanted to go on talking again. 'Of course my problem is that they'll take them away from me.'

'They?'

'The authorities.'

'Surely they wouldn't do that. Not when you're so good about looking after them.'

'They don't like single men. Besides there's the other.'

'The other?' Fenella wasn't absolutely serious about her curiosity, not as much as Austin thought she was. It seemed to her like most things did these days, remote. Nevertheless it was the first conversation she'd held for weeks. 'Do you have another problem, then?'

'It was my boss. In the circus. He tried to accuse me of having a go at his wife, when he knew I'd been nowhere near, and that's why he sacked me. But when he wanted to get rid of her he tried to accuse me. He said I'd needed a woman because my own wife was sick and then dying. And a man like me needed a woman so the court wouldn't believe me if I said I hadn't been near her. He was trying to frame me. Insulting my wife. Just dead. So I tried to strangle him. Not that I really knew what I was doing. They said that in court.'

'Strangle him,' Fenella repeated mystically. 'With your bare hands.'

'They said I was of temporarily unsound mind because of my wife's death. So they let me off. On probation. I didn't hurt him much. He's a strong man too. But that's why they keep nearly taking the children. They had the little one for nearly a year.'

'I see. It must be very upsetting.'

'I'd never been in trouble before. And they see how I look after those two. They're always beautifully turned out. Like angels. Always on time for school. And I pick them up after. They're better cared for than many a child with a mother and a father.'

'I'm sure they are.' Fenella thought about her own mother. She had visited her once before leaving for Canada, but she had been so scared of finding the need to stay that she had hardly dared look at Fenella, repeating with bright untypical confidence, 'Time's a great healer. Nature's cure.' Till Fenella, wishing to end what was painful to both of them, had smiled as widely as she could and talked of her job and the New Life Ahead. Loelia had been happy and gone away. Fenella didn't feel bitter about it for she wanted her mother to be happy but she was saddened by the dishonesty of their parting.

Fenella put her hands out and touched the teapot. 'I'm afraid it's quite cold now. Shall I make some more?'

'Not on my account, thank you, lovey. I expect you see now why your husband's money's such a help to me. I can buy them things they've never had before. That the other children have at school. You know how children like to be the same. Your husband's money makes all the difference. They were thinking of taking them before I got it. I know that, but now it's all right again. They can't say anything when they look so good.'

'Of course not,' said Fenella. She thought that it was odd that Edward's painting should be having such a direct effect on three people's lives. How did one relate this importance with the importance of his painting?

'I'm sorry I've gone on so, lovey, but I don't have anyone much to talk to – except the social worker and she's always in such a hurry. Your husband's a lucky man. And you'll make a lovely mother too. I'll be off now.'

Fenella realized she had been paid Austin's highest compliment and stopped the ironies that came so easily. She thought of Edward's mother. Gunilla's support and interest in her had died almost completely with the death of the baby. She seemed almost to blame Fenella for adding more sorrow to her load and had now retreated to the country. It belonged to Edward and Fenella, she had said, but then retreated there silently, alone.

'I'm glad you came,' Fenella stood up and led Austin to the door.

'The secret is to have them done regularly. Then they don't get so filthy.'

A thought struck Fenella, 'Would the authorities mind if they knew how you earned your money? Posing. With my husband, I mean.'

Austin shrugged. 'It's not their business, is it?'

'No of course not.'

'So I'll come again in four or five weeks time.'

'Thank you. It's very kind.'

'Good-bye, missus.'

Fenella shut the door slowly and only after she had heard the motor bike roar away remembered she had given him no money.

*

Nadia's influence over Edward soon started to show. Even his appearance changed. He had always favoured clothes which had a flamboyantly Elizabethan air about them : capes that swung behind him, wide brimmed hats, puffed handkerchiefs, looped ties, but before they had been put together carelessly, with more regard for general effect than fashion. Now, although the swashbuckling impression remained, the silk handkerchief remained, it was modified to conform with what the world wore so that old baggy sweaters or old-fashioned drain-pipe trousers were dismissed from his wardrobe. Their replacements, mostly chosen by Nadia, were very expensive and fashionable. In fact Nadia was teaching him to take note of the Way of the World. He came in the evening to her London flat.

'I must go to New York next week.' She put down her Vermouth on the mantelpiece and stared in what Edward thought of as her business face. 'I want you to come.'

'To be dragged behind your chariot,' Edward laughed a little nastily. Now and again he liked to simulate a palace revolt although both of them knew their relationship was a case of *Graecia capta ferum victorem cepit*.

'It would do you good. I'd introduce you to important people and you'd enlarge your circle.'

'But I have my circle. Austin. Tish. Monkeys. Tristram. Fenella.'

'Tristram? Fenella?'

Edward smiled and sighed. 'Poor old Tristram. And Fenella's so independent. So brilliant.'

'Austin and Tish aren't enough, Edward. Besides, you want to sell.'

'I want to work.'

'But no great artists ever worked in a vacuum. Find one who didn't long for a sympathetic society around him; for encouragement, for understanding; for criticism.'

'Yes. But I have as much money as I want.'

'Quite.' Nadia was unruffled. 'Even so you'll want an exhibition.'

Edward rolled sideways on the yellow satin sofa, 'Why won't you let me paint you, Nadia?' He was determined to do two pictures of Nadia. In one she would be curled up sinuously in an armchair dressed in one of her clinging silk pyjama suits – there was one a particularly indecent mouse colour that Edward adored; and in the other she would be posed similarly in the armchair but she would be naked. His idea was that she would produce exactly the same response in a viewer whether dressed or nude. This quality of Nadia's appearance fascinated Edward. Ideally he would put the two portraits on the same canvas. He had noticed how people cleverly distanced nudes; their fear of embarrassment or prurience made them change the Woman into Art. Juxtaposition of naked and clothed would foil their game. He had already put the idea to Nadia but she had been unenthusiastic, merely murmuring, '*Playboy* has been doing it for years', which Edward took as no criticism of his theory but a disinclination for her own involvement.

'It's extraordinary you've never been painted. Considering all the artists you've known over the years. You can't be frightened.'

'Have you considered what my husband would think?'

'Your husband!' Edward looked shocked. Nadia had never given the impression that the aged Sir Arthur felt the right to curtail her freedom.

Nadia laughed at his expression. 'No. You're right, that doesn't apply. I'll pose for you when we get back from New York.'

'Nadia nude and New York. Or no nude Nadia.'

'Don't be so literal.'

Edward didn't mind bargains. 'It'll interrupt my picture of Tish and Austin.'

'Tish will kill me. What a combination. Miss Skeffington-Smith and a window-cleaner.'

'He's more representational.' But Nadia had touched on his problem. Edward became gloomily preoccupied. Nudity. It was not much to ask. The combination of Tish and Austin, Beauty and the Beast was not successful. The contrast was too obvious, too grating. The only solution he could see was painting them both nude – nudity brings equality – but he did not dare ask either of them. Austin's horridly working-class morality would be outraged at stripping in front of a woman, while Tish would be alarmed by co-nudity with a window-cleaner. So they stood side by side, immovable, locked apart from each other. Up to now, he had confined himself to sketching their heads. It was pathetic that art should be bent to the command of prudery and snobbery. He glared abstractedly at Nadia.

Nadia came and sat on the arm of his sofa. She put her hand round the back of his neck. 'Do I undress slowly or fast when you paint me?' she said sweetly.

*

Edward's departure for New York upset everybody. Austin was upset at the loss of money for his daughters – he had been saving up to buy a bicycle for the elder one's birthday. Tish, despite her platonic interpretation of Nadia's admiration for Edward, was extremely jealous. Maggie was outraged. In fact, it did her a lot of good. Previously her instinct to anger at Edward's heartless lack of interest in Tristram's plight had been overwhelmed by the uncomfortable consciousness of her own guilty association with him. This final betrayal outweighed their miserable past together. Now she could let go.

Fenella who had come innocently to her drawing-room watched amazed as she stamped up and down, her vast circular dress, for she had not quite relinquished the idea of pregnancy, ballooning round her legs.

'Gallivanting off to New York while Tristram lies mouldering in a cell. Stuffing himself on oysters and champagne while Tristram has spam and fetid water. Climbing the

Statue of Liberty while his oldest friend withers in chains and manacles!'

'He's gone for work,' said Fenella mildly. She would not think of Edward. Or the true foundation of Maggie's anger for him. Her visit was for Tristram. She was offering to visit him. 'Prisons aren't like that any more. There's books and newspapers and television. It's a wonderful chance for Tristram to be serious and concentrate. There're no distractions. That's what I wanted to tell him. I thought it might help.'

'No distractions!' Maggie flung up her hands and whirled round to the drinks table. 'I know it's only eleven, but I need a drink. It's much worse than that. He's humiliated. He's humiliated and destroyed. It's like seeing a stranger. Nothing there of Tristram. You'll hardly recognize him. He isn't even beautiful any more. He looks like them all in there.'

'I can't believe that,' Fenella remembered how romantic he'd looked in the court. How theatrical, with his open-necked white shirt and black sweater. In a way it had been his finest hour. He'd looked like a prince going to execution.

'He will soon. Unless I get him out. That's what Edward should be doing. All that money he's got. Helping to get him out.'

'But you've got money.'

'That's not the point.'

'You need a lawyer.'

'Lawyers. Lawyers. They're all equally corrupt. All in each other's pockets. My solicitor, for instance. For twenty years he's looked after my affairs, doing nothing, taking thousands of pounds for it, and now there's something really important for him to do, he can only find a stupid, mealy-mouthed, heartless barrister who gets my son locked away for eighteen months and then when I say appeal says there's no grounds for appeal, Mrs Brown. No grounds! His job's to find them. That's what I pay them for. And I've told the idiot of a solicitor so or I'll sack them both.'

'Appeal?' said Fenella slowly. She had never thought you could appeal against the miserable injustices of life. She had no one to appeal to; Austin had no one to appeal to.

Maggie, who had by now drunk a large glass of whisky,

subsided onto a chair; it was like the air going out of a balloon; her voluminous skirts folded around her. She looked small and old.

'The trouble is I allowed the solicitor to become too friendly after Johnny died. I was lonely. I was young. I had to see him a lot to clear up everything and he comforted me. You shouldn't let your solicitor get too close or they don't take you seriously. The truth is I'm too old to find a new one. If Johnny was still alive this would never have happened.'

Fenella had never before heard Maggie mention her husband's name. It had been one of her gayest features. She had never posed as the unhappy widow. It showed how low she was brought.

'But I shall get an appeal going. I've nothing else to do.' The bravado was replaced by determination. Fenella thought that despite the whisky and the crazy costume and the ranting and the stamping, Maggie was an admirable woman. More and more she found herself admiring other people.

'If there's anything I can do to help,' she said. But already the urge to visit Tristram had passed into defeated lassitude. She didn't want to be in the same room as Maggie any more, see her small ankles and soft greyish neck.

'Thank you, Fenella,' Maggie said to resurrect her dignity. She smoothed down her reddish hair and crossed her legs under the folds of material. 'I shall certainly call on you, if necessary. But I realize you have your own problems. With your husband.'

*

Edward wandered round his studio. It was odd to be in England. Things seemed smaller, greyer and generally more austere than he remembered. Nadia's flat, which he had previously considered almost vulgar in its luxury, now seemed charmingly simple. His studio was like a monk's cell. He walked once more round the easel before deciding that it was perhaps a good thing after all. It put one in the appropriate self-critical mood for painting.

New York had been a dangerous experience. It was like

taking a crash course in ambition. He might have been corrupted. For Nadia, he discovered, was a minor celebrity in the New York art world and, at her side, he went to every opening, every party, every gathering where success was the *entrée*. Her presence made it look easy. But then he made the much more exciting discovery that the glamour disguised a dedicated earnestness of the sort he'd never met in England. Here were people, not just a few, many people, with as much energy, enthusiasm, determination as himself. His single-mindedness was not unique. He was not the only competitor in the race. And he longed then to be back at work in his studio.

Now he was waiting for Austin to arrive. He looked upwards. He missed New York's brilliant light. He'd wasted most of it in half-lit drawing-rooms and restaurants but on even a few walks down the overhung Avenues he'd noticed its extraordinary clarity. How he'd love a studio at the top of one of those fifty-storey towers. He looked again at his glass roof. Still filthy. He must remind Austin of his promise to clean it.

Austin came in slowly. He was anxious over his children. The authorities were threatening to take them into care. The two weeks in which Edward had been in America had made things worse, for he had earned very little money.

'Morning, chief.' He began to take off his clothes.

'Come and look at these,' said Edward. He was bending over a large folder in the corner of the room. 'I wonder if you can tell how I've developed. It's very strange looking at this stuff I did only three years ago. It's as if I'd painted them with my foot.'

Austin, now undressed, came and looked with incurious obedience over his shoulder. He considered himself paid to obey any of Edward's suggestions during the time he was at the studio.

The pictures were a series of sketches of Tristram. Edward had done them one evening at school. Tristram was nude; standing, sitting, lying, crouching, serious, smiling, laughing. Although the execution was crude and unfinished, Tristram always appeared graceful and appealing.

Edward felt Austin draw away from him.

'Don't you like them? You're quite right of course. They're rotten. Beginner's rubbish. I'll chuck them out.'

'Who is it?'

Austin's voice was stiff and disapproving. Edward almost smiled. For he realized that Austin was shocked by them, although there he was himself quite nude and unvarnished about to be painted in just the same way. Then he remembered the circumstances in which he'd been sketching. Tristram had been so charming then, so gay and obliging. Perhaps in not quite the same way.

'He was a friend of mine.'

'The one who went to prison?'

'Well, yes, as a matter of fact.' Edward turned round surprised. He had forgotten Austin knew about that. He put his hand out quite genuinely meaning to calm him, as you might a sensitive horse. But Austin moved and instead his fingers brushed along the top of his thigh and over his pubic hair.

Austin sprang back with an expression of shock and disgust. Edward stood up slowly but his usually pale face turned a bright red. They stared at each other under the glaring light bulb. Edward was embarrassed and angry, mostly with himself. It was so ridiculous; he hadn't even been making an overture. It was true his mind had been recalling that evening with Tristram, but Austin had a much more important part in his life than that. What could he say that would reassure him?

'I'm sorry. They are dreadful pictures. I'm not surprised you jumped back.'

Austin was miserable. He simply couldn't afford to walk out on Edward's money. If he'd thought he was one of those, he'd never have taken the job in the first place. But there was Mrs Aubrey and everything. It had never crossed his mind. He looked desperately at Edward, hating and despising, but willing him to say something to restore the situation.

'Let's get on with it then,' Edward paused. 'But you know I want you in full gear for this one. I should have said. It's the one with the girl.' He managed a laugh. 'You know how easily girls get ideas.'

It was all right. As Edward laughed more, immoderately more, Austin turned and put on his clothes. 'O.K.' They were men together again. Men shielding the frightening secret of their bodies from the women. Austin could forget those sketches.

'I clean your wife's windows regularly now,' he said, just to be sure.

Edward calmed himself. 'That reminds me. Would you find a moment to do that roof soon. I never know when it's daylight.'

*

Tish stared at Edward. It was very unnerving to be painted by someone, someone you loved, who couldn't hear a word you said, who didn't want to hear a word you said. Nadia had presented Edward with a bulbous pair of earphones, so that he could listen to music as he worked. He had plugged them into his gramophone immediately and was at the moment listening to Boccherini's Quintet in E Flat. What was so ridiculous, thought Tish, was that she herself, with nothing to do at all but stare wistfully at the wall, was much more in need of music than him. But this didn't seem to have crossed Edward's mind. The earphones had become a ritual. Although he couldn't hear, he could, of course, speak:

'Just sway a little to your left, would you, and hold out your cloak an inch or two further. Perfect.' Edward had at last solved the problem of the Beauty and the Beast painting. It had become Little Red Riding Hood and the Big Bad Wolf. Tish stood in a red cape smiling prettily ahead, Austin crouched hairily, hungrily behind. Today he was painting Tish separately.

Tish realized she could hear a very slight squeaking from the earphones. She tried to make out the rhythm of the music but just as she thought she'd got the hang of it there was a prolonged squeak and the arm of the gramophone on the floor lifted noisily from the record and settled back into place. Musicless, Edward still painted on.

Tish shivered slightly. It was a bleak November day and the studio had no heating. Her red cloak, hired from Nathans for the occasion, was only made of silk and her white dress of almost transparent organza was as useless as nothing. She was barelegged and barefooted on Edward's insistence. Even adoring self-sacrifice has its limits. She shivered exaggeratedly. 'I can't stand it much more, I'm afraid.' Edward must at least see her mouth moving. 'I'm frozen.'

Edward, apparently lip-reading with no problem, looked at his watch and then took off his earphones. 'It's three o'clock. I would like to use up the daylight. What there is of it.' He was conciliatory. At his most charming. He came over to Tish and took hold of her arm. 'Good heavens! You feel like an icicle. I'll tell you what, I'm pretty cold myself. Why don't we jump about a bit and warm ourselves up. Just for five minutes and then perhaps you could manage another half-hour?'

Tish was delighted to have so much of his attention. She shivered even more theatrically as he stood facing her and rubbed her arms up and down.

'I'll put on some music. That'll get us going.' Carefully unplugging the earphones from the gramophone, he restarted the Boccherini to full blast. Swinging his arms and bending from side to side, he started vigorously to perform the sort of exercises he had learnt in the school corps. 'One two, one two, one two, one two.'

Tish felt triumphant. The hated earphones were discarded on the floor. Music linked them together in a great rush of sound. She began to do ballet exercises. '*Plié*, two three four, down two three four, up two three four.' She had always been good at ballet; supple, bouncy, even graceful in a brisk kind of way. She began to do *battements*, 'Point lift, point fifth, point lift, point fifth.' Her well-shaped bare leg, still slightly golden from the summer, flashed up and down. Soon she tried a *pirouette* and then encouraged by the success of one, a whole batch of them.

Edward stopped his exercises. 'Magnificent!' he cried. 'More! More! Round and round and round! Bravo!'

Tish panted and stretched and smiled, and her face turned a rosy pink. Her yellow curls fell over her face so that she couldn't see Edward's face but just hear his excited encouraging voice, 'But you're marvellous! Superb! Go on! Don't stop!'

'I'm exhausted,' gasped Tish.

'Come on. I'll help you.'

Tish felt her waist gripped by Edward's bony fingers. 'Go on now. Jump and I'll lift.' Bravely, Tish jumped and felt herself soaring upwards. She had never realized Edward was so strong. It was a wonderful feeling, like flying. And then she was down again, still in Edward's arms but resting on the floor. 'Heavens. I'm exhausted.' But Edward was carried away with a new experience,

'Let's try it moving now. You run across the room, and I'll say one two three. Ready.' And there she was flying again at Edward's fingertips. Backwards and forwards. Backwards and forwards. 'What else can you do? The splits? Can you do the splits? I've always wanted to see that done at close quarters.'

'I used to, but I don't think now.'

'A back bend. You could do that. If I held you. Like this.' Tish felt his arm under her waist and his hand pushing back her head. She was so dazed by now that she couldn't have stopped even if her back had been about to break, but as a matter of fact it had always been one of the things she'd found most easy to do. She put her arms over her head and felt them touch the cold shiny floor. She opened her eyes again which she'd shut as she'd descended.

'Fantastic. Fantastic.' Edward stood over her. He had taken his supporting arm away. He stood astride her. Trapped in her taut position Tish could do nothing but stare. Never had he seemed so magnificent, so dominant. She collapsed backwards onto the floor as he lowered himself slowly onto her.

*

It was harder than Austin had imagined it would be, to get up to the roof of the studio. Although the building was not high, there were no obvious footholds. The fact that it was already starting to grow dark didn't help. Austin grumbled to himself and decided to make sure Edward paid him a proper fee. There was no reason to do someone like him favours. At last he struggled towards the first pane of glass. As he'd thought, absolutely filthy. He'd have to be up and down with half a dozen buckets of water. It was stupid really to have started so late in the day but now he was up he might as well at least make a start. He set his bucket on the flat rim of the roof and pulled out one of his cloths from his waistband.

Tish and Edward seemed to be dancing still on the floor. Their limbs entwined and pointed and bent again. The red silk cape made a vivid backcloth for their pale skin and the torn shreds of Tish's white gossamer dress. The music, nearing its end, crashed and roared about them. One last long chord and it clicked back into silence. But the two figures on the floor had found their own rhythm. The silence was only broken by Tish's mewing cries.

There was an almighty noise above them. Tish who was beneath Edward stared upwards with terror. It seemed the whole glass roof was coming down towards them. The sound of glass shattering and splintering filled her ears. Then it began to cascade towards her. Glittering under the bright bulb of light, it fell like sharp blades of ice, like icicles, like daggers. Tish cried out as the first wave hit the floor.

'Ah. Ah. Ah.' Her staccato screams were hardly different from those before. The shock was too great for more breath. Edward sat up. Crash. Crash. Crash. The glass was falling faster now. Louder. Louder. Edward pulled Tish aside. Tish realized the glass had not been hitting her. Had not been directed towards her. It was falling the other side of the studio. But when she had lain there under Edward looking up, it had been coming towards her. That sharp ice was going to pierce her. Stab her everywhere. She folded her arms protectively and bent her head.

'Ah. Ah. Ah. Ah.'

Edward said, 'Shut up. Be a good girl.' He moved away from her. 'It's nothing really. Just the bloody roof. Falling in. Look, it's almost stopped now.'

And indeed the noise had stopped. Tish looked up nervously.

'Ah. Ah. Ah.' A scarlet face was peering at her out of the black night sky. It was the devil. The devil punishing her. Oh God. God.

Edward began to laugh. But it was only a short-lived nervous reaction, provoked by Tish's expression of lunatic terror. He stopped quickly and looked stern.

'Austin. It's Austin. You see it's Austin.' Since Tish continued her hysterical screaming, he picked up the red cloak and covered her bare limbs. Then he put on his trousers.

Austin stayed on the struts of the roof looking down. He seemed incapable of movement. Indeed it was quite possible that he was actually trapped, now that so much of the glass had fallen.

Eventually Edward looked up again.

Austin said gruffly but without any apology. 'I was cleaning the roof for you.'

'I see.' Edward could think of nothing to say.

'It was even filthier than I expected. Disgusting. Not a proper job for a human being. Disgusting.'

'I see.'

'That's why it happened. I had to rub so hard. To get the filth off.'

'Of course. It was an accident.'

'I've never broken a window before. I've never had to rub so hard before.'

'I don't blame you. It was my fault for letting it get so dirty.'

'You shouldn't leave it so long next time. That's what I told your wife.'

There was a pause. Then Edward reasserted himself. 'I suppose we'd better cover it with something for the night, I've got some cardboard that would be better than nothing.'

'It doesn't look like rain.'

It took them some time to cover the hole but in the end they managed a patch-up job. In the course of their work Tish's screams changed to sobs and finally she became silent. Soon afterwards, she picked herself up, dressed and left the studio. Neither man talked to her. When the night was blotted out and Austin had descended into the studio Edward said, 'It's not such a big hole really, now it's filled up. Not to give so much glass, I mean. It will be still light enough for our session tomorrow.'

Austin did not hesitate. The punishment had equalled the crime, his children must not suffer, 'Right, chief. Ten o'clock.'

Edward took up a broom and began to sweep the glass into a pile.

12

1969

Nadia had fixed the day for the first exhibition of Edward's paintings. March the twenty-first. She had not meant it to be so soon, but a blank four weeks had unexpectedly appeared on the gallery's schedule.

Edward was at first surly about the prospect. He had just bought a house in Camden Town and the enthusiasm needed to plan the decoration was taken from his work.

Nadia, legs curled under in her large armchair, thought how young he still was, how foolish. She said firmly, 'Forget all that.'

'But you told me to buy it in the first place.'

'This is work.'

'But I haven't enough paintings to show.'

'Don't you want an exhibition? You've got nearly three months to collect more.'

'The trouble is you're taking up far too much of my time.'

Nadia, as she had promised, was allowing Edward to paint her, but insisted on his bringing paints and canvas to her flat. 'Why won't you come and sit properly?'

'I've told you; it's freezing in there – particularly with that great slice of glass missing. Why don't you get it mended?'

'I like the patch. It reminds me of the frailty of life. Anyway I can't find anyone to do it.'

'Inefficiency isn't convincing in you.'

'How many paintings do I need?'

'Minimum twenty oil paintings plus any sketches or drawings you may have. You can't, of course, exhibit me nude.'

Edward turned away from her. He didn't say anything.

Nadia went on, 'Arthur's ill. It would not be tactful.'

'I can't possibly paint six more pictures in three months. One a fortnight. You'll have to find someone else for your gallery, Nadia.'

'Arthur and I have always got on so well together it would be a pity to spoil everything now.'

'Make him unhappy.'

'Quite.'

'Is he very ill?'

'When you're his age, any illness is serious.'

'And you wouldn't want to lose his affections at the end.'

'There're more charming ways of putting things, Edward.'

'I can't possibly paint enough pictures.'

Nadia leant forward from her chair and took a cigarette from a marble box on a low table in front of her. It required quite an effort of will to execute the stretch gracefully. She wished this conversation wasn't taking place when she was nude. She knew Edward's theory of her as the same clothed or unclothed, and although she was flattered she gave that impression and studied to do so, she didn't always feel it. Not with someone Edward's age. She was too conscious her body was almost twice as old as his and uncomfortably aware how he would relish the first sign of sagging line or varicose vein. The control she must exercise over her body made her less free to argue forcefully. How could she convince him that she genuinely did not want to hurt her husband who had always been kind to her, when Edward only saw him as an old buffoon. Oh, the beautiful arrogance of youth! On the other hand she was now passionately keen to see Edward's pictures hanging on the wall of her gallery – before someone else took him from her.

'Poor Arthur. He'll get such a shock.'

'Perhaps he won't be well enough to come to the exhibition.'

'One condition. My name mustn't be on the picture.'

'I don't care about names. Call it double-faced if you like. A Two-faced Lady.'

Nadia laughed unconvincingly. Sometimes even beautiful youth went too far. 'No, thank you.'

'When I've finished your painting, I'll go to the country and stay with my mother. It will occupy her to pose and I've a whole group of sketches to work from. I won't be disturbed there.'

'No,' agreed Nadia resignedly. The exhibition was the most important thing now. 'Tish and I will start drumming up support.'

*

Maggie couldn't believe her eyes when she received the invitation. Scrawled across the gallery's name was a handwritten note saying, 'The artist suggested you would like to come to this. Nadia Gore.' Although Maggie hadn't seen Fenella since her visit several months ago she immediately telephoned her.

'Have you seen this invitation?' she cried wildly. 'What can Edward have been thinking of? Doesn't he know? It's been fixed for ages. That's the same day as Tristram's appeal!'

There was a long pause, then Fenella said very quietly and very slowly, as if she wasn't used to speaking. 'I haven't seen Edward for a long time. I've been waiting for the spring. It's so late this year. The leaves have hardly begun to shoot. But I feel more hopeful now the daffodils are here.'

'Didn't you hear what I said?' screamed Maggie. 'Tristram's appeal's the same day as the opening of Edward's exhibition. It's impossible.'

'I wish I could help,' said Fenella vacantly. 'I believe he's staying with Gunilla.'

'But you must know about it.' Maggie waved the card in front of the telephone and then stopped with it triumphantly aloft. 'It's you on the front. A picture of you on the front. It's you all right, though hardly flattering.'

'Oh, it is me,' agreed Fenella. 'It was painted at his parents' home, where he is now in the country, before his father died. It's called "The Lunatic".' Fenella smiled to herself wanly.

Maggie returned to the attack, 'So you've got an invitation too. Then why are you pretending not to know anything?'

'Tish and Lady Gore are organizing it. I expect they chose the painting of me for the cover. Tish has always thought it one of Edward's best. If I were you, I'd ring Lady Gore or Tish. But of course I shall come to the funeral.'

'Funeral?' Maggie was momentarily silenced. It was such a horrid slip of the tongue. In fact Fenella sounded altogether odd; she lowered her voice. 'Are you all right, dear? Not ill, I mean?'

'No, thank you. I'm working. But I'm glad you told me about the appeal. It will be very cheering to see Tristram again. To see him free. I'd rather go to court than the opening. You see I know a lot of the paintings.'

'Of course,' said Maggie, now quite mollified. 'Perhaps we can get something to eat first.'

'If you like.'

'And we could always see Edward's paintings another day.'

'So we could.'

Neither of them realized that it would have been quite possible to attend both the Court of Appeal and the opening of the exhibition as one would be over soon after four and the other didn't begin till five-thirty.

In both their minds the two events were mutually incompatible.

*

Austin also received an invitation to the opening. The idea of gathering people together to look at paintings and drink wine at five-thirty in the afternoon was quite outside his experience. However, he resolved to go. Firstly because Edward's stay in the country had seriously depleted his supply of money and he needed to make immediate contact for more work before, once again, he felt the authorities threatening to take the children. And secondly, it was the girls' Easter holidays, so he could combine business with an outing to London for them. Hiding under the second plan was the hope that Sharon and Louise washed and brushed in scarlet ribbons and shining white socks might woo Edward's artistic eye. After all they were a great deal prettier than he was. Austin didn't feel capable of answering the invitation, but spent the last of his money in the local street market on two brightly patterned dresses for his girls.

*

Tish and Nadia had been heaving pictures about since early morning. They'd been doing it the day before as well.

'I can never understand why I find myself working like a navvy, when I actually pay navvies to do the work.' Nadia, lean and efficient-looking in a denim trouser suit, accepted a picture hook from Tish who stood below.

'It's a labour of love,' replied Tish crisply. 'You know I really don't think we can put the first painting of Fenella, the Florence one, next to the latest. The change in her is too cruel.'

'Is she coming, do you know?' Nadia jumped off her chair and surveyed the hook critically.

Tish turned away guiltily. 'She had an invitation.'

'Well, of course she had an invitation. I wrote on it myself.' Nadia sounded surprised. Since Fenella's unfortunate stay in her house when she had done all in her power to help, she had kept away from Fenella and her problems. Edward never spoke of her. 'I suppose she is coming.'

'There is a difficulty, I think. Mrs Brown rang her. Her son, you remember Tristram, who was convicted on a drugs case, his appeal is being heard today. It's just possible Fenella might decide to go there instead.' Tish blushed at the memory of her conversation with Maggie. She had not been able to convince her that her job required her to stay at the gallery. She had promised to go another day if the case went on, but Maggie hadn't seen the point of this either. She seemed crazily obsessed by the idea that Edward had specially planned the coincidence in some inexplicable savage irony. Tish's assurances that the date had been planned by Lady Gore several months ago had made no impression at all. 'Fenella was very fond of Tristram.'

'It's up to her.' Nadia began to lift a picture up to the chair. 'Come on, darling, give a shove. Muscles are the thing this year.'

*

Fenella wandered across Kensington Gore into the Gardens opposite. Theoretically, she was on her way to the Court of Appeal, but she had not found much use for time lately and felt no sense of urgency. As she'd indicated to Maggie she was more interested in the seasons. She stooped to admire a creamy pink primula – spring was really established at last. Changing direction suddenly, she began to walk more briskly. Her attention had been caught by the Albert Memorial. She had been brought up to believe it the ultimate in artistic vulgarity and yet all at once she was struck by its terrible pathos. That poor dumpy Queen Victoria with her enormous love blocked forever by death only able to find an outlet in this gigantic monstrosity, fated to be the laughing stock of countless generations of snooty schoolgirls. There was true tragedy. Sitting down on a dampish bench opposite the great four-cornered monument, Fenella began to cry silently.

After a while she revived enough to wipe her face with a large red silk handkerchief. It was one of Edward's which had been dangling garishly from her hip pocket. She was dressed in a pair of ugly black trousers wound above by her paisley shawl. Lately she had become obsessional about the shawl, like a small child with his old rug or sock; at first she could not sleep without it on her bed; now she could not bear to part with it for a moment and at night she spread it right over her face.

Despite this, she was, as she'd told Maggie, still working. Collecting illustrations for a book on nineteenth-century explorers. But her earlier round of museums and libraries had shrunk to one, the Royal Geographical Society which was where she'd just come from. It was an imposing Victorian building with a huge echoing hall and a vast staircase. But the library was darkish and not too big and almost invariably empty. That was why Fenella liked it. She had found the glare of people's faces in the British Museum unbearable. But no one stared at her in the Royal Geographical – or almost no one. Once or twice there had been a very sunburnt man crouched over a desk but when she had exchanged a look, it had been to see eyes as wild, as unfitted for social contact as she felt her own. Probably an anthropologist, she had thought to herself, a twentieth-century explorer back from some expedition into a remote civilization and unable to cope with London in 1969. The idea consoled her and if she'd been more confident she would have told him how she too, though not a traveller in time, felt just the same way. As it was, the only person she spoke to was Austin who arrived with what seemed unnecessary regularity to clean her windows. He talked a lot, but seemed to expect nothing more than sympathetic attention from her, so she poured him tea and gave him chocolate cake and even took a curious consolation in his woes. They were so much more tangible than hers. But apart from these visits, she jealously guarded her isolation.

This partly explained her meandering course to the Court of Appeal. She really did want to see Tristram restored to life, she knew it was her duty, she knew it would be good for her, but she was frightened of the human contact necessary. She brought out the red silk handkerchief again to blow her nose and this time the invitation to Edward's exhibition came with it. She stuffed it hastily back into her pocket and jumped up. She began to run across the grass towards the Serpentine. It was not a graceful sight, for swift movement had never been Fenella's style and now that she was so gaunt, her arms and black drainpipe legs flapping in syncopation looked impossibly long and ungainly. Several passers-by turned to stare at her.

*

Tish couldn't shrug off the subject of Fenella easily. 'I haven't spoken to Fenella for some time actually, but I'm sure she would only want what's best for Edward. That's always been her attitude. She'd understand.'

'I'm sure she would.' Nadia refused to be drawn on the subject. 'God, this picture's really too heavy for me. Here, put it down on the floor again. We'll have to get help.'

Tish stared at the picture unhappily. It was the double portrait of herself and Austin. The one she had been posing for the afternoon she and Edward had made love and the glass roof had fallen on top of them, been pushed on top of them. Sometimes she wished her love and admiration for Edward had not become translated into physical expression. The glass crashing, jangling to the floor had spoiled it from the start. Oddly enough it had upset her more than the pangs of conscience over Fenella. After all, Edward and Fenella had never behaved like an ordinary married couple, never really lived together, never used the 'we' about their plans or ideas, always remained individuals with the right to choose any course of action. Fenella must have understood this and accepted it from the start, Tish told herself firmly, stifling the knowledge that even so her behaviour could well cause her pain; it was not as if she was destroying anything. In fact Edward hardly gave her the chance, for their love-making was intermittent to say the least, and had changed nothing in their relationship. Sometimes she excited him – usually after a good session painting – that was all there was to it. Tish sighed and accidentally nudged the picture in front of which she was still crouching. It fell backwards with a bang.

'Oh heavens,' Nadia swung round and then tried to smile as she saw what had caused the noise. 'It sounded just like a gun shot.'

'Sorry.' Tish picked up the picture again. The point was, of course, that Edward's brilliance put him outside any normal rules of behaviour. One simply felt honoured to be noticed. She looked round the room where some pictures were already hung and some were still leaning against the walls. It was a tremendous achievement for someone of Edward's age. Then she noticed one still wrapped in brown paper.

'Is that the one I haven't seen yet?' she called excitedly to Nadia. 'Double-faced, it's called, isn't it? Do let's unwrap it! I can't wait.'

'Stop gushing, Tish. Sometimes you sound just like a silly schoolgirl. Here's Mr Barton, at last.'

Tish recoiled from Nadia's vituperative tone. She'd never before heard her voice raised from its tenor calm. They had to unwrap the picture sometime. Why not now?

Nadia, who never showed her emotions to anyone, was furious with herself. It was ridiculous to shout at the poor besotted girl because she was embarrassed by Edward's portrait of her. In fact it was ridiculous to be embarrassed at all.

The portrait was perfectly accurate and rather flattering. Indeed now that Edward had forced her into public display she would have been rather disappointed if it had gone forever unseen. In her opinion it was one of his best paintings. It was just that she couldn't bear to see Tish's silly blue eyes pop and draw a vulgar conclusion from her nudity. Certainly Edward and she were lovers and she was not ashamed of it but there was no reason to infer that from the portrait. She would have posed nude for him, whatever their relationship.

As a matter of fact Nadia underrated the complication of Tish's attitude. Her conviction that Nadia was Edward's patroness might well withstand a nude portrait or two. After all, in the kind of converse logic she used, she was his lover and yet he had painted her fully clothed.

'Over here. This one first. Where the hook is.' Nadia, calmer now, led over Mr Barton to the picture already unwrapped. Mr Barton, with brown moustache and brown overalls was a very calming sort of person. He'd hung nudes for Nadia's exhibitions over the years and never looked at one of them. Sometimes it was a relief to have people around with no interest in art. The picture was heaved aloft.

'I don't expect Austin will come either,' Tish looked up at his dark face.

'Straight is it?' asked Mr Barton.

'Up a bit to the left.' What Tish meant was that she hoped Austin wouldn't come. His presence always made her uneasy. Her relationship with Edward had nothing to do with him, of course, but he had such a fierce blank face that she never quite knew what he was thinking. It was his big red hand that had pushed in the window. By accident. 'I mean he'd feel awfully out of place.'

'His place. What a snob you are, darling.' Nadia laughed, glad to forget her own portrait. 'You never know, he might like to see how the ladies react to such a fine figure of a man.'

'Oh, no,' said Tish. 'I don't think he's really realized what it's all about. He's much more likely to be shocked by everyone peering at him.'

'Let's have him up next anyway.' Nadia indicated the full-length nude to Mr Barton, who took it up impassively. 'By the door, don't you think? Knock them out as they come in.'

'Oh, no. Not first thing. Put "The Lunatic" there.'

'But it's so sad.' Nadia turned round to see the picture. Fenella's huge eyes stared at her, so did the moon up above and the pompons down the front of her pierrot's costume. It was an unnerving composition. 'Still, it would stop the vice squad closing us down. Let's do that first, Barton. By the door. Low down so it looks as like a real person as it ever will.'

Obediently, Mr Barton put down Austin's hairy body and collected the life-size figure of Fenella. Carefully, eyes peering over the top, he carried her towards the door.

*

Fenella stood looking over the parapet of the bridge crossing the Serpentine; the black waters reflected perfectly the trees around its edges, the tower of the Hilton at the far end and the bridge below her. But try as she might, she could not see her own face. She tried to remember if she could when standing there in the past, whether it was possible at all and she was quite sure it was. Twisting her face from side to side, she leant further and further over the parapet. It was terrible not to be able to see your own reflection. As if you didn't exist. She gave a half jump to raise herself higher.

'Can I help you, miss?'

A hand with five individually pressing fingers landed on Fenella's shoulder. She swung round gasping. A policeman. Tall and flat and blue. She stared at him stupidly. He seemed to be waiting for her to say something.

'I was looking for my reflection.'

'You won't see it from up here, miss.'

'But the tops of the trees . . . No, of course not. It was silly.'

'There's nothing wrong then?'

'No. Nothing at all. I'm going now.'

'That's best, miss. It's still a bit chilly to stand around for too long.'

'Though spring is coming. Well. Here, really. I'll be off then.' Conscious of his watchful eyes, Fenella started away towards Hyde Park Corner and the moment bushes hid the policeman from sight, began once more to run. She flushed now with the embarrassment of the meeting. Ridiculous, too. Obviously he had thought he was saving her from suicide. How ridiculous! She never should have tried to explain about the reflection; that had only made him think she was mad too. Yet it still worried her. It made her feel insubstantial, like having no shadow. When she found a suitable shop window she would stop and find her reflection there.

It was a long way to the end of the park, she'd forgotten how long. Kensington Gardens became Hyde Park and she was still gasping and running. At last there was Apsley House, so scrubbed and bright and then she had to find her way to Piccadilly. She considered the underpasses with distrust; they looked black and cold, but that meant she must face the traffic of Hyde Park Corner and, to make it more complicated, workmen seemed to be digging up most of the pavement. The noise of cars and lorries and buses and drills was terrifying and she could feel her heart thudding in time with her feet as she ran. But at last she reached the safety of Piccadilly. Next down Bond Street. Walking now, but still as quick as she could. It was the first time she had felt hot and excited for months and in some ways it was a pleasurable sensation. She quite forgot to look for a suitable glass window, and instead turned briskly down a small sidestreet towards Nadia's gallery.

'Oh, no! No!' A smart young man ran into Fenella's back as she stopped very suddenly in the middle of the pavement.

'I'm sorry,' he began automatically, and then noticed she was about to fall. 'Here, hold on. Are you all right?'

'I saw myself,' Fenella whispered, eyes tightly shut. She had seen her reflection coming straight towards her out of a great glass window, but instead of being a thin girl in trousers and a paisley shawl she was a brilliantly coloured pierrot with huge round staring eyes and glaring pompons down her front.

The young man said again, embarrassed by her public position in his arms, 'Are you all right now? Can you stand?'

'Yes,' said Fenella, but she still didn't dare open her eyes. But then he let go of her and in order to preserve her balance she had to see. And what she did see beside the pierrot was a fragment of Tish. Fenella smiled weakly at the young man as he moved away. How absurd! How too ludicrous! What was the matter with her today? Of course, that was the picture Edward had painted of her that was on the front of the catalogue. She was dressed in her pierrot costume that had always made her so happy. And now it had scared her almost out of her wits. It had seemed so lifelike.

Slowly she crossed the road to the other side from the gallery so she could see but not be seen. In the park she had determined to visit the exhibition, but now she felt too shattered. She couldn't face Tish's sprightly optimism and Lady Gore's sleek graciousness. There they both were, shadowy figures behind the glass. They had not finished hanging the pictures yet and looked efficient and occupied. She strained to see whether Edward was with them but there was no one tall and fair. That surprised her for in her imaginings of Edward's first exhibition she had always assumed he would be meticulous about the placing of every painting, that he would bang in every nail himself, adjust the lighting, endlessly work at it to perfection as he did his paintings. And yet apparently he had entrusted it all to Lady Gore and Tish.

Well, there was no reason for her to stay any more. They might recognize her lurking figure if she did. She started again walking down the street. The eyes of the pierrot followed her sadly.

*

Edward had just finished giving his mother lunch in Rules. Gunilla leant across the table and fixed her large eyes on her son. They were extraordinarily like his.

'And now you have to show me the house.'

'But that is the point, mother.'

Gunilla smiled gently, 'And the exhibition.'

'Oh, that.' Edward signed the bill and then looked round at the heavy oil paintings that lined the walls of the diningroom. 'People have no judgement. Gawping ignoramuses.'

'How about the critics?'

'They'd write better about monkeys in a zoo.'

Gunilla continued smiling and, taking Edward's thin white

hand, patted it reassuringly. She saw he was nervous, for she had always known he was ambitious. Now that he and Fenella had separated, he had no one to talk to. Gunilla still smiled. Constant mourning had hardened her and made her selfish. She was not happy that the marriage had failed, that Fenella, who she'd always admired, must be suffering, but she could not be very unhappy.

Edward withdrew his hand from his mother's, though not before admiring her fine blue veins and elegant diamond ring. The gesture would have outraged him in anyone else but she was his mother – part of himself. Besides, he wanted to show her his house.

'We won't have long before the opening,' Gunilla stood too as Edward pushed back his chair hurriedly. 'And I want to change and do you justice.'

'You always do.' Edward bowed gallantly. It was true. In the six weeks he'd stayed alone with Gunilla in the country, he had come to feel a more than filial appreciation. Her stern pale face and her tall thin frame appealed to his visual sense, while her calm detached mind soothed his nervous spirit. She did not impinge on him, she did not try to influence him, she did not try to reveal herself to him; he never quite knew what she was thinking. In many ways he was reminded of Fenella as she'd been when he'd first known her – before their marriage. His mother's vagueness, which had always seemed affected to him, had now become diluted by sadness. Moreover, he discovered that it actually disguised a surprising organizing efficiency. He was glad she had decided to come to London for a while. She could help him decorate his new house. She could cook for him when he needed to eat and provide a home for him when he needed a home.

As they left the club, he put an arm across her shoulder, 'You're so stalwart, mother. So tactful. So dignified and just the height a woman should be too !'

Mother and son looked at each other and laughed.

*

Maggie sat in Court Five of the Royal Courts of Justice. Tristram's case hadn't appeared yet. It was named on a typewritten list pinned up outside as the fifth to be dealt with that day and they were still only on the third. But Maggie didn't dare move, whatever her lawyers advised. It was a small room and she was seated in the second row from the back, but she looked round constantly because she was expecting Fenella any minute. The doors banged often but it was usually an inquiring black face come to see British justice or otherwise a party of small Japanese. Maggie thought it very nosey of them, and frowned disapprovingly as they shuffled out after a bare five minutes. So far she had seen a car thief have his sentence reduced from four years to two and an unsuccessful bank robber have his sentence upheld. Now it was a sniffly little man on a charge of forgery. She hoped Tristram, who had been brought from Wormwood Scrubs (so awful to see that name beside his on the notice) to await his turn in some cell downstairs, was not as impatient as she was. Where was Fenella? It would be lunchtime soon. In fact it was already. The central of the three judges stood up and the room emptied. Maggie looked round almost tearfully. She didn't want to have lunch with her solicitor and the new young barrister – too young perhaps, she feared. But she wouldn't use again the Q.C. who had failed her. She wanted to talk to someone who *loved* Tristram.

'No. No. I'll go to the cafeteria,' she protested, as they tried to persuade her.

'But it's so gloomy.' The young barrister, who had a fresh complexion and thick ginger curls, grimaced charmingly.

'So am I.'

There was a greenish underwater atmosphere about the cafeteria; the mumbled conversations rose and fell like waves breaking on a beach somewhere above, the steamy smoky air swirled like underwater currents, the smell was of decomposing seaweed. Through this unattractive haze, Maggie only just recognized the crouched figure of Fenella.

'You're here!'

'I'm sorry,' Fenella said, when she saw who it was. 'I couldn't face the court. It's so cold. So cold, you'd never guess there was spring outside.'

'It doesn't matter,' Maggie was too relieved for complaint.

'His case hasn't come up yet. I am glad you've come.'

'It's so dreadful here,' Fenella spoke in a low monotone, eyes staring into the tea-leaves at the bottom of her cup. 'I really can't bear it.'

'It is rather frightful,' Maggie looked round. 'But I suppose they do their best. You can hardly expect the Ritz.'

'I don't mean here. This is all right. That's why I came in. It's the great mountains of stone, the imposition of it all. There's no hope for anyone here ...' Her voice died away.

'The great hall, you mean,' Maggie was bracing. 'It is ridiculously large. Apparently they use it to play racquets in the evenings. The lawyers. I wonder if they wear their wigs.' Her laugh sounded hysterical in the gloom.

'They play games there? Games!' Fenella looked up with a horrified expression on her face. 'Is that all it is to them? A game!'

'After the courts have closed.' Maggie looked at Fenella, puzzled, and realized through her own emotional blur that there was someone even more disturbed than herself across the table. 'We'd better eat,' she suggested hopefully.

'No, thank you. It's built for us. The Law is built for us. This place. For the people. But it's so ugly. It's pathetic it should be so ugly. And the attendants. They're all crippled. Did you notice? The people are crippled. I asked a man the way and he had a leather hand and a funny horrid wink, as if he was laughing but he wasn't really. He just couldn't help himself. He wanted to be nice to me, he told me there might be a murder case in Court Eleven if I was lucky. "If I was lucky," he said. Then he winked.'

'Poor thing.' Maggie hadn't the strength to fight Fenella's macabre imaginings. She had hoped for help from her. 'I must get something to eat.' She stood up. 'They start again at two.'

When she returned with a plate of liver and mashed potatoes, Fenella seemed to be a little brighter. 'I wonder what Tristram will be eating,' she said almost gaily. 'It must be extraordinary to feel freedom within his grasp.'

Maggie was troubled. 'But we're not appealing against the conviction, darling. You do know that, don't you? We'd never win that. It's just the sentence. We want it reduced to a year. The judge was far too severe, you see.'

'Not the conviction.'

'Of course he's served so much already that with the remission for good behaviour, he could be out very soon.'

'But not today . . .'

Fenella's wild look quite frightened Maggie. 'He doesn't want to stay in. Only a little while.'

'Then there's no point in me coming. I can't lead him out. He's still trapped.'

Maggie looked at her watch. 'We should go to the court now.'

Fenella was biddable suddenly. 'If you like.' It was just that the great stone corridors had depressed her so. She remembered Edward's attack on the modern wing of the Old Bailey and wondered if this would appeal to him more. It probably would. To his sense of the dramatic. Those bomb warnings pinned along the walls, 'On hearing blasts on a whistle'; what did you do? Run. Run. But where was the shelter? Fenella gave a sudden shrieking laugh. She wished she'd brought a whistle to try it.

They began to climb the stairs to the upper corridor and Court Five.

'Have you looked down from the balcony?' Maggie asked, when they reached the top. 'There's just time.'

They leant above the great hall. Its shiny flagstones glistened far below. There would be no reflection from them, Fenella thought, but they looked hard enough to smash a bushel of coconuts.

'Come along now.' Maggie pulled her away.

Just before the court room, Fenella stopped again. She stared at a large oil painting of a judge robed in scarlet and hung with silver curls. 'Sir Edward Clarke Q.C.,' she read out, '1841–1931, by Solomon J. Solomon. Presented by Sir Edward Clarke.' She paused. 'He was ninety,' she said, 'and he gave the picture himself. It's horrible. Isn't it, horrible? Age. Conceit. Age.'

'Yes. Yes.' Maggie was impatient now lest they be late. She didn't want to interrupt the proceedings like those insensitive foreigners. And they might have put Tristram in earlier than expected. 'Hurry, dear, do.'

Fenella followed unnoticing. 'When I first came in, I saw those horrid models of judges in robes. Behind glass. A sort of costume exhibition.'

'Here we are.'

'It was their faces. The faces they'd been given as appropriate to the dealing out of justice.'

'Law, dear,' said Maggie pulling open the door. 'Not justice. Law. That's what my solicitor always says.'

'Their faces are savage. Like vultures. Grey and cruel with thin mouths and hard pointed noses . . .'

'Ssssh now.'

They stood side by side in the narrow bench as the three judges entered the court.

'You see what I mean,' whispered Fenella, passionately.

But to Maggie, who had watched them all morning, they looked like three elderly gentlemen, one with pince-nez, who seemed quite a bit more genial now that they had lunched. She was glad, after all, that Tristram's case had come later in the day.

'It shouldn't be too long,' she said encouragingly.

But Fenella realized she couldn't stay there now and watch Tristram destroyed further by these old men. Ninety years old. They should be dead. People shouldn't outlive their beauty. So ugly. Everyone was ugly here. In the court. Look at that girl, her scarlet lipstick slashed across her stupid face. How could anyone be so absurd. She probably thought it improved her appearance. Poor girl. So pathetic. She couldn't sit here and watch that poor unloved girl. Scribble, scribble. After work she probably went home and sat all by herself, planning the shade of her lipstick for the next day. It was terrible. Insupportable. Tragic.

Fenella rose sharply and shuffled clumsily but quickly towards the door. Maggie started up to snatch her back but was too late. She looked after her despairingly. She couldn't leave herself, there would be too much noise; what if the judge knew who she was and held it against Tristram? Decided he came from an unstable family? Was better locked away? She subsided again. Perhaps it was as well Fenella had left. She had never known her so dispirited.

*

Austin had intended to arrive early at the exhibition, but the girls had taken much longer to get ready than he'd expected. Their hair had to be washed and dried, their shoes polished, their dresses buttoned, their white socks drawn up, their cardigans smoothed neatly on. It was worth it, in the end, they looked so clean and pretty, blue eyes, long yellow hair in neat bunches – no one would have guessed they had no mother. If only she had been there to see them. But perhaps she could. Austin wished that he could be more convinced that death was not the end.

'Come on, now. No dawdling.' A child on either hand, he walked proudly to the bus stop. Fussily he straightened the furry hoods of their identical coats and then looked at his watch. Three-thirty. He couldn't break his promise to give them tea in Piccadilly Circus first so it would probably be six before they arrived.

In fact it was well after, and the gallery already seemed crowded to capacity. The noise of people talking reached the street. Austin suddenly felt nervous. In his determination to present Sharon and Louise at their best, he had not thought of the impression he might make. Now he realized that he was wearing an old imitation leather jacket over a red sweater and jeans. But there through the glass front he could see a collection of smart suits and fashionable dresses. He hesitated outside and might even have retreated except that he suddenly saw the life-size painting of Fenella dressed as a pierrot. It reassured him instantly. Clothes, her wide clever eyes seemed to say, are not at all important; just look at me, look at my rig-out, ludicrous really, but if people like to laugh, I like to help them. She was his friend, Austin thought. How pleased she would be to see his beautiful girls who he'd talked about so much. He would find her first thing.

'Coats off, Louise, Sharon,' he said firmly. 'That's right.

I'll hold them. In we go.' He pushed open the heavy door and let them in under his arm.

Lady Gore, despite her preoccupation with critics and guests – she knew it was going well, even better than she'd hoped – had time to be surprised by Austin's entrance. She couldn't see his daughters because they were hidden by the crowd and she soon lost sight of him also. However, she turned gaily to Tish who appeared for a moment with a drink in either hand. 'Do give one to that window-cleaner, won't you? He can't have come for anything else.'

Tish ducked her head and disappeared again. She had been avoiding Nadia ever since she'd seen the portrait of her. She didn't want to make a comment. It had shocked her, not made her jealous, nor made her draw any conclusions, just shocked her. She thought there was something decidedly unappealing about that thin unclothed body, more like an animal than a human being. An animal, if not actually old, no longer young either. She thought that Edward had humiliated Nadia by it, and was glad he had never asked her to pose nude. She was not surprised it had a Not For Sale mark on it. Nadia could never have let it hang in some stranger's drawing-room. So embarrassing. Tish blushed to herself and shivered. It was all right to paint someone like Austin nude who was employed strictly for that purpose, but it was quite different in the case of a friend. So intimate. Austin was selling very well, as it happened; she had placed little red circles on almost all of his pictures, in fact they were so markedly popular that she couldn't help wondering if it was anything to do with the sexual tastes of the men present.

Banishing such disloyal thoughts, she went to look for the man himself. It was not a task she relished.

Austin pushed a path through the noisy crowd. Behind him, holding onto his coat flaps came Sharon and Louise. He was searching for Fenella and only aware of the people hiding her from him. It would not have occurred to him to look at the walls even if the pictures had been visible. Halfway across the room, he met Edward.

Edward stood with his mother. He was dressed in his father's white tuxedo and a pale green bow-tie which his mother had bought him that afternoon. Gunilla stood beside him. She had bought herself a dress at the same time, the first since her husband had died; it was pale grey chiffon, fold upon fold, rippling across her thin frame.

Edward saw Austin. 'This is my model,' he explained to Gunilla. 'He is indispensable. Austin, this is my mother.'

Austin and Gunilla shook hands. Then Austin said, 'These are my kids.' He pushed them forward. They giggled and hung back.

Gunilla looked at the two spotless squirming girls and said, 'But how beautiful! How lucky you are!'

Austin glowed and Sharon took heart. She held out her hand to Gunilla and curtsied. Louise quickly copied her. Gunilla laughed and Austin could hardly believe their perfection. It made all the days of working and scolding and nagging and fighting the authorities worthwhile.

Gunilla looked round. 'Is their mother here?'

'No, I'm afraid she's passed on.' Austin saw this wasn't a place to talk about death.

'I am sorry.'

Edward began to be restless. 'Austin is a paragon,' he said. 'A saint. He's bringing them up all himself.'

'Just a father,' Austin was dignified. 'I was looking for your daughter-in-law,' he addressed Gunilla, because she seemed so sympathetic. 'I've told her often about the girls and I wanted to show her.'

'Daughter-in-law?' Gunilla at first seemed to question the term, and then turned to Edward. 'But I haven't seen Fenella here tonight, have I, darling?'

'She was asked,' Edward spoke immediately. All around him there were conversations, evaluations of such importance to him taking place that he could hardly be expected to pin himself down to such petty problems.

'The pictures you've done of her are the most moving,' said Gunilla carefully.

'Yes.'

Sharon and Louise tugged on Austin's hands. 'We'll go and look for her ourselves. Good-bye, ma'am.' He shook hands with Gunilla and let the girls pull him away. They were not so overawed now and becoming rather less virtuous.

'Can I have a drink, Dad?'

'There's a lady with sausages on sticks over there. I love sausages on sticks.'

Then Tish found them. She handed over a glass of wine, but Austin held it uncomfortably; the thin glass with its narrow stem didn't feel safe in his big fist.

'And here are your children too. How lovely! What would they like? Orange juice?'

'Sausages,' said Louise firmly, 'on sticks.'

'Sssh,' Sharon giggled.

Tish had been sipping at every wine glass that passed through her hands. She felt exhilarated and had lost the uncomfortable tenseness she usually felt in Austin's presence. Ignoring Louise's request, she waved her hand at the wall, 'Well, how do you think you look, exposed to the public gaze? You're selling awfully well, you know, better than anyone.' She came close to Austin, pressing forward her wine-flushed face with an expression partly flirtatious, partly malicious.

Austin backed away, still without looking at the walls. He did not understand why this normally stand-offish girl had suddenly become so intimate. He was very aware of his daughters' round curious eyes and afraid they might take Tish for a girl friend. He remembered pushing the glass onto her naked limbs as if in a dream.

'We're looking for Mrs Aubrey,' he said in a stupid voice.

Tish became still gayer, 'Senior or junior? Senior seems in command at the moment. I can lead you straight to her. But junior may present a bit more of a problem.'

'But she must be here.'

'In effigy all over the place. But for the actual living breathing human flesh, you'll have to try elsewhere, I'm afraid. You'll have to excuse me too, now. But don't leave without looking at yourself. I'm sure your children will be fascinated to learn how you earn your living.' Smiling delightedly, she disappeared into the crowd. What pleasure she took in torturing him in front of his children and yet it was nothing to what he'd done to her! She remembered painfully the jagged splinters of glass raining down from the roof to where she lay with Edward. Nothing would obliterate that memory.

Now that Austin saw that Tish had been trying to be unpleasant all along, he felt better. Her reference to his posing still didn't sink in. He was quite accustomed to people being nasty to him and able to cope. Her hatred of him was the natural reaction to his disapproval of her immoral behaviour. In the circumstances, he didn't necessarily believe that Fenella wasn't there. The mistress would hardly be objective on the subject of the wife. He wished he hadn't even asked her.

'Louise wants to go now,' said Sharon, hiding her own wish behind her little sister's.

'We'll just find this nice lady.'

But instead Austin found himself approached by a very elegant woman who smelt strongly of expensive scent. He had never seen her before but she took his arm and said warmly, 'You must be Austin, the famous window-cleaner. I'm so pleased to meet you at last. My name is Lady Gore. I own this gallery. And you in a way,' she laughed brightly, glancing towards the walls. 'And are these your beautiful daughters?'

'Yes,' said Austin shortly, he didn't want these women hanging over him any more. He wanted Fenella's sympathy, her real warmth. Without thinking what he was doing, he handed Nadia his still full glass of wine, 'I'm looking for Mrs Aubrey,' and so that there could be no mistake he added, 'The young Mrs Aubrey. Know if she's here?'

Lady Gore's manner changed abruptly. Too many people had asked her that this evening. Besides, even with one Mrs Aubrey gone there seemed another to replace her. She stood back from Austin, looked past him, smiled at someone beyond him, mouthed to someone at the right of him. 'Mrs Aubrey. No. She was invited, of course, but I believe she was busy elsewhere.'

Austin stared. Suddenly he had the conviction that there was a conspiracy against Fenella. It didn't make sense her not being here. Nor the reactions to his inquiries. How could she be busy elsewhere on an occasion like this? He didn't understand, but he suddenly felt a dreadful anxiety on Fenella's account. It took hold of him; it tightened his chest so he could hardly breathe. He felt very hot and faint. The room was stifling him. Grabbing a child in either hand he started to push and shove his way towards the door. Just before he reached it the crowd parted for a moment and he was faced, without any warning, with his own life-size naked body. He stared horror-struck for only a moment and then, shielding the girls behind him, he pressed on. But the glimpse had been enough. Tish was right in thinking he had never imagined when posing the situation in which his body would be seen openly by the public. His instant reaction was to feel even more intensely that the gallery was a corrupt and dangerous place. It must be, to show a man like that. No wonder the woman seemed so strange, so excited. With a great gasp of relief he escaped at last through the door now standing open to the street and emerged into the cool evening air.

'I want to go home now, Dad,' said Sharon.

'That lady never got me any sausages,' complained Louise.

Thank God neither of them had seen the portrait. Austin wiped his face with his handkerchief. It felt smooth and silky and looking down, he saw it was one of Edward's. He stuffed it hastily back into his pocket.

'We've got to go somewhere first.'

'Somewhere nice. I'm hungry, Dad.'

'Very nice. There'll be biscuits. And cake.' Austin had to find Fenella. The whole visit would be pointless without seeing her. Worse than pointless. He must see her. He would go to her flat. He had to find out why everyone was so strange about her. She might be ill.

'Come on. We'll find the underground. You know you like the underground.'

It was dark by the time they reached Fenella's flat and Austin saw immediately she wasn't there for there was no light showing. However, he was determined now and by ringing someone else's bell he got into the building and dragged the unwilling girls upstairs.

'It's dark, Dad.'

'It's cold, Dad.'

He banged on the door energetically but no one answered. Sharon played with the handle and suddenly the door was open.

'Wait here now, just a moment.'

'I'm frightened, Dad.'

Cautiously he went into the flat; he didn't want to be accused of breaking and entering. But they had broken nothing. He switched on a light. Looked round. But there was no one. Meticulously neat.

'Come on in now. Sharon. Louise.' He couldn't leave them standing out there. Someone might hear them chattering. 'Come in. Off with your coats. That's right. Neatly. Sit on that sofa and I'll find you something to eat.' They were impressed by the prettily decorated flat and sat quietly. Austin went into the kitchen. He found a slightly stale chocolate cake in the bread bin and brought it to them.

'You won't mind staying here for a little while, will you? I won't be long.'

'Alone Dad?' Sharon looked serious though her mouth was filled with chocolate cake. 'You never leave us alone.'

Louise began to grizzle. 'I want to go home. I don't like it here. I want my dollie.'

Austin looked at Sharon. He appealed to her, 'You're a big girl now. You can see after Lou, can't you? Just for a little while. You're such a grown-up girl now. And if you're very good I'll buy you a little present.'

The mixture of flattery and bribery won Sharon over. She put an arm round Louise. 'Don't be such a cry baby. But don't be very long, Dad.'

Austin kissed them both and went out into the night. He didn't know what made him so sure that he must find Fenella, made him break all his rules as a father but he couldn't give up the search now. You couldn't leave people when they were in trouble.

Edward's studio was the only other place he knew to look. Feeling the single pound note in his pocket he ran to the main road and found a taxi.

It was completely dark by the time he reached the small

building, but this time light flared out from the roof. Austin went to the window but the curtain was tightly drawn as usual so he could see nothing. There was no sound either. Yet he felt positive she was inside. Although he didn't know what she would be doing there, as all the canvases were at the exhibition.

He would have to climb onto the roof to find out. He took off his jacket and left it in a tidy roll under the window. There was no ladder to help him. Athletically, he sprang upwards.

Thanks to his efforts, the glass was beautifully clean so he saw Fenella almost immediately. The sight of her draped dangling figure caused him to lie flat and shut his eyes. He was above her and she was turned from him, so he could not see her face, but the angle of her head told him without doubt that she was dead. At first he felt nothing but a sickening horror. Then he was reminded of the moment his own wife had died – but that had been in peace. Horror changed to misery. Death was the same in peace or violence.

Being a man more used to physical reaction than mental, he rose into a crawling position once more and began to edge along towards her. Slightly to her left was the board that he and Edward had pinned across the hole in the roof. He would lever it up with his knife and go through.

This turned out to be rather harder than he'd supposed, but eventually he managed to pull up a corner and slide inside. Still managing to avoid seeing Fenella's face, he tried to crawl along to the part of the great black beam from which she hung. He held the knife in front of him ready to cut through the rope. And then he saw with a further thrill of horror what she had used to strangle herself with. It was a rope made of all Edward's silk handkerchiefs first knotted together and then plaited. The cardboard box he had always kept them in lay upside down on the floor. It must have taken her a very long time. She must have sat on the floor and slowly created the rope to hang herself. Austin did not imagine further, but as he reached the top of her head, he realized he could not go through with cutting her down. Not by himself. In this glaring cold empty room.

He swung himself down hurriedly and, in doing so, knocked her shoulder so that she turned a little. There was a rushing sound of soft material sliding and the dark paisley shawl which was wrapped round her shoulders descended swiftly to the floor. Austin, crouched below, turned sharply away. A fringed tassel settled gently over one of his feet. His face was rigid with shock. Under the shawl she was naked. Eyes averted, he ran to the door. He would find a telephone box and call the police.

The poor thin body of Fenella swung like a white skeleton in the middle of the brightly lit studio.

13

Fenella's last hours were easily reconstructed at the inquest. Maggie gave evidence. She described her disconnected state of mind, how she rushed out of the court without even waiting to hear the happy outcome of her son's appeal. Tristram's sentence was reduced to a year and he would be out in a few months. 'If she'd known that, it might have stopped her ...' Maggie broke down and returned to her place.

Then one of the Courts of Justice attendants described how he'd noticed her because of her odd behaviour. She had become involved with an old drunk they'd let sit in one of the stone alcoves by the main door. He often came in out of the cold and they didn't interfere as long as he sat quietly. But under Fenella's obvious sympathy and staring eyes – she had stood opposite him not speaking but watching eagerly – he had become over-excited and begun to shout, silly slogans, 'Justice is the Law!' 'Protect the children of the poor!' 'The people have been conned!' 'You are the Law!' 'Meaningless unless you're drunk or in a nervous state.' The attendant's evidence was given a curious emphasis by a tick he had in his left eye, which made him seem to be telling everything as if it were a joke. 'Of course, when he started shouting we had to throw him out, his voice echoed round the great hall. You can't have that sort of thing. But the young lady had become very upset. In fact she tried to stop us, grabbing first the tramp and then me and my colleague. It didn't last long, she simmered down quickly enough, once I'd got a good hold of her and the old man had gone out of the door. Then she left quite peacefully herself. We didn't think much of it at the time, for in the courts you often get people upset. People with relatives. But when I saw it in the papers I recognized the picture. The poor young lady.' The attendant returned to his seat and as he went he caught his left hand and put it in his pocket. It was made of brown leather. Several people in the court wondered which hand he'd used to get a good hold of her.

Another member of the public who came forward to give evidence had also recognized the young woman by her photograph. He was a jeweller with a shop in Chancery Lane just round the corner from the Courts of Justice. It appeared that Fenella had been attracted to his display of antique rings and come in to see if they could help her. The jeweller seemed genuinely concerned about the incident. 'She was so nervous, she nearly left as soon as she got in without saying anything at all. Our shop is very small and I think she felt trapped. But I asked her what she wanted so she took a ring from her pocket, a big black and gold ring, a man's ring really, with a lock of hair in it, and passed it across the counter. She said it didn't fit her any more and could I make it smaller. I saw at once it was impossible. She had such thin fingers, no flesh on them at all and the ring, like most mourning rings, had so much ornamentation on the front that there was no way I could take a piece out of the back and keep it circular. I explained this but she wouldn't accept it. She became hysterical, half crying, saying it had to be done, so in the end I thought it wiser to say I'd do my best, though I think she realized I was just saying it. She left then anyway, quieter, but I couldn't get her out of my mind.'

It seemed that after depositing the ring Fenella had walked straight down Chancery Lane, turned right at the bottom and caught a Number 19 bus to King's Road. An *Evening Standard* had been found in Edward's studio and the newspaper seller outside Chancery Lane tube station next door to the stop had also remembered her when the police had approached him. It was the day he'd scribbled on his board, 'Ten children burnt alive'. He wouldn't forget her because she'd stood for ages looking at it. 'Dreadful, she'd looked, muttering to herself until I thought she must be a relative.' She'd noticed him looking at her and in the end bought a paper, but he'd swear she had no intention of opening it. 'She'd seemed in too much of, well, a sort of trance.'

The policeman who had moved Fenella from the bridge

over the Serpentine and whose suspicion had suggested suicide as a real possibility, did not come forward. Even so, it was becoming obvious what the coroner's verdict would be. A report was read from the doctor who had attended her miscarriage; she had seemed 'out of proportion distressed,' he concluded, 'for a young and healthy married woman'; in his opinion it was likely that she had been suffering from acute depression brought about by the physical effects of her miscarriage.

Loelia did not attend her daughter's inquest; Fenella had unknowingly chosen to commit suicide the week of her remarriage. Once more she was forced to realize the foolishness of looking for happiness in life. Nevertheless or, in a contradictory way, because of this feeling, she decided not to come back to England. Let people who were shocked and surprised by misery and death attend its valedictions, let them try and understand it; they needed ceremonies to help them but she did not. Nor did Fenella. She was dead. Sitting down at her new modern writing-table, she wrote a stiff note to Edward. Its last words were, 'I'm sure you were prepared for this.'

Edward was at the inquest. He sat with his mother. They both looked stern and beautiful, like statues carved out of ivory.

Loelia had also written to her husband. An equally stiff note. Roger Frith-Peacock came to the inquest. He knew no one except the officials. He was a stranger at the scene of his daughter's death. Even her husband did not know him and he had no idea why she'd died. He was frightened, bewildered, big, red-faced. He recognized Edward from the newspaper photographs, but although they brushed against each other as they found places, he did not introduce himself. But although he knew least, it was his decision to have Fenella cremated without a service, without ceremony. He looked along the row to Edward and Gunilla and thought they would not be concerned. Their hardness frightened him. He wanted to go back to the country. Like mother, like son, he thought. Or like daughter.

Inwardly, Gunilla was worried about her son. She knew

her own cold exterior had gradually taken over from her softer vaguer self after her husband's death. It had always been there within her, but for fifty years she had controlled it. Now she was old; it didn't matter any more. She couldn't hurt anybody by it; there was no one who needed her warmth.

But it was unnatural in someone as young as Edward. In his twenties. She, his mother, couldn't even tell how much he was suffering or whether he was suffering at all. Perhaps he was in need of warmth, but she was very aware that their new relationship, which was the only pleasure left to her, was founded on a dignified respect for each other's privacy. She did not dare jump the divide now, even if she could have found the way.

Edward was outside himself. He felt his life merging with the imaginative part of himself which was usually reserved for painting. Fenella's suicide on the night of his exhibition both eclipsed and enhanced his own triumph. It had become a symbolic act instead of a personal tragedy. She had chosen to die at that moment as a superb act of defiance; she had always known how to inspire his imagination. Edward sat in the court and even smiled slightly. All this talk to prove that she was unstable, unhappy, of unsound mind, was conventional nonsense to try and fit her into one of the world's categories. She was above such things. She had chosen to die magnificently. Edward admired her in her death more than he ever had.

But now, the coroner, an absurd irrelevant little man, was giving his view, '... took her own life while temporarily of unsound mind.'

Such a fool. Such a fool. Edward tapped his fingers. Gunilla sighed; it was best like this. Both scorn and sigh were interrupted,

'She wasn't mad! She was more sane than any of you! She knew what she was doing all right!'

The screaming voice came from the back of the court. Roger Frith-Peacock became a deeper red and put a shielding hand across his face.

Edward turned round eagerly. Absolutely right! He absolutely agreed. How extraordinary someone else should have the sense to understand. Who could it be?

'She didn't take her own life! She wasn't no suicide!'

Austin standing up there and shouting defiance. The vessels in his purple face stood out like snakes and his blue eyes popped idiotically, but he had understood. Edward bent forward and said, 'Here, here,' under his breath.

'What?' said Gunilla nervously.

'It's Austin.'

'Who? Oh, darling.' She swayed backwards. For now Austin had sprung down from his bench and was rushing towards them. When he was opposite Edward he began to shout again and point his short thick finger.

'Murderer! Murderer! You killed her! Murderer! Guilty! Guilty!'

Edward had just time to notice the little black hairs on Austin's finger and remember how long they'd taken to paint before he was hustled away.

'Can we go now?' Gunilla clung to his arm.

Edward stood up impassively.

The night of Fenella's death had been tragic for Austin. For it had led to his daughters being finally taken into care. Poor Sharon and Louise. It was not really their fault, but when their father didn't return for over two hours, they were frightened and Louise began to cry. Sharon did her best, as the eldest, to comfort her, but soon she was wailing just as loudly. It was not long before the neighbour who had let Austin into the building overheard them and came to investigate. But by this time they were both past rational explanation and, still only trying to help, he rang the police.

The sight of a policeman immediately silenced Sharon. She gulped and tried to say they were quite all right, their Dad would be back any minute. But it was too late. Their swollen tear-stained faces told a pathetic tale of abandonment. 'Terrified out of their wits, they were,' said the kindly policeman afterwards, who was a grandfather himself. 'What self-respecting father could do a thing like that, leaving them all alone, at night, in a place they didn't know! Shocking, it was. He had no right to be allowed to look after them.'

Of course the circumstances of Austin's apparent betrayal were known soon enough. It was midnight before he could get back to Fenella's flat and by that time the police had already taken it over. Austin, who had spent most of the evening in one police station, now found himself directed to another.

'Dad! Dad! Dad!' The girls threw themselves into his arms but their fate was decided. For one thing Austin's nude modelling was naturally discovered by the authorities and though, of course, as they said to each other, there was nothing actually illegal or even wrong about such a way of earning money, they couldn't believe it was the right background to bring up two little girls. He had even, it appeared, taken them to an exhibition to see the pictures. Now that was definitely not right. And then his close involvement in the unfortunate suicide, being the actual one to discover the body and so on, though looked at it in one way his action deserved commendation, looked at in another, it was not the kind of thing they liked to happen to a single father.

The girls must be fostered.

When Austin saw the way things were going, he didn't argue but relapsed into a mood of sullen ferocity. The day they took the girls away he bought a bottle of whisky and drank it straight. Since it made him feel no better he took to his bed. The next day was the inquest.

Tish did not learn about Fenella's suicide till the day after it happened. After the party at the gallery, she, Nadia, Edward, Gunilla and two male art critics, friends of Nadia's, had gone out to dinner. The restaurant was an expensive one, flashy and ostentatiously French, the sort where no one goes, except on an expense account and most of the food is cooked in flames at the table. Tish was surprised at Nadia, who always seemed the acme of sophistication, choosing such a place. But their guests, she soon noticed, seemed delighted to be there and found male friends at almost every table. She saw that as usual, Nadia knew what she was doing.

Nevertheless the heat and the noise after the long tense day made her head ache. The wine she had drunk began to depress, instead of exhilarate. She looked round the table for any sympathetic echoes. Edward's pale face glinted in the candlelight; one of the critics was talking to him excitedly, waving his arms about; Edward accepted the homage unemotionally, for he was still dazzled by the sight of all his paintings around a gallery. Gunilla, beside him, certainly looked tired but her polite manner and set mouth gave no indication of giving in to it. Nadia, whatever her feelings, was still playing the role of the organizer, the hostess. Tish wondered at her energy. Probably she hadn't been drinking.

Tish felt herself falling asleep. Except that her brain was too filled with images to let her sleep. Nadia's naked body; Austin's bewildered eyes as she'd taunted him; Maggie complaining, bewailing; Fenella's reproachful pierrot eyes; the glass falling, clattering, crashing.

'I'm awfully sorry. I'm afraid I don't feel too well. I must go home, Nadia. It's so silly. I am sorry.'

So Tish didn't hear the news till she read the papers the next morning. She was only looking for Edward's reviews – her hangover was horrible – and might have missed it altogether if the word 'painter' hadn't been included in the headline. 'Painter's Wife found Hanged.' 'Fenella Aubrey, wife of Edward Aubrey, the painter, was found hanged last night in her husband's studio off King's Road, Chelsea. Foul play is not suspected. She was twenty-three. Mr A. Puffett, a friend of the family's who happened to be passing, found her but she had already been dead for several hours. Her husband had not been in his studio all day. Mr and Mrs Aubrey had been married two years and had no children.'

That was all. Tish read it through several times. There was so little information, but all the facts she knew about were correct. The names were right, the place, the ages; it all had a horrible ring of truth. The only thing that gave her hope was the reference to a family friend, Mr A. Puffett. She was sure they knew no one called that. Desperately needing to know more, she rang Mrs Aubrey's number. Gunilla answered the phone.

'Yes,' she said, to Tish's half-gasped question. 'It was Fenella. Edward is at the police station now. We will know more later.'

Feverishly Tish asked about the family friend. Surely they had got it wrong?

'Well, yes, in a way,' said Gunilla in measured tones, 'that was the window-cleaner, Austin.'

'Austin.' Tish rang off. Austin had found her. Austin had been looking for her at the party. Austin had found the flesh and blood Mrs Aubrey junior, only she wasn't living any more. She remembered only too clearly her own teasing answers to his questions.

Tish sat on the floor staring blindly at the report in the paper. Could it really be true. Then, seeing it was nearly midday, she dressed and ran out to buy an evening newspaper. It was much worse there, because they had had time to find out all sorts of details. Also they had printed the portrait of Fenella dressed in her pierrot costume. This meant that they had discovered where Edward had been during the suicide. Tish was so overcome by the public exposure of Edward's behaviour, that she stopped trying to imagine Fenella's suffering. Any minute, she expected to read her own name. She put the *Standard* to one side of her and the *News* to the other. She read again and again.

'... Ironically, it was Edward Aubrey's first exhibition, a review of which appears on Page 14. However Mrs Aubrey, although living separated from her husband since she lost a child last year, was said to be on good terms with him and very happy about the exhibition; the portraits of her were shown there with her full approval. The only reason she did not attend was because the appeal case against the sentence on a drug's charge of an old friend of hers was due to be heard that day. It seems likely that this case coupled with her miscarriage had preyed on her mind.'

Even now, Tish found she had to know the reaction to Edward's exhibition. With eager shaking hands, she turned to the review. It was ecstatic, talking about 'probing the human psyche', 'a depth of understanding remarkable in so young an artist', 'put across with a deceptively crude force'. It had obviously been written before the suicide was known and made no reference to it.

Tish made herself a cup of coffee and continued to sit

among the papers. Later she went out to get the afternoon editions and then the evening, and from them discovered the time and place of the inquest and the fact that Fenella had used knotted silk handkerchiefs to hang herself. She listened to the news on the radio and the television, but the radio said nothing and the television had film of the house where ten children had been burnt alive. She switched it off quickly.

At about seven the doorbell rang and Maggie appeared. Although she had been so angry with Tish she could think of no one else to mourn with. Soon after her arrival she explained that she was almost certainly the last friend to whom Fenella spoke.

Tish nodded and handed her a cup of coffee. Thereafter they hardly spoke at all. It was strange to see Maggie silenced. She didn't even have the heart to tell Tish about the reduction in Tristram's sentence. They sat together, joined in unavowed guilt, till nearly midnight.

The next morning, after a night in which she had not even attempted to sleep, Tish rang her parents. She announced she had taken a fortnight's holiday from work and was coming to stay with them. They quite understood. So did Nadia. 'Don't come back till you're quite ready,' she said. 'The gallery will run itself now.'

*

Nadia went to the gallery daily. It did not, after all, 'run itself'. For Edward's exhibition had become news. Not on a big scale, but in the sense that there always seemed to be a reporter sniffing round somewhere. They wanted Edward, of course, but also copies of his portraits of Fenella. Horribly aware of her own naked portrait hanging on the wall, Nadia almost lost her nerve and closed the whole exhibition. But fifteen years of striving to launch painters who had never had half such talent as Edward's won through. The reviews had been almost uniformly good. In a humiliating compromise – she blushed far more to see Mr Barton take it down than she had when he put it up – she had her own portrait removed. Then she instructed that anyone inquiring about the pictures of Mrs Aubrey should be sent straight up to her office.

Nadia looked old. Not in any obvious grey or wrinkled way, she was too much a product of artifice for that, but her thinness suddenly lost its elasticity and became brittle like rusty wire. She sat behind her desk, as sinuously dressed as ever, in trousers, wide shoulders hung with falling folds of material, and seemed immovable. In terms of the gallery, she had only good news to deal with; the exhibition had already ninety per cent sold. A New York gallery wanted to mount an exhibition of Edward's works as soon as he could paint them or, failing that, show some of those from her collection to arouse interest.

Nadia talked to them on her push-button telephone, appeared animated and even cast her mind forward to the organization of the next artist she was showing. But she looked old. She felt old. It was a relief when it was suggested to her by her doctor in Hereford that her husband was ill enough to require her presence.

She had not seen Edward since Fenella's suicide. It was Fenella's suicide that had made her life shabby. But she held it against Edward. He shouldn't have married a girl who understood so little about him. It was not fair to her, Nadia. Or perhaps Fenella had understood more than she. It was over thoughts like these that Nadia became old.

So she was relieved when she made the decision to go to the country. However, not being a cowardly woman, she sent her secretary with a note to Edward's studio asking him to come to the gallery. Although she'd had no personal contact with him since Fenella's death, she knew he was working there. Nothing stopped him painting. But she would not go there now. She had always considered herself a cold-blooded person, but she could never go there now.

Edward appeared the next day. He burst into Nadia's office early in the morning when she had hardly settled behind her desk. She was immediately amazed by his youth. In a week she had quite forgotten what a boy he was. It was a perfect spring morning and the sun streamed in on his smooth white skin and his silvery yellow hair. He was dressed in pale blue trousers and a blue and white houndstooth check jacket which she'd actually chosen for him herself. He had the air of a schoolboy, pure and innocent, no cares, no guilty secrets. He even carried a kind of satchel under his arm.

'You do look happy,' Nadia found herself saying almost gaily, which was not at all the sort of approach she had planned. But it was impossible to reconcile this glowing angel of light with the daemon figure she had been imagining over the last week. Nevertheless, the fact remained. The truth remained. He had caused a girl to kill herself. Only a few days ago. At the inquest which had been reported fully in the papers, a man had jumped up and shouted 'Murderer!' True, the man was only a poor semi-illiterate window-cleaner who understood nothing of Edward, but nevertheless the word had been cried out publicly and printed in the daily papers. Nadia determined not to forget these things as she talked to him. If he was blank to emotion, she would not be; even a great painter must follow some rules of human conduct.

'I'm sorry,' she said, beginning again. 'Fenella was a talented girl. It is very sad she couldn't understand the ...' Nadia's voice stopped abruptly, 'understand the rules', 'play the game', 'exist without you'. She looked at Edward and he looked inquiringly at her. She couldn't say these things to Edward. His clever brilliant face made them seem like ageing clichés. After all, there were different standards of behaviour for someone like him. It would be disingenuous, dishonest, to pretend otherwise. 'I'm sorry for Fenella,' she said simply.

Edward stood in front of her; he made no attempt to find a chair. He was looking round her office as she spoke. When she stopped he pointed to a large brown paper parcel in the corner.

'Why did you take down my picture of you? We made a contract. I came to New York, you hung that picture.'

Nadia looked round astonished. It had been down for a week now. She had forgotten about it. Now that it was safely hidden it no longer seemed very important. She had not considered it would be exactly prominent in Edward's mind either.

'I want to talk about business,' she said weakly. 'That's why I asked you here. There are things to discuss. I have to go to Somerset. Arthur needs me.'

Edward stood with his back to her looking out of the window. For a moment, she thought he tensed into unusual rigidity when she said she was leaving London. And he stayed silent for some time. But when he turned, his face was as vigorous and charming as ever.

'Is he very ill? The philatelist extraordinary. I'm sorry. To be ill at his age must be dreadfully depressing. Quite without point.'

Nadia looked surprised; this was almost sympathy; and yet his judgement on sickness in old age was strange.

'But surely it's better to be sick when you're old and not functioning so well anyway?'

'More usual, not better. It doesn't mean anything when you die then. You don't make any statement.'

'But you can't want people to die young,' Nadia was shocked.

Edward looked with a blank expression of utter conviction out of the window. 'Death means something then,' he said eventually.

Nadia looked at him with horror. His appearance was not deceptive at all; it was the truest thing about him; he was a child, with a child's idea about the drama of life. He had no understanding of suffering at all; it meant nothing to him; he had never suffered. The direct simplicity of his pictures, the almost childlike naïveté in which he presented the nudity and violence of Austin, the sexual nature of herself, the doll-like optimism of Tish, the drowning beauty of Fenella, was based on a total lack of understanding. It was a five-year-old, with the skills of an adult, painting a murder. The blood was red paint to him, the victim's distorted face the mixture of an artist's palette. Those who saw Edward's paintings gave them their depth of meaning.

Nadia felt sick. She felt as if there was a monster in the room. With a great effort of will, because she couldn't think of anything else to do, she said, 'The exhibition has been a stupendous success,' and she told him about the plans for the future.

He listened excitedly. And at last when Nadia was finished, he burst out with what was obviously concerning him most at the present, 'I'm doing a painting! A great painting. The most extraordinary thing I've ever attempted.' He wanted her to come to lunch so he could tell her all about it. He had some sketches with him but he didn't want to show them here. He was carried away by the idea, but he couldn't tell her now. He wanted a bottle of wine, he wanted to talk. He'd talked to no one for days. He was desperate for someone to talk to. His brain was bursting with his idea. Surely she would come to lunch.

Nadia declined. She was going to the country.

'But now now! Immediately! It's hardly midday. You need a drink before the desert. Nadia, when I need you, don't abandon me!' He flung open his arms to her; he seemed prepared to drop onto his knees.

Nadia said no, she was sorry, she had to go. She had promised Arthur. And then Edward became petulant and said what had happened to everybody – even Tish had gone to the country. What was wrong with London suddenly?

Nadia didn't try to explain. 'It must be the spring,' she said dourly. 'Good-bye, Edward. Any message about business will reach me through this office.'

Edward went away at last. Bounding down the stairs. But he was still determined to have his lunch. The temporary receptionist Nadia had employed to sit at the desk in Tish's place had recognized his face. She smiled sympathetically at his eager irritation. 'But not till twelve-thirty, Mr Aubrey. Lady Gore is very strict about times.'

'Please don't worry, Hazel. I'll manage,' Nadia, now only wanting to be rid of him, called down the stairs.

'Portraits are living things,' said Edward, as they passed the large painting of Fenella. 'Living things but without the prospect of death.'

'I'm so sorry,' said Hazel nervously, who only knew what she'd read in the papers.

14

Edward had never before made preliminary sketches for a portrait, but he had never before tried to paint someone from memory. The absence of the living model made it a much greater challenge to his imagination. He had painted Fenella before, of course, but then she had been alive. The remembrance of the process helped him but only to a certain extent. Besides, he was not only painting a dead person but painting her dead. And he had not seen her dead. She had already been removed to the morgue when he was escorted to the police station, and no one suggested he should go to see her.

Edward had been dazed; it was after four in the morning, he had drunk a great deal, he had come to the studio from Nadia's bed; he had difficulty at first even in understanding what the police were telling him. They disapproved of him; he could tell that by their curt manner. But he would have been disgusted if they had presumed to give him the sympathy due to a bereaved husband. For at last he understood that Fenella was dead, had killed herself, and then he had wanted to be alone.

But this, apparently, was not allowed. There were questions, endless silly questions about where she was. He tried to explain that they lived individual lives and didn't follow each other round like elephants in a circus. At this point, faced with their blank stupid faces, he had even banged the table with the flat of his hand.

But the policeman had only straightened his piece of paper and written in an illiterate hand, 'Separated'.

So then Edward decided to despise them all and concentrated on putting up barriers between them and himself. This was not difficult, since their approach to the situation found no point of contact with his. They didn't, for example, describe to him exactly what had happened until he forced them to by a series of his own leading questions. Only after nearly an hour did he discover that it was Austin who had found her and that, rather than take her down himself, he had rung for the police. This deference to authority interested him. Austin, himself, had been sent home from the police station some time ago.

Next, he had asked about his handkerchiefs, for he had found the empty box turned upside down on the studio floor which otherwise gave no indication that anything unusual had taken place there. In this way, he discovered the means Fenella had used to kill herself and it was then that his imagination had been properly stimulated. And he had begun to grasp the magnificence in Fenella's action.

He had gone home through bright early morning sunshine, to his mother's house which everyone seemed to think suitable, and lain down for a few hours until the police called him back again. This time he asked more questions than they did. He found out the exact position of the dangling body, the space between her legs and the floor, and finally that she had been naked. The policeman looked away with embarrassment as he told him, but thought the husband had a right to know. Seeing he could ask no further detail without scandalizing the force, Edward then found a young policeman who didn't know why he was in the station. From him he discovered the appearance of the face and neck of a hung person. The policeman was keen on his job.

'The neck would be broken, you see. Much more likely than strangulation.'

'You mean it would go slack?'

'Yes. You know, hang on an angle. All the muscles gone. Like a puppet.'

'Like a puppet's. A puppet!'

The young policeman looked uneasy at Edward's excitement, and said he'd better be off now. He plonked his helmet solidly onto his head, straightened the chin strap neatly. He hoped he hadn't been talking to a murderer. Stupid idea, of course. A man inside a police station. But his pale eyes glittered so oddly.

'Good morning, sir.'

Edward smiled distantly. For now he was beginning to appreciate fully the compliment Fenella had paid him. She had killed herself for him. Hung herself till her neck snapped for him. She had always meant more to him than anyone else and now she had assured her position forever.

There was only one way he could equal the tribute she had paid him and that was by making a picture out of it. A living portrait of her great dying. Feverishly, he recalled every famous scene of death. The Victorians, particularly, understood its inspiration. The Death of Chatterton, Millais' The Drowning of Ophelia. It was a tradition in which he was proud to follow. How well Fenella had understood him.

He had already started the series of sketches by the time of the inquest. He therefore took no notice of Loelia's continued absence in Canada or the news that Tish had gone to the country. The sketches made these formal affairs of the world seem as meaningless as he and Fenella had once agreed was the wedding ceremony. She would live on his canvas. She had no need of inquest or funeral.

Edward locked himself in his studio which had itself become part of his imaginative world and he had no interest in seeing how his exhibition was doing. The gallery delivered reviews to him which he read with a fascinated disbelief and then put aside. In fact he'd assumed Nadia's note was one of these and had not opened it till he needed a rest from work. Then he'd seen her handwriting as if coming on their relationship again, and he'd pushed all the drawings of Fenella's body into a bag. Perhaps he needed to talk it out more, to clarify his approach before daring the white canvas. Then it struck him that no one had come to him since Fenella's death and that he had talked to no one except his mother with whom he stayed occasionally. So he became a little aggrieved and thought he lacked a coterie to cheer him on. It seemed odd to lack a coterie at a time when he had just been recognized by the official art world.

Nadia's rebuff, because he saw it quite clearly as that, although it did not hurt him deeply, made him feel the lack even more. His lunch with the receptionist had served no purpose. She was a stupid girl. He thought of taking Gunilla into his confidence; but lately her coldness had turned from dignity to disapproval; she did not flow with his enthusiasm as she had, when they'd stayed together in the country. Her irritating vagueness had reappeared and she even made the patently ludicrous statement, 'You ought to mix more with people of your age, darling.'

Edward spent even more time in the studio. Two weeks passed, but although his file of sketches increased, he still didn't feel ready to broach the canvas. Then one day, Gunilla told him that Tristram would be out of prison the following week. Edward jumped out of his chair excitedly. He realized that, all unknowingly, this was just what he was waiting for. Tristram knew Fenella as well as he did, they would talk about her, they would recall the beauty of her presence when they had first known her in Florence and during the summer they had spent together at his parents' home. At last he would be inspired to do her justice.

Maggie had managed to tear herself from Tristram's side the evening Edward called and was out. Edward assumed there had been no separation. Tristram stood holding the door open, leaning slightly against it, silent but not disagreeably so, his slanting graceful attitude reminiscent of Hillier's portrait of an Elizabethan nobleman. Painted on ivory; his pallor was remarkable, even by Edward's standards. Then he saw his hair. The tumbled curls had been cropped pudding basin round.

'Exit the cavalier. Enter the roundhead!'

'It's all the rage,' Tristram moved ahead of him into the drawing-room, 'wherever have you been, not to know that!' He glanced over Edward's longish waving hair. He grimaced with mock disgust.

Edward laughed at his flirtatiousness. 'It suits you,' he said. 'Not roundhead at all, but very sacrificial lamb.'

Tristram pranced about the room waggling his hips. 'Oh yes! They carved me up for a tidy morsel where I've been.'

Edward frowned. This seemed a little vulgar.

'Loin of lamb for luncheon, rolled and stuffed lamb for *le diner*. All with a sauce *ravissante*!' Tristram kissed his fingers to his lips.

And his hips seemed a little bigger. Edward decided to introduce the reason for his visit. He was basically not in dallying mood. 'Fenella would have appreciated you. The sacrificial you.' He spoke quite sternly.

Tristram turned sharply away. 'Ah yes. She always had her masculine side.' His voice was hard.

Edward feared that, after all, he had been coarsened by his experience. Delicate insinuation had been previously his most attractive gift. Nevertheless Edward saw no other option but to persevere. 'Shall we have dinner?'

Tristram sat on the sofa then; he put his feet up.

'What very old gymshoes,' Edward commented. Tristram said nothing. Edward sat down opposite him. 'I wanted to talk about Fenella. I wanted your help.' Edward did not fear a rebuff but he was rather taken aback to see Tristram at close quarters. He was wearing an ugly orange-ribbed sweater which did not suit him at all. His languor had a sickly attitude about it. He had been mistaken to liken him to the Elizabethan nobleman or a sacrificial lamb. In fact he was more like a follower of Cromwell – the ugly man – his nose was redder than the rest of his face, the whites of his eyes were yellow and he had a nasty-looking boil on the side of his forehead.

'I don't like crowded places,' he said, answering the question about the restaurant with apparently no concern for Edward's close stare. In fact he spoke in a loud self-mocking tone of voice, 'They frighten me.'

'Don't worry about that. I just want to talk.'

'At your service – as the choirboy said to the bishop.'

Edward decided to ignore Tristram's absurd compulsion to play the whore. There were more important things to occupy them. He opened the bag he had brought with him and took out a pile of sketches. He waited patiently while Tristram insisted on putting on a brilliant overhead light. 'We must not lose the execution in gloom!' Edward then pushed forward one after the other, forcing them into Tristram's hands, under his eyes. Excitedly, walking about now, he began to explain the tribute he was planning to pay Fenella. How he had discovered all the details of her position, her colouring, the exact angle she had hung at – here Tristram had given a quickly stifled cough as if to cover embarrassment – but how he could not, he could not, he just could not begin the oil painting. He swung round dramatically in the middle of the room.

'She was naked, of course, you knew that, a naked white skeleton.' He stood looking down hopefully at Tristram.

Tristram was very casual about the matter. One gathered he had greater things on his mind. 'No problem,' he said flatly. 'Just those elegant bones, strung together loosely like a puppet.'

'That's what I thought,' Edward grew agitated. 'But it's no good. Look at that sketch and this one. There's no magnificence. It looks absurd, like a toy hanging in a car window.'

'Shining with luminous paint.'

'Yes. Yes,' said Edward impatiently. 'Nothing like Fenella at all.'

'With red glass eyes.'

'But there's something right about the puppet. Head hanging down. Great mournful eyes.'

'The dong with the luminous eyes,' Tristram spoke into his lap, and before Edward could retaliate even more crossly, he added quietly, 'the dead Pierrot'.

Edward started up. He shook Tristram's arm excitedly, not noticing how he cowered back, as if such force frightened him. 'Of course ! Of course ! How ridiculous to have taken so long. The pierrot. Clothed in the jester's uniform, poking fun at the world, at the world's concept of death ... !'

Tristram rubbed his forearm while Edward rushed about the room. He tried to pretend he was somewhere else. He felt very ill, as if he might be actually sick. These theatricals frightened him. Edward seemed like a madman. 'Wait.' He bent down to collect the sketches for it looked as if Edward's enthusiasm might carry him away without them. And he wanted no such grisly trophies. But they were waved aside imperiously.

'I don't need these any more. They were red herrings. We must talk again very soon. Very soon, Tristram. Now you're around again. But I needn't explain. Such a hurry now. You see how it is.' Grabbing his coat from a chair, he ran from the house.

Tristram listened to the door slamming without more reaction than a slight expression of relief. The lassitude which had always been part of his nature now seemed a cancer to eat up his life. He could not even summon up the energy to hide Fenella's naked bones which still lay scattered across the floor, though he had to close his eyes to avoid the sight. He curled up on the sofa and waited for Maggie's strength to carry him through the rest of the evening. Again he thought that Edward was a madman. It gave him some consolation.

*

Austin set out for Edward's studio one windy June afternoon. The wind irritated him, it buffeted his motor bicycle so it needed all his strength to keep on a straight line. It also blew clouds across the sun, so that one minute he was staring into a grey vacuum and the next minute he was half-blinded by brilliant sunlight.

However he did the journey quickly and parked his bike neatly at the kerbside. Then he blew his nose, for he was suffering from a lingering summer cold, and knocked on the door.

Inside, Edward was painting. His easel with its large canvas was set up under the great black beam. Edward was wearing a long white overall and his ears were covered by headphones almost as big as boxing gloves. He was listening to Beethoven's Choral Symphony. Every now and again he waved his brush like a conductor's baton. He didn't hear the knock at the door. In fact he was planning to go out for a break. Buy some freshly ground coffee. The intermittent sun which had annoyed Austin was also making it hard for him to get the colour balance right. He wiped his brushes, stuck them in a pot of turpentine and flung a sheet over the picture. He still protected his unfinished pictures against the world.

Austin gave up knocking and turned the door handle.

'It's me, chief,' he said, as soon as he saw Edward. His blue eyes were bright from the ride, his hair windblown.

But he was outside Edward's line of vision and he could hear nothing but Beethoven.

'I've come back,' Austin said, not angrily but louder and with emotion. He rubbed his itching nose with his hand. 'I wanted to see you.' He moved further into the room and Edward saw him.

'Austin. How are you, Austin. Come in.' He could barely hear his own voice above the rising crescendo of music. But his energy and good humour – the picture of Fenella would be finished in two or three days – could easily incorporate Austin's presence, even though he hadn't seen him for months. 'Come looking for work, have you?' He pointed to the chaise longue. 'Would you mind awfully waiting a moment while this record finishes? The music. It won't be a minute. I can speak to you, you see, but I can't hear you speak.'

Austin sat down obediently, although he kept jerking his head about in a rather unusual manner. 'I've got a shocking cold,' he said, since he thought Edward looked at him oddly, but Edward shook his head. Then he put his large red hands on his knees and sat silently; his bulky thighs were tightly covered by a pair of faded jeans and he wore an unpleasantly bright ultra-marine T-shirt. Edward thought that he was less like a gypsy now, with his oiled hair blown back from his forehead by the wind and his dreadful old shiny imitation leather jacket over one shoulder, and more like an old-fashioned teddy boy.

Then as the music poured through his head, he remembered what Austin had shouted at the inquest. But instead of hearing his livid face screaming murderer, which might have given him some warning, he only recalled his passionate words about Fenella, 'She wasn't of unsound mind! There was nothing wrong with her mind! She knew just what she was doing!' The music reached its climax and changed abruptly to silence, but Edward forgot to take off his headphones. He was too excited. Here in this studio was the very person to appreciate fully his painting. The only person outside himself to have really understood that Fenella had chosen death. Moreover, now Edward strode towards Austin, smiling widely under his great earphones, here was the only person, apart from the police, who counted for nothing, who had actually seen Fenella hanging here from that great black beam.

Edward began to talk loudly, haranguing Austin, waving his hands about, explaining his inspiration, what he had planned, asking for his appreciation. And since he still wore the earphones, any interruption Austin might have made went unheard.

Austin listened with an anxious puzzled expression on his face, which gradually changed to a stupid frustration. He didn't understand. Talk of pictures and symbols and form and colour in conjunction with the death of a woman made no sense to him. It was nonsense. Like putting paint on a wound.

Austin stood up, leaving his jacket carefully behind him. His motives for coming to see Edward were still unclear to himself, but if Edward had been interested in anything but his own ideas he would have seen that his usual stolid front was under the influence of something else. Austin was drunk. For the second time in his life he had drunk a full bottle of whisky at a sitting. He had started it as medicine to clear his cold, but after a couple of glasses he had found no reason to stop. The idea to visit Edward had come on him suddenly with no preconception – in fact, he had thought he could never bear to see the studio again. The churlish wind had made him irritable in body as well as in mind.

Now he came closer to Edward, for he could not fully take in why he had become deaf all of a sudden. He thought Edward was playing some trick on him.

'I've come back!' he shouted, as Edward ranted on, 'to tell you what I think of you!'

Edward smelt the whisky from his gaping mouth and moved back a little. The whisky mixed with his body smell and the smell of unwashed clothes. His shoulder brushed the draped canvas standing behind him. He swung round excitedly, still ignoring Austin's frantic mouthings. He never really heard what Austin said anyway. 'For you, I'll make an exception. I'll show you. For you, because you'll understand!'

Austin turned round with him. He had never seen Edward like this before. So emotional, so flushed and garrulous. It encouraged him to loose further his own slipping bonds of self-control. Above them, the sun, in a patch of sky without clouds, poured down through the glass, magnifying the heat beneath minute by minute. Sweat started on Austin's face; then on Edward. Austin sniffed; the heat made it difficult for him to breathe through his stuffy nose. He snorted angrily.

With a showman's flourish, Edward swept the covering from the picture. 'There, you see! You see!'

Together they stared, black-haired, white-haired, tense with concentration, both reaching the same climax of excitement.

This was only the second time Austin had deliberately looked at a painting. The first had been his own naked body in the art gallery from which he fled as if it were the devil. And now what he saw hanging in front of him was more terrifying still. This ghastly hanging body, just as he'd found her, except that now she was dressed in that strange red costume with the huge fluffy pompons down the front, like captured rabbits' tails. It was the same outfit she wore in that painting in the art gallery, but now, instead of that sad sympathetic face, there was a face disfigured by a weird kind of suffering in which the lips even seemed to smile. Only the angle of the head, hanging limply, was anything like what Austin had seen that dreadful night. It reminded him, as he stood there, incapable of looking aside, of a visit he'd paid to Madame Tussaud once with Sharon and Louise and the foul guilt he'd felt when they'd glimpsed the Chamber of Horrors. He'd rushed them away at once, but they had wanted to stay. Already he had corrupted them. Thinking of the girls, who were his no longer, made him ache with rage and desperation. Yet still he looked at the picture, and this time the huge bulging eyes reminded him of the circus owner's when he'd tried to strangle him.

Then Edward gave a little squeal of satisfaction.

Austin turned to see his triumphant crowing face. At last his limbs could move again. With a clumsy lurch he passed Edward and snatched the picture off the easel.

'What's the matter?' Edward cried out. 'For God's sake! It's still wet! Don't touch it!'

Like some great beetle with his huge white extensions to his head, Edward danced about Austin. 'Oh, please. Carefully, please. No! No! Please!'

Austin held the picture and looked above it wildly at Edward. And then, as he saw Edward prepare to make a rush at him, to lunge and grab it back with his long, thin, pincerlike arms, Austin realized what he must do to protect the poor dead lady. Kicking the easel into Edward's face, he pulled his penknife out of his pocket and began to slash at the painting. It was only canvas to him, easy to destroy but to Edward it was a living thing. A picture he had created. A living Fenella who had always meant more to him than anyone. Fenella, the magnificent! At each cut, he screamed with anguish and despair.

'No! No! No! Stop! You can't! You're destroying my painting! You're murdering it! Murderer! Murderer! My Fenella! You're murdering Fenella!'

But his shrieks only made Austin more ferocious than ever; he slashed and hacked; the knife grew streaked with paint.

'Not the face!' Edward wailed. He ran at Austin. He wrenched at the frame, at the tattered canvas. Sweat ran down both their faces. Austin's nose ran too, dripping through the black hairs of his nostrils to his panting red mouth. Although Edward looked so pale and slender, he was much taller than Austin and made strong with fury, so that even Austin, with his heavily muscled body, could not control him easily. Besides he was still trying to rend the canvas further.

At length, they could keep their balance no longer, and they fell on the floor, grappling together in a passionate embrace, rolling over and over each other, smashing across the remains of the picture and bringing down a heavy table across their legs. All this time, the earphones stayed over Edward's ears, so the fight was taking place for him in near silence. He even used them like clubs to batter Austin, and then he heard reverberating thuds like cannon fire. The silence helped him, for it made the scene seem oddly removed, came between the pain from his knocks and bruises. It was like a dream or nightmare. Except that now he could feel the wet heat from Austin's skin.

Edward felt himself smothering in the disgusting smells and liquids of Austin's body, but he fought still; like a woman, scratching and biting, wrenching at Austin's oily black hair that slid through his fingers like buttered spaghetti. He even clutched onto his revolting nose, trying to push him back off his picture. His picture.

Then Austin's frustrated rage turned from the picture to Edward himself, and he gripped the handle of his penknife more securely. Now at last the wires caught in their thrashing bodies and wrenched the headphones off. All of a sudden, Edward was in the middle of a great bellowing brawl – snorts and shrieks and thumps and groans, ugly animal noises like bulls penned too close together.

Panting, gasping, struggling, shuddering, hot, sweating, one on top of the other. How it revolted him, this animal activity, this making love, this degradation of the human soul !

Austin too thought of making love and remembered Edward's hand on his naked body. He pushed the knife with all his strength into Edward's high pale forehead. It didn't go very far so he took it out and tried again. Then again and again.

Edward felt Austin's hot foul-smelling breath on his face and then warm sweet-smelling liquid began to gush over his face. He was blinded by it, suffocated by it, entirely smothered by it. He was a fountain of blood. The grunting and panting gave way to a curious inward lowing. Like a cow's. He supposed it came from him. Such an unpleasing undignified noise. There should be more ecstasy after such a fight. After so much passion, so much hatred. So near love. There should be ecstasy in the prospect of death. For a man can't become a bloody fountain without dying.

> Death is the privilege of Human Nature
> And life without it were not worth our taking.

The lines came easily, although he hadn't thought of them

for years. But he could not now remember the meaning or even when he'd known it. And still that dreadful lowing would not be drowned out. It was a relief when, quite shortly, it stopped.

*

Austin was exhausted; he crouched a few yards from where Edward's body lay. Sprawled out on its back. The blood had run across his face and through his hair to the floor, so that there was a largish pool like a red halo round his head. Austin stared stupidly. That meant that his long white overall should have been relatively pure. Pure like a winding sheet. But it wasn't. On the contrary there were spreading crimson splashes all down the front of it from collar to hem. It was horrible. He was bloody everywhere. Everywhere. Dazedly, Austin wondered how it had happened. Even he, with Edward's scratches, was hardly red anywhere but on his arms and face. So it had not come from his wounds. The only real stains on him were a dirty mixture of paint from the canvas. He focused his eyes more clearly. It was paint, red paint, wet and glistening just like blood. Edward had rolled on the tube of crimson he had been using to paint Fenella's pierrot's costume. He had helped to paint his own death scene.

Austin continued to crouch in the corner like a harmless monkey. And then in macabre imitation of a human being, great tears rolled down his cheeks.

Recently published fiction

Susan Hill

A Change for the Better

In the Prince of Wales Hotel and the shabby terraces and
tearooms of Westbourne retired lives run
their course – all, in their different ways, anticipating a crisis.

Gentleman and Ladies

Miss Faith Lavender would not have cried at her own
funeral. And indeed no one attending the service shed a tear
– neither her two sisters, nor the handful of neighbours, nor
the strange man in black boots holding stolen snowdrops ...
'A remarkable writer' – *The Times*

Alison Lurie

Only Children

Using the same stylish, tender and comic approach as in her
bestselling *War Between the Tates*, Alison Lurie turns her
attention to the goings-on one weekend on an idyllic Upstate
New York farmhouse, when the Hubbards and the Zimmerns
– plus their children – come to stay with Anna.

Barbara Pym

Excellent Women

Mildred was quite capable of dealing with the stock
situations of life. In fact her handling of births, marriages,
deaths, jumble sales and garden fêtes ruined by the
weather was masterly. It is the introduction of new and
exotic neighbours that pulls her up short.

A Glass of Blessings

Wilmet Forsyth is fairly young, good looking, well dressed,
well looked after, suitably husbanded and rather bored.
Her interest wanders to the nearby Anglo-Catholic church
and its three unmarried priests and on to Piers Longridge
whose enigmatic overtures are rather intriguing.

Look out for these from Penguin

Elizabeth Troop

Woolworth Madonna

This is the story of a woman – working-class, a loving
mother, a not-so-loving wife.

Elizabeth Troop's heroine is more than that though. Faced
with the demolition of her house, the slow sliding of hopes
and dreams into middle age, the onset of high-rise living and
flabby flesh, she still remains a force to be reckoned with – a
force that is truly and unbeatably feminine and unforgettable.
'I couldn't fault her book' – Auberon Waugh in the *Evening
Standard*
'An outstanding first novel' – Martyn Goff in the *Daily
Telegraph*
'A rare discovery' – *New Statesman*

Philip Roth

The Ghost Writer

A celebrated blend of sympathy and pitilessness were the
trademarks of E. I. Lonoff's work.

It was to this great Russian-Jewish author that Nathan
Zuckerman turned for support and inspiration. Only to find
when he visited Lonoff's rural retreat the disturbing presence
of an enigmatic houseguest haunted his imagination. Yet it
seemed impossible to Nathan that America's most famous
literary ascetic should keep a mistress. But there she was. The
beautiful, gifted, utterly desirable Amy Bellette . . . or was it
Anne Frank?

Savagely funny, ironical and wise, Philip Roth exposes the
paradoxes of art and life, the artist as voyeur and poseur and,
not least, the problem of unrequited lust.
'Very funny and very shrewd' – *Daily Telegraph*
'Skilful and moving, well constructed . . . beautifully written' –
Listener